Near where Roger Moss lives is a pink pagoda, a
burned-out church, and a grand manor house—
some of the always present settings inextricably linked
within the twenty-six "model games" in

The
Game of
the
Pink Pagoda

It is here, in this village near Essex University where
he has taught literature since 1977, that Roger Moss
has created his provocative, unique, and ultimately
inspiring first novel, a work that, when first
published in England, prompted one reviewer to call
it, "an extraordinary first novel, impossible to
describe in any convincing detail," a book that has
taken the ordinary and made it powerful.

In Roger Moss's hands, the pink pagoda of his village
has become a Holy Grail, the object of The Quest; the
church has burned in some mysterious way, the
grand manor stands above the gravel pits. And there
are always a wealthy landowner, a businessman, a
beautiful woman, a charred body, a seeker of fortune,
a faithful dog, making their constantly shifting moves
in *The Game of the Pink Pagoda,* a game of life
you will never forget.

The Game of
the Pink Pagoda

A Novel

ROGER MOSS

Ballantine Books • New York

Library of Congress Catalog Card Number: 86-91557
ISBN: 0-345-34179-1

Cover design by James R. Harris
Cover illustration by Tim Jacobus
Text illustrations by Hannah Firmin

Manufactured in the United States of America
First American Edition: March 1986
10   9   8   7   6   5   4   3   2   1

The Game of
the Pink Pagoda

A Game for Twelve Players,
with a Board and Six Pieces.
Accounts of Twenty-six Model Games.
Also included: a Note on the
Origins of the Game. The Only
Authorized and Comprehensive
Handbook.

For Susan

The lyf so short, the craft so long to lerne

Contents

Object of the Game

The Game of the Pink Pagoda has several Objects:

The first Object of the Game is to get to the Pink Pagoda without them catching you.

This is not as hard as it sounds, provided you remember that they are all playing their own Games, with aims and rules that may differ in some respects from yours. The hardest thing to remember is that they are also anxious not to be caught by you. You will of course want to be silent, since this is the only way to appreciate the sound of running water, or to feel the full shock of the weight of pheasants lifting themselves out of the grass beside you as you pass, and it is, of course, also the only sure way of knowing that the footfall you heard was not yours but another's, and that you have heard them before they could hear you.

The second Object of the Game is to get to the Pink Pagoda as if it were for the first time.

Do you remember that first time? The low rich autumn sunlight. The tightly held knowledge that where you were was private. The trophies hanging pinned to the barbed-wire fence where the path turned. The sound of running water. Splinters of pink through the trees before the whole thing came into view.

It is, of course, in truth impossible to re-create the sensation of that first time. It was something born of expectation, and the expectation was born of knowledge (the kind of knowledge, admittedly, that came from books and so was of no use in itself, the kind of knowledge that only deadens the sensation of knowing) – so that even the first time had its own flavour of re-creating a time before. There had been a time when the corner had not been turned, and a time before that when another path had been pursued in vain.

There had been a time when one particular book had first been opened, and yet this too gave on to earlier books and on to a long-standing habit of creating desires for things out of half-remembered images, of words merely. So there never was the thing seen purely for the first time. This is arguably the source of the Game's unending fascination.

The third Object of the Game is to become the Occupant of the Pink Pagoda.

The attentive reader will notice that the second and third Objects of the Game are logically incompatible. This indeed would be the case, were it not that one of the chief lessons of the Game is this: the perfect Visitor and the perfect Occupant are One. The best point of entry and the surest sense of having always been there are One. The stealthiest entrance is by the front door.

The fourth Object of the Game is to discover the underlying purpose of the Game. You keep playing in order to find out why.

Introduction to the Model Games

The Pieces

The Pink Pagoda, of course. It is not really a pagoda. It is, in fact, a cottage without special interest converted into a pretty extravaganza. The verandah gives on to a stream. There are two outbuildings also painted pink. You could not really call it a pagoda as a whole, and it has in its time been called by other names. It may not always have been pink. There is a gravel pathway around the side of the cottage, and a gravel driveway leading from the door. At the far end of the lawn is a bridge across the stream, trellis-work on one side, crumbling brick on the other. Gates lead into the adjacent fields. The person standing by the bridge, unable to see either an entrance or a gateway, is the loser of the Game; the person standing on the gravel, a bunch of keys in one hand, and unable to see either an intruder on the bridge or a cloud in the sky, is the winner.

The Big House. Five bays with slightly projecting wings; a substantial pedimented white doorway at the rear, and a larger one with stone pillars and a curving double staircase at the front. The usual circular sweep of gravel. Out of sight, on the roadway, the usual wrought-iron gate with crested eagles. Deer in the park, an artificial lake created from the stream at the foot of the slope, and from the rear doorway, a view southwards across the estuary and towards the open sea. It is this that gives logic to the position of the house, the illusion of ownership.

The Quarries. This Piece can best be seen as a negative landscape, gouged out of the surface of the Board. Obviously this spoils the appearance of the Game and give to the Quarries their invariably negative associations. You would sometimes think that there is no stopping the expansion of the Quarries. Even now, they have begun to bite into a size-able portion of the landscape that once belonged to the Big House. However, each Player should understand that, without such damage being inflicted, there might be no Game at all, since it is on the strength of the sale of wood-chippings, sawdust, sand-ballast, gravel and clinker that the survival of the other Pieces, perhaps even of the Pink Pagoda itself, depends. These holes in the ground are therefore like the visible foundations of the Game, strengthening the fabric of the Board even as they dig into it once more. And it is also true that when the Quarries have finally ravaged the entire Board, what will be left will not be a multitude of lifeless craters, but of thriving lakes – the land will have been returned to water, and the Game given back to the birds (who, as will shortly be seen, may or may not be true Players).

The Burned-out Church. Here is a Piece of genuine mystery. There was the time when the present cottages and the inn grew up around it, and it was renovated with a nicely balustraded gallery. A more distant time when it first stood, new and admired, and a long period of time when it wore itself well down into the minds of those living nearby. There was the time of the fire, and the farthest time of all when nothing stood in the place of the Church but a mound, and a landscape hardly recognizable.

The good part of it is the floor where the black and terra-cotta glaze on the tiles – doubly fired – still holds. Some of the stonework is delicately, indelibly pink from the blaze. It is worth remembering this when the pinkness of the Pink Pagoda becomes intolerably sweet. The Church was burned down, so the local Fire Inspector reported, in the 1960s from an unknown source. It seems to have started close to the altar (where someone still comes every week to place flowers), even though the great fifteenth-century door was securely locked at the time. Local teenagers ob-serve their deconsecrated rites in the former vestry, and litter the floor with dog-ends and Durex.

The Game Wood. Rather than being buildings in a landscape, the Game Wood is a landscape with attendant buildings of wood and mesh covers provided for the Birds. Barbed wire marks the limits of the Wood, and there is a path around the perimeter fence. The whole thing, of course, is open to the sky. But this does nothing to reduce the absolute sense of territory when something emerald-green and brown struts shrieking on to the path, or something heavy, compact and mottled rises effortfully into the trees. The dense plantation is not meant for human Players, it is intended for the Birds – a piece of nature carved out and intensified by men for the sake of the Birds. If only the Birds knew the meaning of their privilege. Because the Game Wood that is theirs can, and inevitably will, as suddenly belong to a noise of muffled blasting that sounds from within, and the orange droppings of cartridge-cases that lie amongst the dead leaves.

Home. In most games Home is the place of safety or neutrality. In the Game of the Pink Pagoda they know better. Home is the last Piece and the place of last resort. Why go to the trouble of getting the Board out at all if you wish only to be at Home? By all means stoke the fire, plump the cushions, make yourself a corner in the candlelight, pour a second whisky. But as soon as you begin to play the Game – as soon as you begin to think to yourself, Now I am comfortable what shall I do next? Shall I perhaps suggest the Game of the Pink Pagoda? – you are announcing to yourself your own restlessness. And that is why there has to be the Pink Pagoda, and why Home is there for the defeated. We are all defeated when the Game is over. But in the meantime this desire for novelty, what is it but the longing for another Home, perhaps for that first Home? But in any case for place and time and identity, all to be renewed in an intricate pattern of moves.

These are the main Pieces in the Game. You will already have noticed others: the River Estuary, the Island, the Village and the Village Inn. You will have been able to guess the existence of others: the Ballast Quay, the Home Farm, the Stables, the New Church. It is a Game where the background decoration of the Board is more than usually indistinguishable from the Pieces designed to stand on it. At its farthest edges the Board merges into sea and cloud and rocks that come and go with the movements of the tide. The noise you hear is the breaking of waves and not on this shore only. What you had thought was a flat Board in fact shares the curvature of the earth. Its scale is the same as the earth's. Bear this in mind: it is not going to be like other board games.

The Players

You. The Player. It is your move that opens play. Weary as they are, the other Players turn from whatever they were up to once they hear that you have had your first move. Hauling themselves out of the hammock in the watergarden, or away from a little light wood-chopping, or from their desks, like sleepwalkers they foregather. But this is the limit of your power. From now on the other Players are only intent upon your defeat. Playing by their own rules, even infringing rules that they themselves have only just made up, they enter into secret alliances or take advantage of the revised Rules of Identity (the rules which state that nobody need be what they seem to be, even to the extent of their existence in time and space). And all this for the sake of preventing you from concluding what you have begun.

You do have one power, however, which the other Players do not possess, the power not only to alter or conceal your identity, but to start out as any number of different things. You can be the Solitary Walker, the Wanderer, the Loafer, the Questing Knight, the Penitent Pilgrim, the Hermit, the Groundling, the Foundling, the Founder of Cities, the Fool, the Younger Brother, the Yearning Lover, the Sailor Back from the Sea, the Seer, the Queer, the Pioneer, the

Lion-hearted Battler, the Left-handed Bowler, the Fat Controller, the Swashbuckler, the Suspect Butler, the Baddie, the Lad, the Jack, the Pawn, Mr Fun the Faker, the Joker, the Poor Potsherd, the Patch, the Pious Shepherd, the First Watch, the Wretch, the Last Man Left Alive, the Little Orphan-child, the King of the Wild, the King of Kings, the Keeper of the Ring, the Thing.

The Dog. This is an optional Player, and unusual in that it is permitted to accompany you throughout the Game. Like the Game Wood and Birds, the Dog is also there to bring an illusion of the wild into a Game otherwise entirely given over to the hideous regulations, and the equally hideous repudiations, of civility.

The Owner of the Big House. The Player of the highest face-value, bar one. Disinclined these days to move very much, and consequently of lower practical value than his official worth might suggest. His main strength is not so much his knowledge of the Rules (he is inclined to forget them), or any inclination to bend them (a concept that he neither can nor needs to understand), but that he is in touch with the very men who make the rules, and with the paraphernalia of underlings who keep them polished and working. When he moves, he moves amongst such people, addresses them by their Christian names (probably went to the damn christening himself), and is addressed by them in turn with a deferential familiarity. When the need arises in the Game, he may be known as Sir Henry Vestibule, King Henry the Numberless, as Lord Vestibule and his late wife, the Earl of Vestibule, sir Henri de Vestibule, or as the Last of the Vestibules, Vestibulum Tyrannus, Gentleman rather than Player.

He did his stint in the Commons after soldiering, married well, and now surveys his estate with ease through the good offices of a hired surveyor, serves on the Board for one thing or another, attaches his moniker to a variety of cases, usually on advice, opens fêtes, knows how to make an entrance still, despite his legs, winters in the Canaries, finds words a problem when they disappear, and confuses his secretary with his wife.

There is hardly a move on the Board the Owner cannot make if he chooses to, but he bides his time, or is it that he is past caring, hating the world as he finds it whenever it finds him, hating Germans like the plague and still suspicious of the Jews – and having no more than a perfunctory sense (inherited like everything else) of the world to come. He in turn is hated by his eldest daughter for everything he represents, and cannot come across her when in drink without his fist involuntarily clenching and a deep growl confusing his speech, remembering so well the time when his large fingers could grasp around her narrow thigh and she wore plaits – grasp around her thigh and she would wriggle – and knowing himself to be an upholder of the decent ways. From his chair by the window, from which he hardly ever moves, he cannot see the Pink Pagoda, but hears more clearly than any current conversation the voices of his father or his grandfather lamenting its sale, and remembers voices raised in fury better than he remembers the pathway there. Damned stupidest thing I ever did, he is given to saying, and thumps the little table by his side, as if it were he himself that had done it, and they assume he means the Pink Pagoda.

The Owner of the Quarries. A versatile and useful Player, a cheerful, cocksure, pugnacious, thieving fellow. Call me Lobby, squire, Harry Lobby, and the pleasure's all mine. He's installed his brother as manager, and a cousin runs the hauliers he employs. His wife's sister married the Borough Planner, and there's a nephew on the local paper. A close-knit family, all sewn up, and thick as thieves. He brakes hard and late on the gravel by the site hut in one of his three cars, and whistles as he jingles change, walking round the perimeter. He periodically gets done for speeding, beds his secretary as often as his wife, and calls his men by their first names. He hates with equal force a man who is idle, which includes one who joins a union, and who won't laugh at a joke about niggers, coming up as he did from scratch, though saying very little about the way he did it, and only mentioning End Green Tech or 159 End Green Lane to make a point. He likes equally a good laugh, a good meal well served, the smell inside a new car, and more than anything he dotes on a white poodle bitch named Sally.

It will become obvious that there are versions of the Game in which these two Players, according to the Rules of Transferability or the Rule of Conspiracy (or according to the ancient Feudal Rules), can be made interchangeable, or in which a single Player can take on the value of both, and so be in a position to control all the major Pieces on the Board. Such Games, however, are rare. More often, the relationship between the two owners is played out under the Rules of Ambition. The Owner of the Big House will proclaim his aim of restoring the Pink Pagoda to its rightful place as part of the estate, and seeing off the little sandpit-digger, as he likes to call the Owner of the Quarries. His rival will freely admit in an otherwise empty bar that his long-term aim, regardless of financial common sense and in the face of cautious backers, is to buy up the Big House. For him, the Game of the Pink Pagoda is no more than a practice run for this bigger Game, and he has no intention of allowing the uninvoked but oppressive Rules of Class and Inheritance to forestall him.

The Beautiful Woman. What game would be complete without a Beautiful Woman? Everyone has her in their Game, and she may come to command as much as the Pink Pagoda itself the moves that are played according to the Rule of Desire (the rule which states that a Piece or Player in the Game is valuable in proportion to its power of making other Players play according to imaginary rules – the rule, therefore, under which no valid play can take place at all, but under which at least half the Players at any one time are likely to be playing). None of your nonsense about the temptress versus the goddess; the Beautiful Woman is of value in the Game only really when she combines the features of both, as she generally does.

The Friend. The Friend is of indeterminate age and sex, a good companion, especially over a bottle of wine, amusing and easy to talk to, unpredictable, honest, a little vain, gentle, and very critical of you, the Player. The Friend, like the Dog, may be an accomplice in the Game, keeping up with you and helping you through the tricky moments, suggesting moves and willing to talk over at length the plan that is formulating in your mind. Or the Friend, like any other player, may be one of your competitors, striving for the same goal as you. At an extreme, if the Rule of Deceit is invoked – the rule of extremes, by which all other rules become unworkable – the Friend may appear to fulfil all the functions of an accomplice, and be in fact the Betrayer, contemptuous of you and of all that your intimacy has allowed him to know of your likely moves and past failures. In this, as in all play between you and the Friend, the mysterious Rule of Desire is always touched upon and yet never openly invoked.

The Charred Body in the Burned-out Church. As the Fire Inspector and the Police Chief both agree in their reports, the Body remains unidentified, even its sex cannot be specified. Therefore with this player there is endless possibility for play according to the Rules of Transferability, according to which the identities of two Players may be conjoined, either as a wholesome means of increasing the pleasure of the Game, or in the more negative form of the rule of Conspiracy, as a secret arrangement between two Players for their mutual advantage. Despite its inactivity, the Body has great value under both these rules. It may serve simply as a barrier to the Pink Pagoda, placed on the Board at a judicious moment to cause another Player to lose several turns in fruitless thought, or as a warning of the dangers of presuming to enter. You can never quite remove from your mind the disturbing facts. The door was locked. There is still someone who brings flowers to the Church. The key was never found.

The Figure in the Grounds. The only Player directly associated with the Pink Pagoda to have an active role. All his moves are furtive, and he is only ever half seen on a pencil's width of lawn between two trees arranged just so, always about to go in hurriedly through an unseen doorway, and always with his back to you – assuming it to be a man. Perhaps it is the Occupant of the Pink Pagoda himself? Herself? Or is it one of the other Players who has got here before you, and is trying to throw you off the scent? But when nothing can be ruled out, why cannot the Figure in the Grounds be also the Body in the Burned-out Church, with only the Rule of Time altered to make it so? Why cannot he in fact be you, the Player, with the Game concluded according to the Psychic Trickery Endgame? – so that your entrance to the Pink Pagoda is forever halted by a mirror-like delusion in which one of you always steps out from the garden as the other walks into it, and both of you at the same pace. Who can tell, indeed, if the Figure in the Grounds, whom you saw entering an outhouse a moment ago, does not now appear behind you silently on the path from the opposite direction, and turn out to be . . .

The Man with the Gun? He is always silent, the Man with the Gun. He does not need many words. Usually he is employed by one of the two Owners, and his job is the protection of their Game Wood, their Quarries, their Big House, their Pink Pagoda. But there can be changes in the rules which suddenly give him an independent lease of life, or death, and there are coincidences of moves, which effectively put him outside the rules entirely, and turn him from Protector into Hunter. It's all very well saying, keep the Dog close by you at all times, but the Dog has his own Game to play, and in any case the Man with the Gun often has a Dog of his own, answerable only to his call, coming back again and again through the water, leaving your Dog pinned to the ground, feeble with admiration.

The Shooters. The Birds in the Game Wood look up in alarm. Don't worry, they are harmless enough. They only come to claim their bag, and then they'll be sharing lifts home. They may be here at the invitation of the Owner of the Quarries, or as old friends up at the Big House. Like any Player whose interest in the Game is marginal, their real importance lies in the way they can be used by other Players to distort or delay the progress of play.

The Three Old Men and the Boy. These are the Shooters in another, more permanent, guise. Like them, they have the value of only one Player in all known versions of the Game. Their ambit, however, is wider than that of the Shooters, and the Rules of Transferability freely apply to their appearances on the Board. They turn up anywhere. When you meet them you always give them the time of day. They are usually in ones or twos along the paths over-looking the Estuary. They all talk with the same thoughtful creak and yawn, chewing over the same pleasant clichés. The boy hangs back fiddling at the branches, looking at you through screwed-up eyes. He barely speaks a word, and when he does it is with a stammer. They seem to pose no threat to the progress of your Game, unless it is that as they speak (about the state of the tide or the state of the nation, the upkeep of the paths and the downpour of last night, about the sighting of a kingfisher along the ditches – the first since the heavy winter of two years before – or the sit-ing of a new estate across the meadows) their eyes do in-deed glance upwards to catch the pre-arranged signal from a figure in the distance, and they will claim their fiver later at the Village Inn for a job well done that you hardly knew was being done at all.

The Occupant. This Player is not to be confused with the Owners of the Big House and Quarries. The Occupant is the Occupant of the Pink Pagoda, and remember: it is occu-pancy and not ownership that counts. Like the King in chess, the Occupant is therefore the most valuable of all the Players, with almost magical properties. Like the King in chess, he cannot be taken. Unlike the King, however, he cannot take. He is, in fact, rarely seen in any version of the

Game. Play continues only in the mutual assurance that such a player does really exist. Is the Occupant then not like the King so much as like the Joker?

The Birds. Are they in the Game at all, or outside it, playing according to their own rules of exclusion and possession? There are too many of them for us to know how they might participate in any Game. Should they all be given the value of a single Player? Or divided into groups: the game birds in the Game Wood, the river birds on the River Estuary, and the small birds everywhere? But what then of the gulls that come up from beyond the confines of the Board? What of the swans whose singing wing-gait as they pass can cause a Player to lose a succession of moves in admiration (you always feel the urge to hear its passage into silence)? What of the single kingfisher in the ditch? The single woodpecker, flashing red and green, in the pathway? What of the other birds who spring free from any groupings we contrive for them, so that there are always more Birds than the Game can contain?

Perhaps that is the point. Perhaps the commentary that the Birds offer is not one of criticism of our moves or our aims, or even the distant commentary of another Game played out according to rules beyond our understanding, but one that reminds the Players of our Game of a world of play beyond games, where the rules are neither broken nor obeyed, nor even ignored – but where play is endless and the players are inconscient of rules, circling in the air, and then as suddenly dropping down into a sideways gust, according to a rule of desire that they have neither adopted nor named. Without them, the Board would be unnaturally empty. Without them, the long moments between moves would be frighteningly quiet.

Although the Rules of the Game are here explained, the Players are never able to understand them, either before they play or even after their first Game. What this book does is to start from the basic Pieces and Players, and then to show them in action – which is to say, in their various guises – in a selection of Model Games, many of which are adapted from world-class matches.

A final word of warning: in recent years, since the worldwide popularity of the Game became established, a number of so-called aids have become available, promising to help participants to achieve greater preparedness for, and so greater satisfaction in, the Game. Remember: there is only one book that can give you authoritative information on the Game, and you are reading it. Nothing else will do, and you only play into the hands of unscrupulous merchants if you imagine that anything more than this straightforward guidance, coupled with your own skill, tenacity, imagination and experience, will ever advance you in the practice of the Game.

*The Game of
the Pink Pagoda*

1

The Pleasure Gambit

First, nothing. Then an Old Man made water: the stream feeding the large river, the large river feeding the sea, the sea the sky, and the sky feeding the secret springs out of which the first stream ran.

Then another Old Man pinched up the earth between his fingers, and made hill-tops from which the river could be seen, slopes descending to the river, and he filled in the gaps in his work with sandy beaches and mudflats, so that there was always room for argument between the water and the earth.

Then a third Old Man scattered life on the water and under it (birds and plants and fishes), and life on the earth and under it (grass, worms, insects and everything with feet), so that everything was occupied.

When they had finished, the three Old Men lay down to rest. And they began to talk in an idle way about why they had done all this from nothing. The first Old Man said, 'Surely we did it for pleasure, to make ourselves a toy.' The second Old Man answered, 'No, we did it to make ourselves a home, a place we could call our own.' But the third Old Man said, 'We did it for a sense of achievement, so that we could say, Look at what we have made, and so that we could feel pride in ourselves and respect for each other.'

But by this time the first Old Man was feeling bored with the argument, and he began to fiddle with some pretty pink stuff he had with him and gradually folded it into an odd little shape. 'See here,' he said, 'I will prove my point. I have made a Pink Pagoda, that is what I shall call it, and I shall set it down by the stream as a place of delight and pleasure, and I will put an Occupant in it to enjoy all the good things that belong there.' So he set down the Pink Pagoda beside the stream, and stocked it with fine wine and good food and good books and all the accoutrements of joy. And the Occupant lived in it in endless pleasure.

Then the second Old Man stood up and said, 'You have proved nothing. I will build a Big House on the top of the hill as a place of safety and repose, and I will give it to an Owner who will enjoy his rights in it for the whole of his life, and will die secure in the knowledge that it will pass to his children and to his children's children in perpetuity.' And he built the Big House and gave it, with all the necessary documentation and a sizeable staff, to the Owner, who lived there in some splendour.

Finally, the third Old Man stood up and said, 'I will show you both. I will dig Quarries out of the earth, and fill them with workers, and give it all to an Owner as a place of enterprise and profit, so that the Owner will make his living there and go home tired but proud in the evening.' And he dug the Quarries, giving them and a site-office and a bank loan and several sharp suits and ties to the Owner, who immediately started to dictate a letter.

The first Old Man then said, 'I grant that you have given your Owners some kind of pleasure, the satisfaction of ownership and the joy of achievement. But think what you have given them besides in anxiety and fatigue. Whereas I have given the Occupant of the Pink Pagoda pleasure pure and unalloyed. If you recognize the importance of pleasure, why mix it in with troubles?'

The second Old Man replied, 'On the contrary, you have given your Occupant a home, but no security. You have given him pleasure, but taken away from him the respect of his neighbours.'

The third Old Man said, 'Neither of you is right. The

4

pleasure that the Owner of the Quarries takes from his work is the pleasure of something known inch by inch, something built up hour after hour. Whereas the Owner of the Big House simply sits inside something spacious, something which cannot fail, and leaves it to others to make it work. As for the Occupant of the Pink Pagoda, his pleasures are so idle that he hardly notices their existence. His eyes are too bleary from fine claret to read his beautifully printed first editions. The Mozart is turned up so loud that he cannot hear birdsong in the garden. He may be envied by some of his neighbours, but most of them despise him. And even he finds the dangers of boredom so threatening that he has begun to build up a collection of antiquarian maps, glancing through catalogues and telephoning agents. What is more, his self-indulgence will almost certainly bring him to an early grave.'

And he was right. The Occupant of the Pink Pagoda died comparatively young and alone. A few friends came up from London for the funeral – gallery-owners, wine-merchants, gossips and critics – but most were, as the Occupant had been, too listless to bother. His affairs were left in an incomprehensible confusion. The books and maps were auctioned, the wine-cellar was bought up cheaply by a local dealer. It seemed inevitable that the Pink Pagoda would fall into a state of disrepair. There was no family, and nothing had been done to secure its future. Even a manuscript on local topography and customs, at which the Occupant had occasionally worked over many years, was in no state to be published as it stood.

But it was not entirely different for the Owner of the Big House. He was older when he died. Horses were his pleasure and brandy was his vice, and a drunken fall from his favourite six-year-old roan was what killed him. His greater age had done little more than give him time to conclude that the world to which he thought he belonged had passed away, and that of his heirs none was worthy or willing to take up the estate which would survive. His wife, whom he had not loved for thirty years, lived on, and much of the value of the property was eaten up in the ensuing years in fruitless litigation between her and the hated children. To have one thing he could rely on, he made provision in his will for a monument to be erected to his memory in the local church, and for the endowment of the church with generous funds. It was a gesture of defiance against the irreligion and disrespect of the world at large, against the family who called him a mule and the local people who called him a parasite. The executors, his sons, moved as slowly as they could to do anything at all about the setting up of such an ugly mock-Gothic folly. Even the rector, fashionably mindful of local feeling against it, temporized. So that it was barely in place, and the detailed carving only just begun, when the church was burned down in a mysterious fire.

After several years of spectacular expansion, the Owner of the Quarries was ordered by a specialist to take things easy. He entrusted more than he thought wise to junior partners and managers, and financial failure followed. This coincided with his wife leaving him – for God's sake – for a former friend, a schoolmaster, because, she said, she needed someone who would show her affection. For two years, he was laid low by all this, but then suddenly sprang up and began to invest in a local car-hire firm. A year later, he had bought out the original owners, merged with a second company, and was back on top. Much of the business was done from home, which gratified his doctors, and enabled his estranged children to come for embarrassing weekends of silent and extravagant shopping expeditions. Some people said he was overdoing it again, others that he needed a good woman. He turned his back on doctors, friends and women alike, and put all his energy and too much of his ingenuity into the firm. A local reporter, who bore him a grudge from way back, began to enquire discreetly into the business, noticed a pattern of inconsistencies in the log-books of some of the cars, and handed his researches over to the police. A car disappeared from the fleet one evening, and six days later a farmer found the Owner's body, his skull shot open, in a field adjacent to the old Quarries.

Each life has its pain and failure. Each place you inhabit has its poisoned well. It is perhaps time we need above all, time to stop drawing at the well, and to sit by it instead, imagining ways of getting our water from another source. The well itself is too deep for its waters to be easily purified, except in our imaginations.

In this Game, because it is a game, pastimes and imagination are given pride of place. It is these along with pleasure and refreshment that come first. You will have noticed that the three Old Men, whatever their disagreements, are much inclined to rest, and that their disagreements only take shape when they are resting, as a form of relaxation. As the first Old Man said, it is pleasure of a kind that everyone is after, the two Owners as much as the Occupant of the Pink Pagoda. But the pursuit of pleasure has dangers of its own – let that be clear. In the Game of the Pink Pagoda, all we can say is that game-playing and delight, horse-riding and holidays, fantasies and weekends, take on an importance across the Board, which they may not usually have. From the viewpoint of the Game, work and ownership themselves appear like games. Doubtless, these things are told differently in the stories that come from the Big House and the Quarries. Supposing that in those places they have time for stories.

7

2

The Play of Godly Desire

It was the time before the Board was inhabited by Pieces
or by Players, and there were only powers that lived above
the Board where the clouds are. Chief of the powers was
Hoos, and where his voice could not be heard was ruled
by the Power of Darkness, Quari. Between them, they
ruled everything, and their voices were the rules. But
between them, there was also a ceaseless enmity.

Hoos loved a woman. This was always happening, and
Hoos's queen was very jealous. This woman was beautiful,
as pale as the clouds, and as fresh in the ways of love.
Hoos built for her a pale hiding-place on the surface of the
Board, where a fresh stream ran and flowers were. The
woman lived there, and Hoos invited her in secret whenever he could.

But his jealous queen discovered the truth. Perhaps it
was Quari who told her to make mischief. In any case, the
Queen went to Quari to help her.

'Be careful,' said Quari, who was really a cowardly
power. 'You know the strength of the King. You know he
cannot be touched.'

'Do nothing to him,' said the Queen. 'Kill her, she is a
mortal. Kill her, so that he may find his way back to me.'

Hoos came to the woman's hiding-place, full of his love
for her. She looked at him with many blushes, and took
off her white robe. Hoos stood before her naked also, the
tawny man and the blushing woman.

Quari came covered in darkness to the spot where the
lovers met, and waited in the garden listening for voices.

Presently he heard the murmur of their love-making rise above the murmur of the stream, and he came to a window.

Was Quari transfixed by the gentle beauty of what he saw, unknown to him in the dark world from which he came, so that he stood there quivering with delight, his spear useless?

Some say so. They say that the love-making of Hoos and the woman was sweet and long, and that the pale colour of the place where they lay took on the colour of the woman's blushes, or of the virgin-blood she shed, so that it was transformed from white to pink. They say that Hoos in his happiness crested the building with a high roof to mark it out. And they say that all the people of the earth came first from the love between Hoos and the woman, between a power and a mortal being. They add that Quari returned to the Queen empty-handed, and that she in her anger made darkness forever rule over the actions of lovers.

But others say that Quari was excited both by desire and by hatred as he stood by the window; that he rushed in where Hoos and the woman lay, and pierced her with his spear, delighted to see his weapon enter her pale skin and sink it under the weight of Hoos's body. They say that the pagoda changed its colour through the spilling of her innocent blood, and that Hoos built up its roof as a grave-stone to the woman. They say the teeming people of the earth sprang first from the drops of the woman's blood as they touched the soil and mingled themselves with its dust. And they say that Quari returned to the Queen triumphant, that she took him for her king, and that Hoos to this day wanders the world in despair, seeking in vain for a love that is pure and strong and filled with brightness.

The people of the earth know both these stories, and at different times believe each of them to be true. They think that if they could return to the garden of the pink pagoda they would know how it gained its colour and its shape, and whether in the end it is pleasure that is triumphant, and the darkness and concealment at its edges are only

9

the vengeance of those who live without pleasure, or whether it is death that triumphs, and that all pleasures go hand-in-hand with the realm of darkness and perversity.

3

War Games

There were in later times two kings in the land, Loggia and Lobi, fierce men and famous for their victories. Before their coming the whole land had been ruled by the Queen of the Pink Pagoda, and the water from the river, the fruit from the trees, the building stone and the deer meat, had been shared by all in peace. After their coming all this was taken away. They came from outside, the two kings, from the abandoned wreckages of other lands – Boards where the Game had gone out of control – and they brought their greed and ferocity to a place where these were unknown. That at least is how the story was told by the subjects of the Queen, for who would want to claim such men as belonging to their own kind?

Loggia came first from the north, and his warriors took the high land above the river. The people tried to fight, but it was hopeless. Loggia's men could see them coming from so far afield that they had the leisure to prepare cruel and intricate deaths for those who came. There were bodies never again found for burial, and anonymous limbs and blood-clotted handfuls of hair which the mourners quarrelled over. The Queen's eldest son, who had led the fighting, was returned to her spiked through on a costly pewter bier, like roasted meat served up at a feast. And so the high land was taken and Loggia built a fine castle there to defend it for all time.

Lobi's coming was more secret. He came from the west and made his first encampment on the far side of the river.

Then he sent spies amongst the armies of the Queen and of Loggia, and sowed rumours amongst them, that the army of Loggia was preparing a final assault on the Pink Pagoda and that the army of the Queen was plotting a last desperate rebellion against the enemy to the north. The Queen's army was told to expect Loggia's men at any time. Loggia's men were told that the Queen's army planned a night-time assault on such-and-such a date. On the night in question Lobi moved his army silently across the river in their canoes. The few of the Queen's army who were guarding the west were quietly slaughtered from behind with wires. Then at a given signal some of Lobi's men set fire to the houses of the people in the valley. Loggia's lookouts were confused and took this as the beginning of the rebellion. The Queen's lookouts were still more confused and did not know whether to defend their homes or to face the onslaught that now came to them from the hills. Lobi's men had little more to do than to move amongst the two opposing armies creating confusion. They set fire to the church where some of the Queen's people had gathered for safety, and picked them off one by one as they came screaming from the flames. Most of Lobi's army spent the night digging themselves in at a point to the south, so that by morning they were in a position to force Loggia's army to a retreat. Between the two armies, the Queen's people and her inexperienced forces were bewildered, and half their numbers destroyed. Her two remaining sons went each to sue for peace with the leaders of the opposing forces. But they were taken as hostages; by Loggia because he suspected the Queen's men of betrayal, and by Lobi because he foresaw the possibility of future rebellion. Their swollen and tortured corpses were returned to the Queen as a warning, and as a needless sign of her total defeat. By the following evening Lobi had secured his position in the low lands by the river, and over the months he built his trenches into an intricate underground network of tunnels and chambers, so that his fortress below ground was finally as impregnable as Loggia's above the ground.

It was in this way that the Queen of the Pink Pagoda became the ruler of a depleted and frightened people, who lived in the daily knowledge that the Pink Pagoda itself was the only prize left to be disputed between the two great armies of Loggia and Lobi, and that it must certainly become the object of yet another battle in the future – for it was inevitable that the king of the castle and the king of the trenches would fight. The desperate remnant of the Queen's people – the old or young, widows and mothers, mostly – huddled about their queen so that the Pink Pagoda became a kind of curious hostel, or a convent really, given the disproportionate numbers of women amongst them, for those who dared not return to their homes.

The mourning Queen reserved a small suite of rooms to herself, and did what she could to help. But inside herself she became embittered towards the Pink Pagoda and towards her own glamorous beauty. They were things that should only have been admired and valued from a distance, not used in these ways, and they got in the way when they were put to use – so that there was a hush of admiration from her people when the Queen bent on her knees to scrub the floors, or sat down to talk at a bedside, just as there was a tiptoeing respect for the fabric of the Pink Pagoda. The Queen became almost glad to see the place degraded by the attrition of trolleys and of too many people, and wished that grief and fatigue and despair could have marked themselves more visibly on her own face. From the time that the bodies of her sons had been brought to her, skewered and bruised, when she had felt pass through her own body the shock of seeing so much cruelty and of feeling so much love – and had been unable to grasp these two extremes within herself, or see how they could be held together within the soul of a single species, such cruelty and such love – from that moment, she had come to despise the inadequacy of a beauty that

13

holds itself from others, that is beautiful only by being held apart, and had come to hate every whisper of personal approbation from those around her, and every gesture of respect shown towards her regal bearing or towards the fine panelling of the pagoda's walls. She felt that now was a time to live in rags, in a stinking hut, with the staring passive eyes of the defeated. She maintained her elegance and courtesy only because she knew no other way, and because it acted as some kind of solder for her broken people, whom she had no right to force into the same intimacy with their own despair as she had come to feel.

When the attack came it did so with the relief and terror of a lightning-storm after days of increasing pressure. The plans for evacuation were well worked out. The Queen was ushered swiftly but respectfully down through the same pathways as her people into a circle of yew trees, shaded from the sunlight, where the soft ground was sucked free of other life by the thriving yews, and which had been the planned refuge of the people ever since the great defeat. It was a place with a reputation for sanctity, and once the trail had been covered over by the last to leave it was a place cut off from the world outside. Here they gathered, and their scarred imaginations all too easily amplified the muffled thuds and cries they heard into the din of a terrible battle. Someone claimed to have seen the Pink Pagoda ablaze. No one for a moment imagined that it would survive intact.

It was not clear from which side the battle had started, and it hardly mattered. From then on, there would be a respite in the noise for periods of a day or two together, times of tension for the people in the clearing who would imagine that the two kings had given up fighting each other and had come in search of them. But then the noises would be heard again, almost with relief, and new atrocities imagined by those who had known atrocity at close quarters. There was no reason why the fighting should ever stop, no reason why the small plot upon which

14

the Pink Pagoda stood should ever finally be won by either of the armies. There was every reason to think that the building would be entirely destroyed long before anyone could claim even a temporary victory, but no reason why that should put an end to the warfare. This meant, of course, that there would never come a time when the Queen could return in safety to the land outside the wood and re-establish life there with her people. Inside the clearing, the food would run out, winter would come, and there would not be enough strong men to chop firewood. The old and those already sick would be the first to die. The babies too. It was hard to believe that they could survive their first winter with even half their numbers intact.

In the corner of the clearing that was set apart for her use, the Queen foresaw the day when those that remained would inevitably come from their hiding-place and give themselves up to the appalling degradations that the soldiers of the two armies would inflict on them. They would be slaves in what had been their own land, and their only means of survival would be to learn the brutish ways of their masters. Perhaps in time there would be children born to the younger women whose fathers would be Loggia's or Lobi's men, but who would grow up with the knowledge of an earlier time and of a Pink Pagoda impinging on their minds. Perhaps, as a result of this, some future generation would attempt to rebuild the Pink Pagoda they had heard so much about. It would only be a replica, of course, inexact in many details of its construction and even in its location. And, besides, what use was a Pink Pagoda by itself, without the old days that had been lived around it being lived once more? It would be an attempt to retrieve something that its builders could not really understand, an admission by them only that something had once been lost. Would this be better than to fall asleep under the yew trees, to let winter come, and to accept the sacred clearing as a place of burial? The part of the Queen's mind that had gone cold when she saw the steel thrust up through the body of one son, and the bloated skin on the faces of the others, was willing to accept an effortless defeat. But the part of her that was still Queen to her people knew that something had to be done, and incessantly planned new moves even as the hopeless days dragged on.

Why could there be no rescue? Why did you not come and save the Queen and her people, and restore the Pink Pagoda to its rightful inhabitants? Why do you choose to enter the Game only when the Pink Pagoda is a shadow of reality, belonging to virtual strangers, and there is nothing any longer of real value to be won?

4

The Winner's Tale

After the victories the sense of loss that comes now there is time to remember, even for the winners. The deaths of comrades, the long departure from home, the scarring of a landscape by the junk of war, the obliteration of yourself, your everyday self, in the harsh months of commitment to a cause. And now the loss of that commitment as well. The games that are played after a victory are games of greeting, games of mourning, games of celebration, games of boasting in pubs and telling the children, games of return. But on the way back everything is lost, so that it is you and not you that stands on the quayside, them and not them. There are memories you can never share, just as there are for them, memories that you would just as soon not own, and so in time forget. Cannonfire still thuds and does not thud in your stomach. A chunk of steel still burns and does not burn inside the stomach of him next to you who was your friend (whose fire was soon put out). For them, it is the remembered agony of every morning's post. The game of returning, then, is one in which you lose your way, and come at last to an unexpected place, a place that is no longer your home – if only because it has had to get used to the expectation of living without you.

What made you lose your way? It was first of all the mist coming down over the water, blanketing your eyes just as it reduced the land's edge to a smear that did not distinguish between the treacherous mud and the friendly mooring where the beach is smooth and the crabs come daily into the shallows, good to eat. They would not let you stop and wait for it to clear, your men, but sailed on blindly, hungry for home meats and the familiar bed.

Surely there were also powers against you even before you set sail, powers to whom the chant of a victory song is like a cry of derision, a score that must be settled. There must be gods who push men into doing things that the gods forbid, or who had singled you out, Lewis, perhaps for your moments of pride as a leader of men, perhaps for the grimness with which you faced the voyage home, standing against the merriment of your men, knowing it to be next to the loss of concentration which brings about a mishap. For it was you, Lewis, who saw the shadow rising from the shore and ordered a landing. At that moment you could see that a time on steady ground with dry clothes was needed to restore purpose to the men. So you jumped first off the prow and accepted the laughter, standing there up to your thighs in filth, as the laughter of relief. Once off the beach, you ordered the men into parties, one to unload, one to search out the shadowy building you had seen, and one as a hunting-party to bring back meat to the men.

You stayed to organize what should be taken off the ship before you went to inspect the building. You were doing stage by stage what you thought was best, and in fact you were weaving together the strands of a curse. There were only two men in the building, you had been told, an older and a younger. When you arrived, the boy lay oddly on the straw looking up through unfocused staring eyes. The other faced the wall a little way off. Both of them were tied. The men you had set over them as guards were exchanging smiles and glances. You asked them what had happened. You shouted the question twice, knowing from their bearing that these men were priests of the place (and you knew from childhood the price that was laid on sacrilege, even on sacrilege against alien gods), and guessing what your men had done, when there had hardly been time to do anything. You approached the boy, intend-

18

ing to show your peaceful intentions. He flinched away from you, fearing the worst, and behind you one of the men giggled. You swung round then, and in your fear and fury laid a blow against the man nearest you and ran outside, shouting to your men to stop the hunt, to extinguish the fire that was being built in the lee of the building, and to reload the ship.

The men were slow to understand, and slower still to carry out orders that ran so counter to their appetites. The prohibitions against sacrilege were nothing to them against the expectation of roasting pig meat. Events were now controlled by a clockwork more powerfully wound than anything you, Lewis, had at your command. The first pig was killed before the order to stop had reached the hunting-party. The sacred animal's squeal came up through the darkness just as the wind whipped round, and a gust sent sparks into the eaves of the sacred building. The fire quickly spread to the roof, and there was a madness of fire with the timbers falling in before even you, Lewis, had time to issue new orders. The holy place was sending in its demons against you in an army. The men began to understand your urgency now, and set the ship ready to sail in the briefest time. But your first order was to free the captive priests. The man you sent to do this job came back quickly saying that the flames were already too intense, that the men were lost. You had to accept the story as true, though in the instant in which you heard it, you imagined the old priest in his temple muttering words in a dark tongue to your messenger, words which added anger to his panic, so that the knife which should have been used to cut the ropes was used instead to stop his babble for ever, and then used in a fury of frustration against the whimpering boy. You imagined all the ways in which the curse upon you might have been multiplied and hardened, though all that was certain was that the two men had died, and that the fire by which they had died had consumed with it any witness to the truth.

19

The burning temple was an orange flag on the water as you steered the ship away. You did not blink or turn until the flag could be seen no more. You held yourself stiff in expectation of the coming doom. Already there was a rumour, growing to a certainty, that one of the youngsters in the hunting-party had not been counted back on board, and must therefore have been left to live or die in an alien and empty land.

Dawn brought some lessening of the mist and a feeble horizon of shoreline to navigate by. Then on the path by the water's edge, a woman. They had not seen a woman in all this grey, groaning, untender time, and now on the bank there was real woman-flesh, not just the remembered image of a wife or girl. Her arms lashed the air, her high voice was lost on the wind, and her grey dress was torn as she ran, with the birds scattering from their feeding-grounds across the water. The crew were watching, murmuring their desire, and some of them concluding that the woman needed their help – mixing their desire for a nightlong draught of sweet woman's honey-flesh with the desire to atone for the evil they had done, by coming to the aid of a lone and feeble stranger. You, Lewis, saw her too, and heard the murmuring rise on the ship. You smiled at the confusion of their desires, but you were grim in your knowledge that no curse was so easily redeemed, and that it would only be redoubled if the men were allowed ashore to seek their pleasure with a young, white-breasted woman.

Guided by your firm hand, Lewis, the ship sailed on into the bay. The men had lost sight of the woman, but now they saw the hulks of three, perhaps four, ships still being shattered between the rocks where the sea was heaviest at the farthest edge of the bay. Saw this, and saw ships' timbers strewing the sands all along the beach – and heard too above the waves the imploring tones of men's voices now, so that they scanned the shore more keenly and tried to make things out. Still closer in, and the crews from the shipwrecks could be made out in groups on the sand, pitiful creatures under the guard of other women – dressed like the first woman, who now came running to join them on the beach, still hallooing – standing there with axes, clubs and chains. Around a fire the reddened faces of more women were eating meat still dripping from the spit. Near them lay the hunched-over body of a sailor, clothes wildly torn around the midriff, where the blood was still fresh in the places from which the flesh had been cut. The ship seemed to lurch away from the shore at the same time as your crewmen's faces, Lewis, turned in pale horror as the understanding sank into them. But no understanding, no amount of staring, was sufficient. Here were fellow sailors, the victims of wreckage, and here was a company of beautiful women – both of them recognized by the crew in the most direct and deepest ways. But here were both these things turned into something else, turned by the foul trading of the women on men's pity for their cries into their opposites – into perverse butchers, and into creatures beyond the reach of pity. It was you, Lewis, who forced the ship around, almost by your will-power alone, ignoring the mute appeal of the men on the beach, just as you had ignored the woman's cries, certain in your heart that if there was a curse laid on you, it came from what had already happened and not from what you now refused to do.

All were subdued on board the ship, but a week of clear sailing brought the crew back into good spirits, so that by the end of it they were singing once again the songs of their battles, and adding the verses that were to become the song of the voyage. There was the night when the man who had been the intended rescuer of the two priests disappeared, and was presumed to have fallen or to have thrown himself overboard. But his morose presence, as it had become, was not greatly missed. A few more days and nights of steady progress, and then out of the darkness, unremarked until it was all around them, the ship was

21

caught in a net. A net that was stronger than a net and unyielding, so that it was the ship itself that was forced to yield on the moving waters. The creaking as its timbers tore themselves apart was like a noise of human anguish. In the darkness, you, Lewis, gave the order to abandon ship, and the men swam in fear for the shore, a few lucky ones finding that they could pick their way to land across the solid network within which the ship was held. Your men knew what a storm was and how to face it, but this static self-destruction in the darkness left them and you unnerved and defeated.

Daylight showed you the skeleton of your ship, almost mocking you with the completeness of an outline that had nothing solid in it at all. You looked over the almost total destruction, and at the vicious thing of piers and crossbars, with chains and wires disappearing inland – some giant's fishing-net, or so it seemed – in which the ship had become entangled. Once again, you found yourself dividing up the crew, against your oldest principles. One small party to go inland in the search for fresh timber. The rest to stay with the ship under the command of your trusted lieutenant. You, Lewis, would lead the inland party.

A little way in on the path, and the giant's fist first struck out, taking two of the men by the backs of their skulls and leaving them stone-cold dead in a minute. Then there were other fists, two, three, four, and only you, Lewis, were left, zigzagging through the thorn-bushes as fast as you could, as low as possible, until the roaring sound had died away. In the undergrowth at the edge of a clearing you squatted to recover breath, and then began to make out the details of what seemed to be the giant's nesting-ground – several large pits dug out of the space between the surrounding trees. What you had taken for fists were in fact weapons, guided by no visible hand, that moved in and out of the pits and along the level ground at rapid speed. Then there were none, and all you could see was the solitary figure of a small grey man standing on a sandy terrace towards the bottom of the nearest pit. A shadowing rush of vengeance and rage left you no time to think. The man was clearly in the giant's protection, and allowed by him to enter the heart of his territory unmolested, just as he allowed the giant to prey on other men. You hurtled headlong, like a catapult fired, down the steep side of the pit, so fast that the man had only time to raise his eyes and turn about to see the large flat stone you had grasped in your headlong rush come crashing down upon his face, and to hear your battle yell of terror issuing from a cavernous mouth. Why did you go on hitting him after he had fallen? Was it for the sake of those whom the giant had felled? Was it for the sake of every barrier in the way of getting home, and for those who would never get home? Or was it that some battlefield hunger, which could not be satisfied by the old ways of caution and cunning, was now alive in you and needed its fill of prey? You found the questions on the fringes of your mind, as you came to yourself again, crouching crowlike over the body. Then you knew that you had added another notch to the tally that accounted for your curse, and you wept.

When you were ready to search again for timber, you saw that the wood beyond the farthest pit had the best trees, broad and straight for planking. You found your way around the edge of the clearing, through thick undergrowth, keeping low to avoid any of the giant's weapons that might be loosed upon you. Then, when you were nearing your goal, the sharp point of a spear against your spine told you to stand up slowly, to raise your arms, and to wait. You were prodded out into the open where the pits were, with your mind racing ahead and trying to plan. Someone had seen you kill the man in the pit? You were being taken for trial? Or to a place of execution? Or to where the rest of your men had already been taken by these unknown creatures, and were beyond rescue, with you the sole fugitive awaiting capture? At one feverish moment you even thought that perhaps the whole homeward journey had been miraculously shortened, and that you would walk out of the shadows of the wood to find yourself in your wife's sweet arms and by the remembered fireside. There was a last push from the spear point that jerked you into the sunlight, and then the sound of running footsteps. You turned to see a figure darting between the trees back into the woods. The man with the spear appeared himself to be escaping, and to have left you free.

Instinct told you the quickest way back to your ship. But at the rim of the first pit you came to, a sight confronted you which was at first horrifying, then inviting, then again disturbing, and finally enthralling. Rising above the pit's edge, the giant face of a giant man met your gaze, and as the face moved, imploring your attention, and a giant hand beckoned, entreating you courteously to follow, so it became clear that there were three faces, three giant heads on a single body – and each face was gentler than the face you had seen first, each was the face of an old wise man, and not at all an object of horror. If this was the giant of the pits, the giant of the net, then it seemed as if he had lost control of the weapons in his power. The faces were serene, but also weary faces, like those of prophets or priests who have spent a lifetime telling their fellows things they did not care to hear. Of course, their size alone – faces as tall as your entire body, Lewis – made them also monstrous, but still you followed, and followed gladly, as if the pathway down into the pit was a path towards wisdom.

At the bottom of the pit you turned a corner and came upon several terraces in the sand, layer upon layer above and below where you stood. Here the giant left you, Lewis, but you hardly noticed his departure, gazing instead on the faces of those standing looking back across at you. You saw the face of your great friend, killed beside you in battle; the faces of many comrades, victims of war or of the voyage you had undertaken. You saw the face of the youngster from the hunting-party, and his lips smiled in

24

welcome when your eyes met. There was your father, alive when you had left home for the war; the face of your young cousin, who died before manhood came. And there, in a single group, the two priests from the burning temple, and the crewman you had supposed to be their murderer. These, too, smiling at you as their eyes met yours – even, you suddenly noticed, the face of the small man in the pit, whose eyes you had only seen before as two pinpricks of terror – all of them smiling, so that it seemed as if you had been brought there for their benefit rather than for yours. There were forgiveness and a blessing in every pair of eyes, even in the eyes it most troubled your conscience to meet again. It was as if they were forgiving you, Lewis, having been able to forgive themselves, lifting the weight of the curse from you and wishing you well. It was as if they had gathered there for the pleasure of seeing a true victor, a real hero. And yet it was also as if they welcomed you amongst them before your time. Certainly, they made their own condition seem most welcome. Then, before you could ask them what they intended, or say any of the hundred things that coursed through your mind, they turned away from you, and in a body disappeared along their terraces and out of sight, leaving you alone to climb back to the pit's rim and level ground.

There you felt your human powers return. You were not in any way surprised to find stacks of perfect timber, cut and ready, laid on the ground at your feet. You accepted the gift without suspicion or question, and went back to the shore to announce the good news to your men. They took it in more slowly than you had expected, and even as they obeyed your orders to carry the timber to the ship and to begin repairs, they began to look upon you strangely, as one who has journeyed too far and forgotten the simple homely knowledge of the tired warrior. They accepted your orders to re-launch the ship, but they did not listen to what you told them about the pit without glancing amongst themselves and shaking their heads. One night your second-in-command came to you and announced that he was taking charge. They put you in a boat. It was done regretfully, even respectfully – some of the men were weeping – but the action was as decisive as your example had always taught them to be. You did not protest. They gave you food and water, but no oars, and the new leader called you Captain as he pushed the boat clear.

It was still dark when the weather changed. You knew the signals, Lewis, the increasing humidity in the air and the picking up of the surface of the water. But there was nothing you either could or wanted to do in the face of the coming storm, any more than in the face of your crew's mutiny. When it came, increasing in force beyond each of its successive climaxes, you knew that the ship could not outlast the storm. The smiling faces in the pit came into your mind as you thought of each of your men, swirling water for a final time above the balls of their horrorstruck eyes, and you thought of their deaths with no satisfaction, but with a pity for how unsuited such fierce and fickle men were to the placid world of the pit.

The same storm took up your little boat and brought it unresisting on to a gentler shore. It was the daughter of the king who found you, salved your wounds and clothed your body. The king's men were sent for, and you were immediately imprisoned in the palace. The absurd law in that country was that all strangers were spies and merited execution. As they wrangled over you, the king's daughter came to where you were and pestered you with sweetmeats and curious dishes of drink, when all you wanted to do was rest. She interceded with the king on your behalf. She conspired with the prison-guard. And when the former failed, and the date for execution was set, she turned to the latter, and begging a single kiss, she smuggled you back to the shore one night, furnished your little boat with oars and more of her silly food – and so restored to you the gifts of life and freedom you valued now no more than her delicacies.

You were so tired, Lewis, tired beyond sleeping. The oars were left in the bottom of the boat. You raised your eyes only once when the unmistakable wreckage of your former ship came into view, smashed against the rocks of an unfriendly coast in the storm, as you had guessed it would be. There was a tune in your head, that was all, the melody of the crewmen's song, the song of the voyage. But that song had too many verses now, and you were the only singer. With that tune in your head, you survived another lesser storm which capsized the boat, and left you naked, clinging to the back of the boat in the baking sun. The efforts you made to save your skin when the storm came, minimal and habitual though they were – as if saving your life was a daily task like making a bed – were curious in the face of the careless exhaustion which overtook you when the storm was past. You lay there on your upturned boat laughing, laughing in all humility at the forces that kept you from death, with the tune still running in your head. What was it they wanted from you? Was the curse they had laid upon you this ceaseless chorus of disasters? – so that you, Lewis, the victor, were now alone, your crew were dead, your ship was lost, your body was unclothed, and you were at the mercy of the currents. Or was the real curse that you, who were the only one to know the sweetness of death, you alone were the one who could not die?

You must have laughed yourself asleep. You woke with a dog's snout prodding affectionately at your face and found yourself on an empty beach, where the outlet of a stream beckoned you inland. Oblivious of your nakedness you strode along the foreshore and began to follow the stream. All the time the dog played and followed at your side, as if it were pleased to have its master home. You found yourself in time facing the entrance of a small pink-painted pleasure-house, apparently deserted and with the door wide open. You went inside and up the stairs, and in the first room you came to you found laid out a perfect

27

suit of clothes. Before dressing, you bathed, and then came downstairs again to find drink and plates of food laid out, all perfectly suited to your taste, as if everything had been waiting for your arrival. You ate, and glanced into the garden where the dog was playing, but it was the comfort of the silken bed-sheets that invited you. You went upstairs to sleep.

You have been here for a good while now. Your food, your clothes, your drink, are all prepared for you by invisible hands. They leave your favourite cocktails out at your preferred hour. Sometimes there is music playing from a hidden source. There are books to read in your own language. The garden is an ever-changing source of delight. There is the dog for company. This place is not your home, but there is little more that you could ask for after such striving. One human longing only remains unsatisfied, or seems to be. But even this is not certain, for more than once you have seen a shoulder turn a corner into a farther room, smelt a perfume in the air, or heard dying laughter. And more than once recently you have had the sensation, upon waking, of having awoken from a night of perfect sleep and of the most satisfying dreams, and noticed a crushing of the bedclothes next to you that was not made by your own body. You spend much of your time searching for this other occupant, if she is there. But you have yet to find her. You tell yourself, Lewis, that you have played across the entire Board, and it is time now to take your winnings and withdraw from the Game. But despite the perfect comfort, idleness and solitude of the place – each of which has its own pleasures – already you can feel inside yourself the urgings to know where such perfect beauty as you have known in your dreams might be found, or to know again the pleasures of home, with all their imperfections. At any time, either of these urgings might take its hold on you, and once again draw you towards the waters of the sea, re-awakening in you all the longings, the bottomless longings, of the voyager.

5

The Poor Boy and the Princess

Once a poor man sent his son to bargain for potatoes in the town. He gave him a sack, and the boy took his dog, and set off early in the morning.

As he passed by way of a stone-quarry, the dwarf who lived in the quarry saw him coming, and said to himself, 'Here is a fine-looking boy whose strength I could surely make use of.'

So he called out to the boy, 'Boy! I'll make a bargain with you. I'll turn your dog into a strong mule, and your sack into a good thick overall, if you will work for me for a day. Who knows, but you may find something rare and precious amongst the stones, and anything you find we will share fifty-fifty.'

But the boy said, 'No, I'll not dig for you, not for a mule nor an overall. I'm only on my way to fetch potatoes from the town.' And he went on his way.

Shortly afterwards he passed by way of a great castle, where the wizard who lived in the castle saw him coming, and said to himself, 'Here is a fine-looking boy whose grace I could surely make use of.'

So he called out to the boy, 'Boy! I'll make a bargain with you. I'll turn your dog into a sleek horse, and your sack into a suit of fine clothes, if you will work for me for a night. Who knows, but which of my guests might reward you greatly if you serve them well.'

But the boy said, 'No, I'll not serve for you, not for a horse nor a suit of clothes. I'm only on my way to fetch potatoes from the town.' And he went on his way.

But before he ever got to the town he passed alongside the garden of a pink pagoda, where a princess was playing with her friends. And the boy knew he had never seen, nor would ever see, so beautiful a creature as that princess, who seemed to float upon the ground as she danced and laughed and played. The boy stood gazing, and if he didn't fall in love with her right away, he did in the next five minutes. Sometimes the princess glanced at him, so that the boy's heart leapt and he stood forward as if about to speak to her. 'But,' he said to himself, 'what could I say to her? My accent is as rough as my clothes, my words as poor as my home. I could never come near her without her friends laughing at me, and if she were to come near me, they would laugh at her as well. It is unthinkable that she would ever love me.' And so the boy turned to go away, but not without one last look of longing into the garden of the pink pagoda. And there the princess stood all alone, her friends had gone inside, looking longingly back at the boy. But neither of them said a word.

Now, when the boy came to the turning into town he stopped and thought a good long while. And after he had thought, he returned the way he had come and came to the stone-quarry where the dwarf still sat. And he said to the dwarf, 'I'll make my bargain with you, if you're still willing. Turn my dog into a mule, and my sack into an overall, and I'll dig for you for a day.'

The dwarf leapt up and said, 'I knew you'd see the sense in this.' And he turned the dog into a mule, and the sack into an overall, and set the boy to work. All day long, in the heat of the sun, the boy dug stone from the quarry and fetched it up to the surface in baskets carried on the mule's back. And when he was almost done, at the end of the day, and so tired that his legs would hardly move beneath him and his arms hardly lift either pick or shovel, he found amongst the rocks a stone that glittered. And he took the rock to the dwarf, and the dwarf said it was gold. 'I knew,' said the dwarf, 'that you would bring me luck. Here's half for you and half for me.' And he handed the boy a bag of coins, and the boy went on his way.

The boy came to the great castle where the wizard still was. And he said to the wizard, 'I'll make my bargain with you if you're still willing. Turn this mule that was my dog into a sleek horse, and this overall that was my sack into a suit of clothes, and I'll serve you for a night.'

The wizard clapped his hands and said, 'Splendid, you're just in time for my dinner guests.' And he turned the mule into a horse, and the overall into a suit of clothes, and set the boy to work. All night long, tired as he was, the boy fetched and carried for the wizard's fine guests, and kept himself perfectly smart and perfectly polite however late it became and whatever the guests required him to do. And when he was almost done, and the dawn was breaking, and he was so tired that his legs would hardly move beneath him and his arms hardly carry another tray or bottle, he was stopped by one of the grandest of the wizard's grand guests, who looked at him closely and said, 'In all my life, I have never been so gracefully or promptly served. I would like you to accept this as a reward. And remember, wherever you go, if you deal as politely as you have dealt with me tonight you will never go wrong.' And he handed the boy a bag of coins, and the boy went on his way.

And he came to the pink pagoda finely dressed in his new clothes, riding on a sleek and shining horse, carrying the two bags of money that made him a rich man, and feeling perfectly confident about the way he spoke and what he would say to the beautiful princess. 'Like this,' he said to himself, 'no one will laugh at me. And if the princess found me worth a glance when I was the son of a poor man with only a dog and a sack, surely she will be able to love me now and marry me.'

But in all the magical changes that had been going on, some of the magic had spilled into the pink pagoda, and the princess herself had been turned into a bird – a pink

31

and pretty bird that flew about inside the garden, and perched on the tops of bushes and looked at the boy sideways through pink eyes as if it would speak. But all it could do was sing its pretty birdsong and fly about. The boy was beside himself with fury and grief, and in his anguish he tore his fine suit of clothes into shreds, set his sleek horse loose, and threw his bags of money to the ground. 'I want none of this,' he said, 'if the cost of it all is that she has been changed too.'

So the boy returned to his father without his dog, without his potatoes – without even a sack – and with only a suit of clothes that was so tattered and torn that it was beyond repair. His father was angry with him, and shut him up in his room for three days and three nights as a punishment. But it did no good. When the boy came out again, he had become a stubborn and listless lad, quite unlike what he had been before. He spent his time with strange books and strange men and women in the neighbouring towns, and he spent what little money he had on buying curious pots and jars of stuff which he mixed and re-mixed all alone in his room. His father died a sad and poorer man several years later, without ever knowing that the words that were always on his son's lips were these: 'Is there a magic spell that can turn a bird back into a woman?' and 'Are there charms that can turn an ordinary boy into a pink and pink-eyed bird?' and 'Please, can you teach me the language of the birds?' But the boy's questions were never answered, and he grew into manhood and middle-age and died quite young, with the reputation of a queer and solitary fellow who had never married, despite having been a fine-looking young man, and who had wasted all his little wealth dabbling in nonsensical magic, and all his little spare time hanging around the gardens of the pink pagoda bird-watching.

6

The Way of Uncertainty

You are standing on the path beside the Game Wood when she comes to you. You have already missed several turns by standing there like that in the middle of nowhere. She, the Beautiful Woman, comes to you like a vision, and in unmistakable gestures tells you to follow and to keep silent. She leads you away from the Pink Pagoda. You were nearer than she evidently thought. But what she does, she does as in a vision. And as in a vision, you meekly follow.

She takes you to the brink of the Quarries, to the very edge. Silently again, and in unmistakable gestures, she guides your eyes down into the depths of the quarry-pit. The tipper-trucks are buzzing around the rim of the quarry, yellow, fixed, passionless. With spastic motion they lift their loads of clay, but instead of taking them away they return to the quarry's edge and drop them over. Behind reflecting, mud-stained shields the faces of the drivers can be caught, yellow, fixed and passionless.

You feel as if you are participating in some infantile game, where the game is simply not to do things properly. You look into the muddied water of the quarry as into an oval glass, failing to comprehend the Beautiful Woman's warm smile as she stands beside you. Then suddenly out of the water there arises a face. A greyish-pink and perfect oval face, its hair floating out on the water. In a moment you have corrected your first assumption that it is a reflection, and have begun to see how each load, when it is dropped, brings to the surface in the contrary motion whatever is resting hidden in the obscure depths of the brown water. By this time the face has gone down again, the water drawing over its eyes and finally over its nose, leaving a strand or two of dark hair floating before they too are drawn back into the depths and seen no more. You turn to your guide in panic, but her eyes are so firmly fixed on the surface of the water that yours are forced back downwards in silence. Another load of clay is tipped into the pit. There is a splash, a moment in which the turbulence spreads down into the depths and across the breadth of the pit, and then there rises up another face, a few feet distant from where the first had been, but this time upside-down in relation to you. You look to your guide in horror, and only the impassive smile upon her lips prevents you from crying out: That was the face of . . . that was my . . . that was my . . . But you do not speak, and the realization is born into you slowly in silence.

And now the tipper-trucks are working together in a rhythm, so that load after load falls into the pit from all sides, dislodging from the unseen depths whatever it is that can be shifted. Face after face rises and then sinks back. The knowledge is slowly awoken in you. The third face you see, directly beneath your gaze, is without doubt the face of your father, so that you would have cried out 'Father' had not the necessity for silence been stronger. And so it was true that the other face had been your mother's. And now you see, rising in succession, the faces of your sisters and your brothers, your first school-teacher, your earliest companion, your piano-instructor, a favourite aunt, and the face of a man you thought you had forgotten, who had shown you once, one wasted summer's afternoon in an empty room, how a loom worked – one of the old sort of looms – had stood behind you, guiding your hands with his over the frame and shuttle, until you felt the confidence of its rhythm in you, and began to work the thing yourself.

You catch your guide by the sleeve, the questions burn-

34

ing in your throat, but she is already turning to move away, and you must follow. A last dreadful look back into the pit where already more faces are rising, as heavy bubbles rise in a soup. You make out the faces of your headmaster, the girl you first kissed, the man for whom you worked, and your Friend – him too, there in the slimy water. But the Beautiful Woman has already started on the path, and there is nothing for you to do but follow, your head still turned over your shoulder, your eyes filling with tears of confusion. Stumbling in one direction, you see for the first time behind you, beyond the pit, the distant figure of the Owner of the Quarries. The trucks churn about him, he is clearly in charge, and he looks impassively after you, faintly smiling. You begin to think that the Beautiful Woman and he are in some terrible complicity, that all this is being done to put you into confusion, you who were nearing the Pink Pagoda not half an hour before. All your anxiety, and the pity you feel for those you have seen, focuses on a single question: Whose was the face I first saw, the one I did not have time to recognize, before I even knew there were faces in the water?

She, the Beautiful Woman, is now guiding you back towards the Pink Pagoda. The pleasure of this prospect begins to ease away the pain of the Quarries, although the reason for the detour still troubles you. Already you can hear the sound of the stream, and you sense that in a moment you will be ready to step for the first time into the Pink Pagoda's garden.

The purling of the water grows clearer, and mingled with it now are the sounds of human talk and laughter, the ringing of knives against china, and the music of a small string orchestra – first clear, then losing itself on the breeze. When you come to the bridge, you stand there, your hands next to hers on the white woodwork, and she is directing your gaze once more with hers. It is first of all too busy a sight, too peopled, for you to be able to focus on any single part distinctly. A party is in progress. All is

35

delight, relief and pleasure, as you always knew it would be in the Pink Pagoda. What you first see are the delicate roses everywhere. Roses growing in the garden, but roses, too, on the buttonholes of all the men and on the breasts of all the women. You see the same roses in a ring decorating white cups and white plates. You see fingers lifting these same cups to lips, and fingers wiping away a crumb. On the white ornamental tables that edge the lawn, you see a single rose in a vase on every table. The men are wearing white suits and the women long white dresses. You see mouths moving in conversation, opening in laughter, hands placed lightly to dance, feet moving gracefully across the grass in time to the music. There are children in a dance, white dresses and neat white suits made to size, rosebud posies, and delighted smiles. You see the musicians sitting in the shade of the Pink Pagoda, bobbing gently to the unfolding rhythm of their music. Inside the uneven shade of the trellised verandah, you can make out the figure of the Owner of the Big House, seated on a fine wickerwork chair. Around him there is a constant flow of respectful guests, so that you can never take in the whole of his resplendent white-suited figure at one time, the perfect rose in the buttonhole, the unfailing smile, hair slicked into shape, and large hands comfortably folded upon an imposing lap. A little girl sits there for a few moments of decorous and playful conversation. Somebody brings him tea and returns to the dance.

Following the gestures of the Beautiful Woman once again, you descend from the bridge on to the lawn. You approach the groups of guests feeling abashed, knowing how unsuitably dressed you are. But when you find yourself moving amongst the tea-tables, and weaving in and out of the dancing couples, without any notice being taken, you begin to realize that neither of you can be seen. The knowledge comes to you both as a great relief and as a disappointment. It means that you do not need to feel awed by the prospect of confronting the Owner of the Big

36

House. It means that there was no malice in the unseeing stare of the Owner of the Quarries. At the same time it means, according to the Rules, that you have not truly arrived.

You hear a voice and turn about. Looking across a small circle of intimates talking together, you see, with the same plunge of certainty as before, the face of your mother as she raises a cup to her lips. Not the puffy, soiled face of the Quarries though, but the face you remember from photographs of her engagement and the early years of marriage before there were children, the face you like to imagine leaning over your cot or feeding you. She replaces her cup on her saucer, and tilts her head in the accustomed way to listen to her companion's question. Your instinct is to approach the group, and to say, 'Mother, it's me. I saw you in another place only half an hour ago.' But your guide, behind you, is gently reproving, shaking her head and smiling still. You are nevertheless drawn to the group, to try to hear what they are saying. The figure nearest you, with his back to you, for no reason turns, and you find yourself facing into the eyes of your Friend. And then you turn about and look at all the other faces. They are there again, the faces from the past, all the faces from the dreadful waters of the Quarries – but now refreshed and at their finest. Dancing an elegant waltz, you see your father and the woman who used to baby-sit. Walking amongst the flowers, your grandfather, your employer, your bank manager and the boy from across the street. The group with your mother and Friend in it has now broken up, and your mother is talking happily to one of your schoolmasters, who is asking her to dance. The children playing on the lawn you recognize as your nephews and nieces. And in animated conversation at a table, all transformed by the loveliness of the place, is a group of friends from student days. There are faces you do not remember seeing at the Quarries, as well as faces that were there but you cannot find here. Yet there seems

37

no reason to doubt that all of them were both here and there, if you had stayed long enough to look.

It is this thought which reminds you with a stab of pain of the faces you had seen at the Quarries – pale, detached, bloated, evidently beyond recall. The pleasure of the music, and all this radiant, unaffected happiness, had momentarily made you careless, and now suddenly seems like a terrible falsehood. And then you long for the Rule of Silence to be broken, and for the Beautiful Woman, your guide, to lead you away from both these places and to sit you down to answer all your desperate questions. Even in the sunshine, at no great distance from here, these same party-goers lie buried – no, worse than that, they lie submerged – in a sludge so thick that they are not normally to be seen at all. What has happened? How can they be in both places at once? Is one of them the place where they really are, and one a dream? Or is neither place final, and are both of them true? Will I ever join them, and if so where? And whose was that face I saw first in the pit? The answers, however, are not given, are never given. You find yourself back on the pathway where you started, halfway between the Quarries and the Pink Pagoda, and the Beautiful Woman has gone. For the moment, the will to pursue the Game has left you. You need time to take in this new weight of knowledge before your appetite for play will return, and you retrace your steps until you are on the familiar pathway Home.

7

The Old Game

'. . . and even in much later years, when all these adventures were far behind them, they still often thought back to the garden of the pink pagoda where they had first met.'

With a snap, the master of the house puts down his drink to mark the end of his tale, and resumes his seat. There are murmurs of approval from around the room, more than mere politeness, for the story has entertained us all. The master smiles in satisfaction, and nods his head, accepting the approval. It is that moment of silence that follows the telling of a tale, when the fullness of the tale – however slight a thing it may in itself have been – is weighed afresh by everyone, including the teller.

'And now you, my lad,' says the master. 'Are you ready?' The boy sitting beside him licks his lips nervously. It is his first time in the game, and he is all excitement, proud to be taking part, and determined not to displease his guardian. In time, everyone will take their turn. Not the three old fellows perched on the sofa, looking a little stiff in their suits, but glad to be here all the same, and to have a role in the old custom. They will be the judges at the end of it all, when that vestige of the ritual falls into its allotted place. In the old days, so I am told, all the workers and tenants on the master's estate would gather for the game. It might last anything up to a week to hear them out. It would be a kind of holiday, a special feast in the calendar of the estate, celebrated throughout the district and jealously protected by the participants. Now, with the estate much reduced and the custom no longer held in such respect, it is only the master's family and a handful of employees and tenants who are here, and the day ends with a modest supper. Besides the master himself, and the boy, his ward, there is the beautiful girl by the window, his daughter. It is hard for me to keep my eyes off her. There are the three old men from the cottages, our judges, and also the overseer of the master's quarries. He does not seem the kind of man who would wish to keep up the old ways for their own sake, and from the way his gaze returns as often as mine to the master's daughter, I fear that his presence here has little to do with the game. My friend, the master's secretary, at whose invitation I have come, makes up the party. And myself, the outsider. We have our tales yet to tell. But now, there are encouraging smiles from everyone, and a deliberate stillness, as the boy takes his place by the hearth. In a clear, steady voice he begins.

'One day a bad king was bored with staying in his castle, and wanted to go out fighting. He and his men had already destroyed most of the houses in that country, and the people had fled from the king's unruly violence. But the pink pagoda remained, and a beautiful lady lived there all alone. When the king saw the place, he commanded his men to surround it, and they began to force their way inside. There was nothing the lady could do. She locked herself inside a secret room in the pink pagoda, in the hope they would not find her. She could hear the terrible noise as windows were smashed and doors were knocked down. And she was just about to come out of her hiding-place and beg for mercy, when she heard the even louder noise of a challenge blown on a horn. She heard the king giving orders to his men to answer the challenge on their honour, and she heard the men's horses moving farther and farther away as they followed the sound of the horn into the forest. But as she began to think she was safe, she also heard the terrible footsteps of the king himself, who had stayed behind, coming nearer and nearer to where she was.

'What had happened was that a brave knight and his

brave companion had been passing when the attack started. The knight's companion had blown on the silver horn that always hung by his side, and in this way he had got the men to follow him into the forest where they were quickly lost. The knight himself, meanwhile, had taken the iron sword that always hung by his side, and had gone into the pink pagoda in search of the king. He found him just as the king had come to the last unopened door in the whole building, and was about to break it down. From inside, the lady heard the king crashing against the door. She then heard a cry as the king was struck by a blow from the knight's iron sword, and a thump as his body fell to the floor. But before she could come out of the room in which she was concealed, the knight had left the pink pagoda and gone to help his companion in the forest.

'In the depths of the forest, where the king's men had been lured, the knight and his companion defeated them all, down to the very last one. Then together they returned to the pink pagoda, where the lady was overjoyed to meet her rescuers and thank them. She gave them wine and food and every comfort, and told them that they had rescued not only her but countless numbers of other people in the kingdom. In time, as the news of the bad king's death spread far and wide, the people returned to their homes and re-built them. They made the knight their new king, and very soon the beautiful lady became his queen. Together they lived, sometimes in the castle and sometimes in the pink pagoda. And whenever he was bored, the new king and his companion would go out, not to fight, but to travel around the country, making it safe and helping the people who lived there.'

At the end of the story, the boy sits down. The master takes special care to put an assuring arm around the boy's shoulder, and leads us all in warm applause. He has done well. It is one of the rules of the tale-telling contest, in a sense the only one, that the pink pagoda, the little pink pagoda in the grounds of the estate, should figure somewhere in each tale. The contest was started all those generations ago when the pink pagoda had been built, and the first master had said, 'I have added something to my estate that is neither useful nor grand nor a strong defence, but a place of small pleasures and recreation. And yet I think I am right that it is the glory of the estate. Let us celebrate its completion by telling stories that are themselves of no obvious use and of little consequence, but pleasurable and sweet.' This is what the master's ward has done. He has added his voice to all the voices before him, and has every reason now to feel relaxed and fulfilled. But the rest of the party, and especially our three judges, are already sitting forward on their seats in eager anticipation of the tale that is to come. It is the turn of my friend, the master's secretary, to tell his tale. Like the boy before him, he looks a little apprehensive before he begins, trying to hold the whole of his idea in his mind at once, but settling into the tale once the telling is under way.

'A king,' he begins, 'fell in love with a beautiful country girl, and would have married her, if a wicked man in the kingdom had not succeeded, by stealth, in ousting the king from his throne and leaving him to be hunted, like an outlaw. The usurper's wickedness knew no bounds, and he forced his attentions on the girl who would have been the king's bride. When she refused him, with all her wiles and might, he had no hesitation in making her a prisoner in the pink pagoda where she lived, tying her up, and stopping her ears with wax and her mouth with a gag, so that she could neither hear nor speak. The usurper knew how much the king's will to survive, and the girl's will to resist, depended upon them being able to send messages to each other. "In this way," he said, "no word can pass from you to him, or from him to you, and I shall have my way with you both."

'But the king of the birds, a peregrine falcon, saw all this, and took pity on the king and the girl, and asked a wise old owl to find a way to help them. The owl gathered

42

all the birds together in the woods, and told them his plan. Then a kingfisher and a cuckoo flew to the pink pagoda, and perched on a window-sill high up in the room where the girl was imprisoned. At first, the girl was puzzled to see the two birds, but when she saw the cuckoo pecking at the kingfisher until the kingfisher flew away, she began to understand that they meant to tell her about how the king had lost his throne to a usurper. When the kingfisher returned with a woodcock, that flew in slow circles round and round him, she understood that the king was in hiding in the woods, and she slept peacefully that night knowing where he was. The following morning, the kingfisher returned with a stonechat, and the cuckoo chasing the kingfisher away, by which she understood that the king had been pursued to the stone-quarries. But when she saw the cuckoo fly off, she was relieved to realize that the usurper had not found the king, and had given up the hunt for the day.

'On the third day, there was chaos in the skies. The peregrine falcon and the owl flew high above the rest, so that they could see everything that was happening. The kingfisher returned to her window with a stork. Now, the girl remembered from her schooldays that the stork was Christ, and she guessed that the king had escaped from the stone-quarries and now found refuge in the chapel. But when the cuckoo came, she was terrified that the king had been found in the chapel. The kingfisher and the cuckoo flew busily about, diving and pecking. There was a fight, and when a robin redbreast came, she knew that someone was wounded. But before she had even had time to worry about this, a firecrest settled on her window-sill and the stork flew slowly away. The chapel was burning. Someone was wounded inside the chapel. A black raven flew past her window, with the kingfisher following. She thought to herself that the king was dead, and his body burned to ashes in the fire, and she despaired at the news the birds had brought.

'But then the kingfisher was once again at her window,

43

and before she had time even to feel a moment's hope, the king himself was inside the pink pagoda, freeing her from her bonds, and holding her in his arms. The raven had meant to tell the girl that it was the usurper who had died in a fire of his own making, and the kingfisher that the king had stayed to make certain he was dead, before coming to find the girl. "I knew, you see," said the king, "that you were safe, even though I had heard no word from you. A whitethroat, telling me of your beautiful pure skin, had come to me with the cuckoo, showing me how you had been entrapped. Then a mute swan and a wax-wing came to tell me how you had been gagged and your ears stopped up. So that I knew I only had to free myself from my enemy's pursuit before I could return here to find you, and free you too." And they held each other safely in their arms, whilst the peregrine falcon and the owl, and all the other birds, looked on, and a pair of turtle-doves circled above their heads, cooing softly.'

My friend comes to the end of his story, and everyone is pleased by the clever messages of the birds and the amusing way he has woven his own love of bird-watching into the tale. It is said that the winning tale is always the one that keeps a balance between what is new and different and what is familiar, between what is personal to the teller and what is shared by all. But already I can feel my own difficulty here. For the pink pagoda, around which all the tales must revolve, is no ordinary place for me, nor even a place made special by its ornamented style or its delightful setting. Since only this morning, it has become a place I cannot think about without thinking about her, the master's beautiful daughter. For it was there we met this morning, she and I, quite by chance, and there was something in her eyes, something in the way her sighing harmonized with mine, that gave me hope, and made me believe that, with a moment longer to ourselves, we might have been touching hands. Such thoughts are barely kept under by the telling of tales, and the prospect of telling my own tale raises in me the fear that I will only betray myself. But now, the overseer of the quarries is asked to take his turn, and I begin to wonder how much he will betray, what he will say to give an outlet to his feelings – for it is certain that his eyes have hardly left hers since the game began, and certain that he looks to her for support now as he rises to his place.

'There were three men and a youth went hunting in the woods,' he says, and there is an almost audible sigh of contentment within the room as we all relax into the expectation of another tale. 'They hunted all the morning through, but without success, until they came to a place where five paths met. There one of them said, "Let's each of us take a separate path, and see if that will bring us more luck." They all agreed, and decided to meet again at the same place at sunset to pool whatever they had caught, and divide it equally amongst them. They then cut straws to choose a path, but each time the youth came up the loser, so that he was left with the choice of going back the way he had come, or of following a path where the trees were few and the undergrowth was sparse. He reasoned to himself that if luck was to be his guide, then his luck might change, and he chose the poor-looking path. His three companions each went their way into the depths of the wood, and there they found game in plenty. The first of them found pheasant, the second of them rabbit, and the third wood-pigeon, and they spent the day busily hunting. The youth found only a stream that was well enough stocked with fish, but useless to him as he had with him nothing but a gun.

'With nothing better to do, he followed the stream, and was following it round a bend when, to his surprise, a beautiful pink pagoda came into view. In the pink pagoda's garden he glimpsed the beautiful figure of a woman crossing the grounds, but she disappeared from sight until, as he stepped nearer the pagoda, she stepped out of the verandah door, stopping him short with her beauty, and

45

greeting him in a friendly voice.' There is a glance between the overseer and the master's daughter, I am certain of it. It is nothing that would be noticed by anyone else. But with all the intensity that belongs to a lover's heart, I know now that I will listen to the remainder of this tale as to a rival's words.

'"Hullo," said the young woman,' the overseer continues. '"Welcome to my home. Will you come inside?" she added with a smile. Now, it has to be understood that, if the young woman is as beautiful as can be imagined, the youth too is a fine-looking young man, tall and bright-eyed and healthy. He may be young in the ways of love, and unpractised, but in the woman's eyes he is in readiness. "I have to be at my hunting," the youth answered shyly, "I've caught nothing yet, and I must be back at sunset." "Let me play the huntress," said the woman with a laugh, "I'll gladly be your captor, and still I'll let you go at sunset." "I really shouldn't," said the youth. "Don't you want to?" said the woman. "I promised my friends," said the youth. "Am I not beautiful?" said the woman, and threw back her thick black hair to show him the paleness of her throat. "Come inside. We should not dishonour the luck that has thrown us in each other's way." The persuasion of her answers was almost as forceful as the lure of her beauty, and the youth was quickly defeated. She led him through the beauties of the pink pagoda's rooms to an inner chamber, where they tasted all the sweetness of love to the full and stayed in each other's arms until the evening came.

'At sunset the youth leapt up and said he had to leave. He could not bear to lose the woman now that he had found her. He asked her to go with him, he wanted her to be his wife. The woman, who was as much in love with him as he with her, agreed, and together they returned to the meeting place. There they found the young man's three companions, who had already divided their spoil into four equal bags, each with its own share of pheasant and rabbit and pigeon, and had begun to grow impatient with waiting. When they saw the beautiful woman with the youth, at first they were amused. But when they realized that he had caught nothing whilst they had been hard at work, they began to feel annoyed. "We made a bargain," one of them said, "and you've not kept it." "He caught this woman," another said, "perhaps we should each take a share of her." He meant it as a joke, but the third man did not have his sense of humour. "Equal divisions of what was caught," he said, "that's what was agreed. So let's each of us have a taste of her, and I'll have mine first." The youth stood in his way. "Take back my share of what you caught," he said. "I'd sooner have my share of her," said the man, and pushed him out of the way. "She's a good-looking woman, and her flesh at this moment will answer my needs better than any game meat."

'He was about to grab the woman, and the youth had reached for his gun, when the beautiful woman stepped forward, and spoke. "Stop," she said, and he stopped in his tracks. "Your bargain was to divide in four everything you had caught. Well, let me tell you, that it wasn't your friend who caught me, but I who caught him. He's only a youngster, and I was the huntress, as you'll surely believe. But I'm not part of your bargain. If he caught anything of me, he has caught my heart, which cannot be divided without my death, and he has caught my love, which does not exist except to be shared between the two of us. If there was one other thing he caught of me it was a glimpse of my figure as he came into my garden. And you've already had more than your fair shares of a glimpse of me." And with that, she grabbed the youth's bag of game in one hand, and the youth himself in her other hand, and together they ran off into the darkness and did not stop until they reached the pink pagoda. There, in great contentment, they feasted together, both on the good food that the three hunters had provided for them, and on the newfound love that was theirs alone.'

There are smiles all around the room as the overseer takes his seat again, and even the master's daughter, though her head is lowered, is smiling, as I can see, at the audacity of the woman in the overseer's tale. My rival sits back, satisfied to have finished his tale and to have made an impression on the girl. But there is no time for anything more to come of this, as it is the girl's turn now to tell her tale. The overseer leans across to speak to her. I try to give her a special smile as she rises from her seat. But we are both ignored; the girl is absorbed in the game. I know that I will be unable to listen to her tale for what it is, but will only be intent on any message it may contain for me.

'There was an attractive young widow of modest means,' she says, 'who used to take her beloved dog for a walk every day in the gardens of the pink pagoda.' She pauses as everyone happily smiles in recognition – her fondness for her own dog is known to us all. 'One day a large hound came bounding into her path, frightening her own dog, and nearly knocking the woman over. The hound was swiftly followed by its master, whom the woman recognized as the young owner of the big house on the hill, a man with the reputation of a shameless womanizer and a flatterer. He caught hold of his dog, and was in the middle of his apologies, when he saw for the first time whom he was addressing. Immediately, his eyes lit up, and his speech too seemed to catch a new fire. "I must own myself indebted," he said, "to the uncouthness of this dog of mine, because without it I might never have seen a gentle beauty such as yours." The woman blushed and turned to leave, ignoring the young man's request for her to stay.

'The next morning he was there again, and his compliments were as fulsome as they had been before. The woman wanted none of this attention, but mere politeness demanded that they must speak. "I must, sir," she said, "forbid you to address me further in that manner. If we are to talk at all, it must be on a subject that can do no

48

injustice to the honour of either of us." "In that case," said the man, "what subject do you propose? Might we, for instance, talk of our dogs?" "That would do very well," said the woman, and she fell silent. "Your little dog," the man began, "is remarkably pretty and of very fine breeding." "I am sure," said the woman with a smile, "that your dog outdoes mine in pedigree, and it is only a shame that the same cannot be said of his manners." "He is young," said the man, "and full of friendly feelings to all. He means no harm." "He needs better training," said the woman. "Ah," said the man, "there you are almost right. He needs someone towards whom he can feel protective. He does not feel this towards me, of course, but then neither is he afraid of me." "What sane person would wish to be protected by such a brute?" said the woman. "And yet," said the man, "would it not be a kind of duty, if this were the only hope of curbing his boisterous ways?" "Meanwhile," said the woman, "perhaps you should put him on a tighter leash." "He would only sulk and fret," said the man. "But at least the rest of us could go about in freedom," said the woman. "Would your dog go free if mine were on a leash?" said the man. "I was noticing that you keep your dog restrained even though you speak so highly of her manners." "I am obliged to keep my dog restrained," said the woman, "when there are hounds around like yours." "Is this the only reason?" said the man, "are you not a little afraid of discovering your dog's true nature if you let her go?" "And what do you suppose her true nature might be?" said the woman. "I believe she might enjoy a game with my dog," said the man, "there is a brightness in her eyes that makes me think so." "But would that brightness still be there," said the woman, "after your dog had finished what you are pleased to call his game?" "There are things your dog could learn from mine," said the man. "Such as unsettledness and over-bearingness and noise," the woman said. "Such as fun, and a sense of liberty, and the delights of nature," said the man, "more than my dog could ever learn from yours." "My dog," said the woman, "could teach him decency and prudence and self-respect." "But only if you let her off the leash," the man said, and with that the woman laughed, and slipped her dog from its leash, and let herself be taken laughing into the young man's arms. "It is not your persistence that I yield to," she said, "nor your deviousness, nor yet your brash impertinence. But I am pleased by your wit, for it shows in you a mind that is capable of more than appetite, and a grace that is capable of more than wilfulness." And the two dogs played with endless pleasure and invention on the grass, whilst the two owners walked arm in arm around the pink pagoda engrossed in the happiest of conversations.'

There is no hint, beyond a certain laughter in her eyes as she sits down, as to what the girl has meant by her amusing tale. No glance of encouragement at the overseer of the quarries for his wit, nor of disdain for his brashness; no sign of a challenge to me to do better, nor of a rebuff against me doing anything at all. Nothing to suggest that I might be the young man in her tale, either as a token of her affection or of her contempt, and nothing that can be taken as an invitation to meet her again tomorrow, as we met today, in the pink pagoda's garden. Nothing to make clear her feelings for me or for my rival. Nothing but the neatness of her tale.

And suddenly I am all impatience with the game itself, with all the silly prevarications of the tales, all their beguilements and convolutions. Why do we sit here, surrounding ourselves with these pretences, when there are real things that we might say, when there is a real pagoda in the grounds? It is all a mere passing of the time, for the sake of some time long since gone, and gets us nowhere. And even as these thoughts begin to swell in my head, blotting out all sense of the game, I hear my name called, I see the arm waving me towards my place. I know I must get up to tell my tale. But what can I say when my mind is occupied with one thing only? How can I tell a tale when what I want is not talk revolving round and round the pink pagoda, but to be there? To be there again as I was this morning, and to be certain that what was true this morning is still true, and that from this point onwards we shall think back to the pink pagoda, not as a place of stories, but as where our story first began. How can I play the game, when I know that her eyes are looking at me, and that beyond her head I can see where the pathway begins? – there, through the window, where there is a gap in the white palings, and the land falls sharply away.

8

Country Dancing

With this one, you'd think the Game was over before it had even begun. There they are, the four young friends, lying on the grass, with the doors of the pink pagoda open to the garden. As if they owned the place. And the garden itself so delightful, sparkling with hyacinth and daisies on a bright spring morning, and a single dewdrop left in every petal. The trees in blossom are seething with the year's first butterflies. There are birds in the sky and songbirds in cages; water trickles over the flat stones – tunes all around that interlace and extend each other's harmonies. The sun is warm, but a gentle breeze moves through the garden, so that no one is ever chilled for a moment or oppressed by sitting too much in the sun.

The one who calls himself Meridew has got to the middle of his story. He is a fine young man, young enough for the down on his cheek to be a maytime crop, unripe for the harvest, but man enough for the legs he spreads upon the ground to be slim and long and firm. One pair of delicate ears is attentive. It is nearly the exciting climax of his story, and at any moment there may be the need for a firm, long arm to place itself comfortingly around the delicate shoulders. Go on then, you can be Meridew.

'And the King of the Quarries,' he was saying, 'was a most brutal tyrant, so that there were some working in the depths of his quarries who never saw the light of the sun from the moment they were born to the day they died. They were kept in their place by those who worked above them, and above them all stood the King, never dirtying his fingers or going into the darkness, and deaf to the noise of grumbling beneath him that was like the groaning you hear underground before the eruption of a volcano.'

'I pity those people,' said Jonquil of the dark hair, the attentive ear and the smiling eye. 'But I also pity the King, tyrant as he is, for the folly of his tyranny that is certain to bring about the loss of his kingdom.'

'The two princes,' said Meridew, 'to whom we were bound in service, they also wanted to save the King and his kingdom, for they were the sons of kings, and knew that uncontrolled rebellion was an evil as great as the evil of tyranny. They persuaded the rebel leaders to capture the King, and not to kill him, but to take him bound and blindfolded into the depths of the quarries. When he was brought down to the very bottom of his kingdom, the princes removed his blindfold and showed him the darkness of perpetual night that his tyranny had created. When his ears were unstopped they made him listen to the groans of his tormented people. And at last, when his mouth was ungagged, they made him promise to make amends for all that he had done wrong, and to give his people back the life and the light he had taken from them. All this he promised, and claimed in his defence that he had been kept from the knowledge of the truth by dishonest advisers. The princes were satisfied, and returned with the King to his chambers, believing that out of this attack upon a king, a kingdom had been saved, and by this petty disorder, a greater disorder had been averted.

'But when they reached the surface, and the King sat down with his advisers, it was to avenge themselves against the rebels, and not to reform the kingdom, that they planned. The guards were called, and the princes and the rebel leaders arrested. As they were taken away to the King's fearful prison in the heart of the Quarries, the princes, and we their squires, turned on the guards and fought them, allowing the rebel leaders to scatter and escape. But in that skirmish both Prince Paragon and Prince

Butane were killed, bravely defending their allies, and it is only we, Meridew and Yeovil, who live to speak of their deeds.'

'Oh, gallant princes,' Jonquil said, and for a moment a tear hung in her eye, as pure and white as the single pearl that hung upon her shepherdess's breast. And as an afterthought she added, 'And gallant squires too.'

At a little distance, far enough for comfort, but close enough for their words and sighs to mingle in a single murmur, and for one parasol to serve both couples, Meridew's companion, Yeovil, had arrived at the same point in his tale.

'And it is only we,' said he, 'Yeovil and Meridew, who live to speak of their deeds.'

'Oh, gallant princes,' said Tansy, who had been sitting as attentively, and now sat as tearfully, as her sister shepherdess. 'And gallant squires too. Jonquil and I must work together and weave a garland of flowers for these princes. For, although we are only the orphan daughters of a poor shepherd, we are as able to be moved by bravery and honour as any princesses, and especially by the tragic deaths of two fine young men.' And so she and her sister rose up and began to gather flowers, with the two squires looking on.

Now, the situation is this. Jonquil and Tansy are not really Jonquil and Tansy at all, but Melissa and Quintilia. They are no more shepherdesses in reality than they are orphans. They are the daughters of the King of the Big House, princesses by birth, and heiresses to an entire kingdom. If they appear now in the modest surroundings of the pink pagoda, and in the simple dresses of shepherd girls, it is no fantasy of their own that they are playing at. It is the whim of the King himself, their eccentric father, who has decided to give up all the trappings of power and wealth, and return his kingdom to its primitive innocence. Of course, this is not what has happened. Far from re-creating paradise in the land, he has returned it to its first chaos. The shepherds and the townspeople do no work, but every day for them is a drunken holiday. Nothing grows in the land, and all the buildings, from the humblest cottage to the Big House itself, are fallen into a state of woeful disrepair – as will always happen when rule is thrown aside, and a ruler becomes a rebel unto himself. Fortunately, the princesses are protected from the worst of this, by the comforts of the pink pagoda their father has built for them, and by the names they have adopted, which shelter them from the violence of the people's envy or their lust. The King, in turn, has taken to a hermitage somewhere, to meditate on the world's ills, and find a sanctuary from the roaming bands of rioters that he has himself released upon his kingdom.

What is more, Meridew and Yeovil are not really Meridew and Yeovil either. They are, in fact, the Princes Paragon and Butane, supposedly killed in the battle at the Quarries. The story they told the shepherdesses was all true, up to the point where they told them about the escape of the squires and the brave self-sacrifice of the princes. For it was the squires who were killed, and the princes took their clothes in order to make good their escape. There are still agents of the King in pursuit of them, which is why they have kept up the disguise, and why they were so glad to find a hideaway like the pink pagoda – a place made all the more attractive to their eyes by the presence of two young shepherdesses. The shepherdesses themselves were equally glad to have the company of two fine young men, especially as it made them feel even more protected from the outside world.

All this, of course, adds up to why there is a Game to play, because nobody is here as themselves, and everything is yet to be won. Even within the Rules of Identity, where you play as anyone you like, you can still only win as yourself. But this Game has been joined by Love, which doubles the winnings and increases the urgency of play. You should hear what Melissa and Quintilia say to each other at night, about the fine-limbed Meridew and the handsome Yeovil. You should hear what Paragon and Butane say too, about the eyes of Jonquil and the hair of Tansy. You should see the looks that pass between each squire and his shepherdess, looks of longing, and the knowing looks that pass between the princes, and between the princesses when they think they are alone. When Love is in play, the moves in the Game are minimal and undertaken with intense concentration. The pace of play is slower than a heartbeat, and the glance of an eye can seem to mean that everything is won or that everything is lost. It could have gone on like this for ever, if there had not been other Players in the Game.

One morning there is a visitor to the pink pagoda, an elderly lady in furs and feathers and rouge, who claims to be a godmother of the girls and has come to see how they are. Politely but reluctantly, the princesses make her welcome. But Meridew and Yeovil are fearful in case this visitor, however improbably, turns out to be an agent of the King of the Quarries, and they rush off to find yet a further disguise. The godmother is taking tea with the girls when Meridew and Yeovil re-appear in the only costumes they could find – the white skirts and embroidered blouses of shepherdesses – and are introduced by quick-thinking Jonquil (Tansy has turned away to laugh) as shepherdesses from a neighbouring cottage. 'This,' says Jonquil, turning towards Meridew, 'is Silvia. And this,' turning towards Yeovil, 'is her friend, Crystal.' Yeovil bows to the lady, but Meridew remembers to drop a curtsy. 'How very nice to meet you,' says the lady sweetly, and nods to them both with a smile.

As the day wears on, the godmother's attentions towards Silvia and Crystal become more and more marked, and by the time she is flushed with the sherry that is served before they eat, and the wine they drink with supper, she is full of little smiles and little squeezes for them both. It becomes too late for her to be allowed to leave, and her hostesses are forced to invite her to stay there for the night, and to make a lavish pretence of inviting the neighbouring shepherdesses too.

'Very well,' the godmother says at length, 'I shall accept your generous invitation. But on no account are you young ladies to give up an entire bedroom to me alone. I will not hear of it. Let Tansy share Jonquil's room with her, and I will share Tansy's room with Silvia. Crystal, my dear, you must sleep on the sofa tonight. But if we all stay here for another night,' she adds with a twinkling eye at the whole company, 'then Silvia must take the sofa, and Crystal can share with me!'

'But, godmother!' say Jonquil and Tansy at once, thinking of poor Meridew's difficulties. 'But, madam!' says Meridew, thinking uncomfortably of himself. 'A sensible and generous arrangement,' says Yeovil, thinking only of himself and of Tansy, and of a sofa otherwise unoccupied. 'Not another word,' says the godmother. 'It's all arranged, and I think we should now go to our beds.'

Meridew could only hope to delay his readiness for bed for as long as possible, and comfort himself with thinking that tomorrow night he and Jonquil would be able to take the places of Yeovil and Tansy. But the old lady, it seemed, could not prepare herself for bed with more alacrity, and when she and Meridew were eventually beneath the sheets, she could not stop her chatter. To Meridew's confusion – the embarrassment of any young man who finds himself by accident sharing a bed with an elderly matron – her talk was all of love, and the sweet chances of love, and the pleasures that can ensue from love between partners of widely differing ages. His confusion would have been all the greater had he known the truth – namely, that beneath the carmined cheeks and the wig and the flowery nightdress there lay the improbable and increasingly impatient body of the King of the Big House, prompted by all the urgings of an uncontrolled lust.

The hermitage where he had taken sanctuary had been

discovered by a torch-carrying mob of revellers, who in their drunken fury had consigned it, and very nearly the King as well, to the flames. The King had only managed to escape by snatching a woman's clothes in the confusion, and then passing undetected through the crowd. He had made his way to where his daughters were as the only safe place he knew, and would have revealed his true identity to them if it had not been for the unexpected presence of two enticing young maids. His solitary time in the hermitage had only served to accumulate his fleshly longings – for it will always be the case that the man who has forsaken his responsibility of ruling over others will lose all power to rule over himself – but even he was surprised at the passion which Silvia had excited in his frame. As he spoke about the mysteries of love, his voice would drop into a tone that was honey-thick with lust, an alteration that Meridew ascribed to the effects of drink. He tried not to yawn, and hoped that the old woman would soon reach the end of her extraordinary effusion. Meanwhile, Tansy waited with equal impatience for her sister to fall asleep (dreaming – who knows? – of the following night when she might be enfolded in the long, strong arms of Meridew), and then crept from her bedroom on slippered feet towards the sitting-room where Yeovil was breathlessly waiting.

There were, however, other feet that crept and paused, and crept again, in the pink pagoda that night. An agent of the King of the Quarries, a dangerous man with a pistol in his hand, had caught up with the two escaped princes, and was approaching the room where they would be sleeping in order to take them by surprise. There were horses waiting with an accomplice at the end of the drive.

It was shortly after midnight, then, when Yeovil was about to clasp Tansy to him, saying something pretty about the softness of the skin beneath her breast, and with the King of the Big House about to put an end to all persuasion by plucking off the wig and bodice that were (as he thought) the only impediments that lay between him and a slender shepherdess, when there was a loud bang in the pink pagoda, followed by the shattering of glass. A pistol was fired into the air as the slender shepherdess, to the King's amazement, dived across the bed and brought an intruder to the floor. The struggle that followed was brief. Meridew's gown made it hard for him to fight, and it was not long before the two occupants of the bedroom had been bundled through a broken window, secured with rope, and manhandled on to the backs of horses. Tansy and Yeovil sprang apart from one another in time to hear the sound of departing horses, and Yeovil immediately leapt from his bed, ordered a horse to be saddled, and left Tansy to explain to her sister as best she could why she had awoken, startled, to find herself all alone.

When the agents of the King of the Quarries had time to notice their captives, they quickly realized their mistake with the old woman, and vented their frustration by jeering at Paragon for his choice of bedmate. But when they came to strip Paragon of his disguise as Silvia, the King of the Big House almost revealed his own true identity, thinking he was about to witness a rape infinitely more terrible than the one he had himself been contemplating only moments before. He was deterred at first by the suspicion that his captors were in the employ of his ancient enemy, the King of the Quarries, and then by the unimaginable sight of a manly chest emerging from beneath Silvia's ruffles, and a man's hair from beneath the discarded wig. The confusion of the King's reaction put him into a swoon, which seemed to his captors entirely consistent with the behaviour of an elderly female.

Prince Paragon was taken, for the second time, to the King's prison deep within the Quarries, but this time with no hope of overpowering the guard. The King of the Big House, however, was taken somewhere that seemed to him far worse than prison. He found himself face to face with his old adversary, the King of the Quarries, in his chambers. And worse than that, he quickly found the King showing towards him the same uncontrollable and disgusting affection as he had shown towards the presumed shepherdess. It was like looking into a distorting mirror to see the poutings and ridiculous grimaces on his companion's puffy face. There was nothing he could do; he could not yield to the King's importunings without uncovering his real nature in an even riskier way. His only hope was to defend himself as he before had hoped to gain his victory – by ceaseless talking, parrying the King's advances, and playing the coquette. Tired and confused as he was, he spoke on and on about anything that came into his head – the value of meditation, the proper education of children, the dangers of alcohol – but not a word about love, whilst his would-be lover stalked him round and round the room.

As soon as Prince Butane arrived at the Quarries, he made contact with the rebel leaders and was smuggled by them into the depths he had visited before. This time he had no hesitation about agreeing with the rebel leaders on a full-scale assault on the tyrant's guard and on the tyrant himself. The first part of the plan was to attack the prison, where many of the King's old enemies were falsely imprisoned, as well as Paragon himself. Then the two princes led the rebels and the people in an unassailable march on the King of the Quarries himself. Hundreds of men and women, kept down for years by deception and by force, came out into the sunlight, blinking and marvelling at what they had never before seen. In the face of such numbers, many members of the King's guard decided there was no point in resistance and joined the storming of the last stronghold.

But it was too late. Increasingly agitated with frustration, the King of the Quarries decided that he would listen to no more talk, and made a grab at his sweetheart's shoulders. But at the same moment she made a grab at a candelabrum on a nearby table and brought it heavily down on the back of the King's skull. The King's own weight brought both of them down together. At first the King of the Quarries took it all in sport, thinking it was a part of the woman's impassioned love-making. Together they rolled about in a ridiculous charade, whether of amatory pleasures or of fighting. But it was not long before the King of the Big House's wig slipped in the tussle, his make-up smeared, and his skirt was ripped to uncover a man's hairy calves. At last, the features of the tyrant's bitterest enemy were unmistakable, and then the fighting between them was in earnest. The two large, ageing bodies flung about in elephantine motion. But the blow on his head had weakened the King of the Quarries, and eventually the King of the Big House stood in momentary triumph over the head of his opponent, which slumped sideways like the head of a dead, beached dolphin. But he did not stand for long, and Paragon was at the door, and able to catch the King of the Big House's body in his arms, as it fell to the floor in exhaustion, and the heart pumped life into its flesh for the last time. So there they lay, the tyrant and the lord of misrule, two victims of their own extremes of passion, two monuments to the failure to govern a self or a kingdom.

The princes left the people of the Quarries to celebrate their freedom, and hurried back to the pink pagoda, where they began to tell their extraordinary story to the two young women. Torn between the delight of seeing the two men safe and well, and sadness at the death of their father, they sank down crying, 'Oh, Meridew! Oh, Yeovil! Oh, Yeovil! Oh, Meridew! Oh, Daddy!' And then, of course, they had to explain who their father truly was, who the godmother must have been, and who they were themselves, and how they had not really been orphans until that moment. At which the two princes in turn also had to explain who they truly were, and how the real Meridew and the real Yeovil had been killed before, and how their deaths had now been avenged. Melisa and Quintilia vowed that they would make garlands for the memories of Meri-dew and Yeovil. But for Paragon and Butane they vowed they would make wedding posies.

And so it was. The two princesses married the two princes. Paragon and Melissa became King and Queen of the Big House, and restored order to that troubled land. The newly liberated people of the Quarries, with one voice, invited Butane and Quintilia to return to their kingdom and to become their King and Queen. And sometimes, even now, on fine spring days, they gather on the lawn of the pink pagoda, which is looking a little faded and flaky with under-use, and try to recapture the pleasures of a time when there was nothing else to do, and it seemed as if their game need never be concluded.

9

The Travels of Hal Milepost

Squire Vestibule stood on the broad south steps of Vestibule Hall, and surveyed with pride the park stretching down towards the river. With equal pride he looked towards the garden where his grandson and a young friend played, and he held out a hand towards his daughter.

'No, daughter,' said the Squire. 'Don't stop them in their play. I was bold and gamesome once, and a few honest scratches on a true player's face are better than the unblemished skin of a bore or a coward.'

The Squire's daughter smiled, and left the boys to tumble on the grass. She listened as she had listened before to her father's story, with a willing submission and a smile of encouragement.

'I was not born to a life like this,' he began. 'I grew up as Hal Milepost, and have made the change from wild young Hal to sober Henry in my lifetime, like England's finest king. I was called Milepost because that was where I was found, a tiny crying bundle in the rain. And I was called Hal by the good parson and his good wife who took me in, in memory of their own son who had died. The parson taught me letters, and the parson's wife taught me manners, and I grew up hardly knowing the bitterness of the world since I had seen only instances of its sweetness.

'I came to know misfortune – the misfortunes upon which all my present prosperity has been built – because at the age of sixteen I fell in love with the Squire's daughter, Grace, and so provoked his hatred. Grace and I were forced to meet in secret, and we met one day in the churchyard, where my foolish dog chased her little kitten into a tree, and so in through a window of the church. To please my beloved I set out to rescue her pet, and, climbing in through the same window, I dislodged an old oil-lamp so that pretty soon the church was ablaze. The kitten was safe, and so was I, but a stranger inside the church was horribly burned in the fire, and died. I could not have known of this, and my motives were only those of generosity, perhaps tempered by a little vanity. But I knew that the Squire would see me hanged for this, and I determined to make my escape. I swore my Grace to secrecy. I could not bear to bid farewell to the parson and his wife, nor in the rashness of my youth did I think to trust them with my folly. I stole away at night, and left my home by way of winding lanes and hidden pathways.

'I found work at the quarries, digging stone, but such work as a boy should never do, and forced to it by a master who was both a brute when drunk and a cheat when sober, stealing my few pence from me with his guile. One night, when he lay snoring with an empty bottle at his side, I stole back from him what he had taken from me, and ran off once more. Little good it did me. Passing through a wood the following morning, I was taken by a gang of men with a little drummer-boy and put on board a ship bound for the Indies. Again I was set to work amongst men who were older and harder than I, and that and the heat and the unfamiliarity of the sea made me sick. It was my sickness that saved me, for when the ship ran aground in heavy seas one night it was the rest of the crew, in their miserable pens amidships, who were lost, whereas I was thrown free from the stern and floated on my little bed for two days and two nights. I was rescued by good fortune and by the good captain of another vessel, also Indies-bound. The captain took a fancy to me, thinking I was a lucky charm by the extraordinary circumstances of my deliverance, and he became my friend, letting me get well again, before he put me to work such as a lad could do.

'I gladly worked for him, and worked well for him both on board ship and on his plantation when we came to our journey's end. The man made me his manager, and I would have been perfectly content if my conscience had not begun to trouble me on account of the two I had left behind who were as a father and a mother to me, and on account of the love I still bore another. But my friend the captain would not hear of me leaving, and I loved him well enough to nurse him when he fell sick of a fever, and to mourn for him at his untimely death. When I heard that he had left me the whole of his plantation and all his fortune, having neither wife nor child, my sadness was turned to joy, not at my riches alone, but at this witness to our friendship, and above all at the fact that I would now be able to return to England and claim Grace for my bride.

'I did not then know what a snare riches could be to a young man who was fair of face but innocent of mind. On the voyage home, I became the plaything of some wild young men, who were deeply set in the ways of folly, and gambled away their time and their money – and mine – on cards and on any crazy wager. I foolishly took them as models of what a young man of the world should be, and when we came to Southampton I was happy to bring them all to London and to pay the hire of a suite of rooms for us all in a fashionable part of town.

'I remember now with shame the intemperate and wilful things we did in the name of pleasure. I lied to myself that I was merely taking a holiday before going into the country to find Grace, when in reality I was wasting my fortune and burying myself in a manner of living from which an early and desolate death is the only escape. My rescue came from the least expected quarter. After a night of drinking and gaming, my false friends and I went to the narrow streets where women are bought and sold like so many ribbons, or rather like so many carcasses of diseased flesh. There I set my eyes on a woman of flaming beauty, but advanced in years, thinking in my conceit that a vigorous young man might impress such a woman and learn in her arms lessons that a younger mistress would be ill-prepared to teach.

'In my vanity, I engaged the woman in conversation, and in the glow of wine we fell into talk. She told me how she had come to lead her present life, and I looked and listened with more fascination for her lips than sympathy for her story. "I fell in love," she told me, "with a landowner's second son, who enticed me with promises that were not his to make, and with a charming passion that was to turn into madness. I bore him a son whom I was forced to abandon, and I left that part of the country to make my living variously as a governess, a seamstress and a maid. But wherever I worked, my former lover found me, and demanded me to tell him where his son could be found. He had turned from a selfish intensity of feeling towards an increasingly egotistical mania, and towards a fiery and uncharitable fanaticism which some people mistake for religion. He wanted his son, he said, in order to bring him into the perverted ways that he called godly. And when I tried to shake him off he became wild, and his wildness led him to utter rumours about my past which I was too honest to deny, so that wherever he came I was eventually forced to leave. Unable to make an honest living, I was gradually forced to choose between despair and the entreaties of those who would have me make my living dishonestly. I chose the latter as the only way to survive, and as a sure escape from the persecution of my son's father. And so I joined the flotsam of vice that finds its way inevitably to London, and used the skill of my beauty over a dozen years to keep myself alive."

'After this, we returned to my rooms where we drank more wine and talked to less purpose than before, conversing with our eyes and the pressure of our hands as much as with our lips. My lips desired only to kiss hers, and hers soon yielded, so that by degrees we removed to the bedchamber and then to the naked condition of our universal parents, but not innocently. I held her in my arms and we had ceased to utter words, when she suddenly sat up as if in fear and demanded a candle to be brought closer. The horror in her voice was its own imperative, and I brought her the candle. She held it closely to my breast and whispered in a chilling voice, "The little temple, the little eastern temple! Dear Lord, the little eastern temple!" I glanced down, and she was pointing at a curious pinkish birthmark which had disfigured the right side of my chest for as long as I had known, and which did indeed resemble a temple or pagoda in outline. I took time to comprehend the source of her alarm, but gradually I came to understand that the baby she had abandoned had been born with a pinkish birthmark in the same spot, and that she had abandoned it by the milepost outside my own village. I was that baby, and she – whom I had held in lust but a minute before – was my own mother. We greeted this news with a mixture of pain and joy, of laughter and shameful weeping, that was hard to bear. But whatever pain there was in the first meeting, there was joy in the outcome.

'I abandoned those who had nearly been my ruin, and returned forthwith into my own country. There I learned of the sad deaths of the dear parson and his wife, and I was both bitterly anguished and filled with pride to hear that they had never abandoned their trust in me and had always held up my innocence against all slanderers. Grace's father, the Squire, had also died, and Grace Vestibule had retired to Vestibule Hall to live alone, a beautiful and pious creature, faithful only to one whom she would not name, and an avowed spinster to her dying day.

'My dear daughter, as you know, I persuaded your mother to abjure her vow, and I became by marriage the Squire of Vestibule Hall. And not by marriage only, for I also learnt that the man who had been mysteriously killed in the church, by my hand but not by my will, was none other than the Squire's younger brother, my father – who died, I hope, in repentance and prayer, however twisted the nature of his faith.

'It was my fancy to build for my own mother a home in the grounds of Vestibule Hall. I promised not to reveal the story of her past to anyone, and without a word of explanation to the over-curious folk in the parish, I built a house in the shape of a little pink pagoda. But my mother never lived there. She died in London before the work was done. And that is why the pink pagoda now stands by the stream, unoccupied, a little worse for wear. The parishioners think of it as a rich man's folly, but the rich man knows it to be something much closer to his heart. Shall we take those young ruffians down there for a quiet walk before it is time to go in for luncheon?'

10

A Position of Advantage

My dear Rowland,

I have arrived! My situation is as well as it can be in your absence. The two girls, Letitia and Veronica, are very pretty and ladylike – Letitia taking charge of tea. There is a housekeeper who has been most kind and helpful. I feel sorry in my heart for the poor little orphans, though they are unspoilt and seem to accept their situation. There is an elder brother, Mr Dudley, who returns from the regiment tomorrow. Tomorrow also, it is arranged that I shall meet the grandfather, and make a fuller tour of the house and grounds. I am so busy, but still my every second thought is of you. The interview with His Lordship daunts me rather. I hope I shall make a good impression. You must wish me courage. I will write when I have more news.

Your devoted Bella.

My beloved Rowland,

More news, and so soon! I was taken around the estate, and I find it is not only spacious and grand, it is magical! Tucked away in a corner by the stream is a tiny cottage with a garden, and inside and out it is decked out like an oriental pagoda, and the whole painted pink. Oh, it would have charmed your sweet eyes, as it did mine. I was taken there by my youngest charge, Veronica, and by Mr Dudley, the brother, who is now with us. The interview with His Lordship passed off well. I fancy I made the grand old man quite like me. Tomorrow I begin my duties in earnest.

Your adoring Bella.

My dearest Rowland,

No, you must not come. I will not see you. Cannot rather – for you know my duties here. Our love must survive this interlude, as it surely will if we are patient. If *you* are patient, my beloved. Please do not bring us to ruin through your impetuosity.

I implore you, as you love me, Bella.

My dearest Rowland,

You should not have come, though it was sweet to hold your face in my hands for a moment again. But it was foolish too, and we must not be foolish. It was prudence brought me here after the ruination of your prospects, and it is through prudence we will survive. Of course I find our separation unendurable, but no less so than the humiliation of having to deceive my benefactors with a tale about a brother. You, my brother! I am sure that suspicions were aroused. In the afternoon, to cover my shame, I walked alone to the pink pagoda. Where, to my further confusion, I found Mr Dudley – the Honourable Dudley Vestibule, I must call him. He is to reside there, it appears, when he comes of age. He was all politeness, but I am sure he knew that I was overwrought. Rowland, I beg you, never again. I forbid it.

Bella.

My dearest Rowland,

You are jealous. I love you more for that. But it is all needless. Mr Dudley is a kind member of a kind family, and that is all. It would be as impossible for me to avoid his company, as you propose, as it would be unnecessary – Rowland, my love, he would be a kind friend to you too, if he knew you. I am sure of that, for he is no rigid respecter of class, as his treatment of me testifies. Honourable in nature as in title.

Be assured, Bella.

70

My dearest Rowland,

You came again. I am sure it was you. How sweet and foolish to come like a knight of old in disguise, and such a long way! Was it you? A good fellow, they said, and wanting employ as a gamekeeper. But I do not believe you could fire off a gun, my Rowland, if there were wolves around your ankles. It is I alone you must keep, my gentle boy – I will be your game, your chick, your wild pheasant. Do I speak strangely? It is this place that makes me feel so free. Today Dudley called me a giddy goat for something I said. But I am not so free as to be with you. And what good would it have done to have you here, if we had been as separated as we are now, you a groundsman, me a governess? Think of that. Think of it before you are tempted to be foolish again.

Your prize, if patient, Bella.

My dear Rowland,

No, we cannot meet. You must not issue orders. And in the church, you say. How strange you have become! And such precise instructions you give. How do you know all these things? You cannot merely be guessing. A chill settles round my heart as I ask this question, Rowland, and a foolish thought freezes my brain. I will say it, only so that you can call it a girlish folly and deny it utterly, and forgive me, so that I can banish it from my mind. It is that you are here, Rowland, always here, living alongside me on these lawns, in this park, by the river, along the pathways. Deny it, Rowland, deny it if you can! People in the house have spoken of a stranger in the game wood, and there was a gunshot fired over Mr Dudley's head three days ago as he left the pink pagoda. Letitia woke me nervously the other night saying she had seen the figure of a man running through the grounds. A stranger who answered your description approached Veronica in the village street only yesterday. I have had to chide you for your jealousy and impatience before,

Rowland, but if it is true that you have come to set a guard over me and to keep watch on me, that would be cruel and wicked. Even as I write these words I see them as an idle fancy, a grotesque image of something that I dearly wish – that you should be here with me, and that we should never be apart – turned into a nightmare of itself. I do not entirely know what I am saying. But write to me, Rowland, and tell me that it is false, so that my heart can beat steadily again.

Bella.

Dear Rowland,

You do not answer my question. You merely repeat your insistence that we must meet. Rowland, I tell you frankly, this is unkind. You ask me to do what I cannot do. You continue to do what I beg you to have done with. Please, for the love you bear me, reassure me.

Bella.

Dear Rowland,

I have not written for many weeks. I shall write no more. I am to be married. Mr Dudley Vestibule has done me the honour to ask for my hand, and I have accepted with his grandfather's gracious blessing. We will live in the little pink pagoda. What else could I do? He is a good man, and nowhere more so than in his acceptance of me, a governess of no family, as his wife. We should have made each other free, you and I, long since. But it is too late for regret. Try to believe well of me.

Arabella.

Rowland – I write unwillingly and in haste. Your proposal is as preposterous as it is blasphemous. If, as seems most likely, you have taken up a secret residency in this neighbourhood, I must request you to remove yourself forthwith. It will do you no good, and can only bring me harm. You will do best by returning to the city and forgetting about me entirely. As a former friend, I beg you to do this. As the future wife of my husband, I insist upon it.

In three days time, Mrs Arabella Vestibule.

My dear Letitia,

The city here is wonderful. We have seen so much beauty I cannot begin to tell you. Last night, a masquerade ball and we were brought back to our palazzo through the waterways with music playing! Such happenings! Such happiness! But you have had your own excitements too, as your letter tells me, for which many thanks. A fire you say, at the church. And a mysterious body caught in the blaze. Please be sure to send my greetings to the rector and his wife, and express my shock at the news. Console him if you can with memories of the ceremony that took place there in the morning, and which will always remain as the happiest event in my life. But what of the unknown victim? Was there no clue to the man's identity, nothing at all? Was it for certain a man? Has no one reported a person missing, or any strange goings-on? I so long to be informed of everything that transpires in this mystery. It is quite like an old story. Do write to me with further news. Where, by the way, will the poor wretch be buried? In the meantime, I can hardly wait to see the new furnishings in the pagoda. Please send me any letters that may be waiting for me, if you would. Let Veronica have all this news. My respectful greetings, and Dudley's too, to your grandfather.

Your loving sister, if you will permit me, Arabella.

11

Dead Heat

The Voice of the Charred Body speaks from the Burned-out Church:

It is I. I bide my time. I watch and wait. I have all the time in the world; and all the time beyond it too.

They do not know me, they do not know my name. They do not even know my sex, so thoroughly burned I was, without identity or feature. The first one to find me – they think it was the first – scraped away some ash from around my cheeks to see me better, and found it was my cheeks they scraped away. The bone beneath was shiny black with heat, not ashen. The eyeballs had melted and boiled away. I wish, sometimes, that they had turned to glass, so that I could have looked with a frozen stare (I speak metaphorically) upon my pillagers.

All they found on me was this gold ring. They clipped it off with their long shears, and then someone took it from me. My only remaining earthly possession, the one thing about me that the fire did not destroy. One of them still wears it to this day. For the rest of them, they do not know me, and that is why they can never quite put me out of their minds. But one of them thinks she knows, he knows. One of them has something to remember, and wears a ring with the hallmark still cut through by the trace of a line. That mark will never wear away. Who took the ring? Who wants to remember? Who cannot help remembering what they would just as soon forget? Who wears against their skin the little cleft that will never disappear? Was it you?

Or was it you? Or was it you? One of you has picked it up and put it in your pocket. It was you? It was really you, my darling? Am I getting warmer? Oh, I think I'm very warm indeed. I think I'm burning.

Come on then, gather round the dying embers, my body, and listen to the tales. See her with the sad withdrawn look, idly fidgeting with her hand, always fidgeting, turning, turning, turning, trying to smooth it away, trying to forget, but never letting go of what, in the end, will remind her. Let's say it was she who took the ring. The dishonoured daughter of the local squire. Or the adulterous wife – no, better, the incestuous wife and her stepson. The wickedly beautiful lady plunging the stonemason into despair. Or plunging the knife into the mason's heart, and dragging him through the rainsodden pathways on a moonless night to the threshold of the church. It is rainwater that channels down her skirt, down her forehead with the perspiration. Water and fire, woman and man. Plunging the knife up to the hilt into the stepson's beauteous breast, in a moment of madness when he threatens to betray, threatens to fall in love with the simpering child of a local family, threatens to go away to war. She has pleaded with him in the chandeliered hallway, a tempest as violent as anything outside. Our love, the fineness of our love. But he is cold to her demands, silent in the face of her screeching. Too young to know how to answer the fury of her passion, just as he was always too young. Or too awed – it is the mason now – by the splendour of her words, the gleaming in the crystal, and stands in front of her, tongue-tied and adamant. Or she faces the last pleadings of her desperate husband, and names the price of her fidelity. It is then that the knife goes in, the face aghast at the strength within his ageing arm. Drags the body to its final rest, weeping, sweating, rainsodden. Or drags himself in the uncomprehending blackness of despair to the altar to pray. Muttering for mercy, for vengeance, for a hasty end. The candelabrum grabbed, totters, the sparks begin to spread along the

75

altar-cloth. Then to his, to her, blazing eyes Christ goes up in radiance.

Waits till the morning, when all has died down, and goes to the church to see. Pushes past the little crowd that has gathered, standing amongst the remains, amidst the wisps of, is it mist, or is it smoke, rising from the chilled charred ashes, and finds what he is looking for, a token of their love. And still to this day he wears it on his hand, and sits aside from any group like ours, fiddling, fondling, half remembering.

Start again. The stranger who has been seen around the grounds for a day or more. The escapee, the onlooker, the fanatic. Say that he was on his way home, say that. When the burden fell upon him finally, guilt, pride, hopelessness, one of these or all. He could neither go this way nor that. Or that he has arranged all this, as their final assignation. Seeks out the coolness of the nave – cool, notice that – even in the certainty of his unbelief, seeking only the smell of the church, the quiet, the echoing floor-tiles, cool underfoot, the faded beauty of the walls. Lets the door close heavily behind him. Or, in the fury of his belief, her belief, slammed the door, challenging his soul, his God, or hers, to a last battle. He does not know that there are already dark eyes watching him from the shadows. Or dark eyes that are always alert to secrets watching his dark head as he bows in prayer or anguish. Something makes him turn, her scuttle from behind the pillars. In a moment she has gone, or he has raised his arm, the candelabrum grabbed, totters, or this time a more deliberate pyre lovingly built at the altar-rail. Muttering, is it prayers, or a lunatic laughter through the nose? Only a believer could devise such perfect sacrilege. And later, in the rubble, dark eyes search out a souvenir. Or the one to whom he was no stranger comes to remove the only evidence, and then cannot quite bring himself, herself, to see it disappear.

What now? You want the one about the madwoman

from the moor and the bastard child (her priceless ring is her only possession, and her dying secret)? Or the generations of ancient mystics and their deliberate rituals (a jewelled youth dies each year, but the ring always finds its way back to their vaults)? We can do it in costume, king's men and commonwealth men, and the seal that too late identifies a brother. Or the witch daughter of a monk who carries the secret on; or the slave's armlet that becomes a legionary's wedding-band. You only have to say. All of them are there, tales waiting to be told at the fireside. All of them to go into the fire's all-consuming flames.

Nothing else remains. So what's the point? Why all these guessing-games and tale-telling games and games of secret messages? They all come out the same. We are none the wiser. Nothing we can guess makes any difference. None of your feeble questions – was it him or was it her? was it suicide or was it murder? – can be answered. Take it from one who knows: we do not make such distinctions here. All your petty fuss of he and she counts for nothing with us. And from all our long experience – for, after all, we have nothing else to do – we know that in every case the suicide is driven by someone else, or by you all, and that is murder. And we know that the murder victim – I admit it – always draws the killer on by provocation, complicity, or weakness. That is suicide. None of it matters.

So what does matter? The ring remains on the finger. The fidgeting persists. It is this that matters, rather than what it might recall, or what is buried beneath recollection. The finger gets a swelling where the rubbing is. She, he, tries to kick the habit, can't. Soon the swelling is calloused and hardened, and the ring can hardly be removed. It would have to be taken off, if at all, with shears, she, he, learns with a shudder. The little tumour grows and rigidifies, rings itself with a whisker or two, embedding the gold band farther in. And still she, he, twists and turns it, twists and turns. Before it all begins, the unintelligible chaos of what happened; then the ring is taken from the hand; then the fiddling begins; and so in time the lump grows bigger, acquires a colouring and a crown of thick black hairs, stands like a beacon on the hand to say: Once I knew a man, a woman, a stonemason, a witch's daughter, wore this ring, and in the church she went, he went, and there I took him, her, anyone, whatever – all the tales gathering around the point of irritation, round and round and round for ever, to make it better, or make it worse. It is the saying that matters, the token, not what is said.

And so I live on. You cannot destroy me. You cannot put me aside. For me, what they say is true, when they talk about ashes to ashes, dust to dust. It was embarrassing on the day of my funeral, with the coffin-bearers trying to stagger in the accustomed way, when all they were carrying was a cupful of my dust. In the normal course of events it's more like slime to slime, and smear to smear. But even when my coffin had bloated itself on rainwater and exploded long ago, and been sluiced away, I still remain, a thin hard dry line, like a seam of coal, that nothing will ever unsettle. I will never go away. And the rest of me – for there was a good deal left behind amongst the wood-ash and the nails that had melted down like candles – is scattered like everything else, blown out through the blank window-holes into the graveyard, and from there to the fields and houses beyond, across the world. Some of me still hovers and returns in the air. So that I cannot be beaten. And when you think you have won, and idly run your finger along the top of the mantelshelf in one of the precious rooms of the pink pagoda – is it the finger that wears a ring? – some of the blackness on your fingertip will be me. I was there before you. Grains of me still swirl and eddy within the walls of the ruined church, in the hallway where you killed me. You cannot avoid me. You thought you had destroyed me. You thought you had won. But I will survive you all. I am always in the air. I am here, and there, and everywhere. You must keep listening to me.

(The Voice crackles and fades, and disappears.)

12

The Weight of One Bluebird

On another Board far away from here, there is a Big House so big that there seems to be no end to its walls and towers on the hillside where it stands. Its grounds extend so far that, even by standing on the highest point of the tallest of its towers, you still cannot see the limits of the Owner's domain. It is the size of it, compared to the Board we know, that makes you think that this one is the original, and ours only a replica, rather than the other way round.

The Owner himself, the Emperor, is exceptionally large as well. So large that the last time he had a gown made for himself, the piece of cloth was too big for the skinny tailor's workshop, and the silk thread with which the women embroidered birds and flowers upon it was too long for the standard size of bobbin. The tailor had to go to the Emperor's Master Builder and request an extension to his workshop, and the women had to choose someone to go to the Emperor's Quartermaster to see if larger bobbins could be found. Both of these officials in turn had to report to the Imperial Planning Committee, who handed the relevant papers over to the Budgeting Sub-committee, and waited for the Emperor's signature, before an architect could be appointed, or letters to manufacturers sent out. After the Building Inspectorate had satisfied themselves that the plans for the workshop were up to standard, and the Management Committee had obtained clarification as to whether the bobbins were to be placed on regular or on special order, it was nearly time for the making of the gown to begin. Not only is the Emperor himself of an extraordinary size, he also possesses, as you can see, the largest bureaucracy that is to be found in this or any part of the world – a factor which makes the Games that are played here amongst the longest and most laborious that can be played.

The Emperor is almost as fond of his bureaucracy as he is of the magnificent gown that was eventually made. But he is fonder far of his daughter. And who would not be? For she is young, not at all fat, she has shining eyes above pink cheeks that make you catch your breath, and a little lock of dark hair hanging over her brow that makes you want to hug her. It was for her fifteenth birthday, nearly a year ago, that the gown was made for the Emperor. And on the same occasion the Emperor gave his daughter a bluebird in a cage, which is now her favourite possession, and which she keeps in the little walled garden behind her apartments that has always been her favourite place. The Emperor has promised his daughter that, when she is sixteen years of age, she will have not only a garden but also a Gardening Sub-committee, and not only a bluebird but also a Curator of the Imperial Aviary, all of her own, for her to consult and direct as she pleases. She has said politely that she would much prefer to leave such things to the wisdom of her father, whom she loves far above her pet bird and far above her garden. But whether she loves him far above one other possession of hers, a possession which no one else could have given her, is perhaps a question best left unasked. For the Emperor's daughter possesses the heart of a good young man, as he possesses hers, and this is her greatest love, as it is also her best-kept secret.

Now, you will be the first to ask why the love of a good young man, who is very tender and agreeably handsome, who is as deeply in love with her as she with him, and who is also really quite well-off, should be a secret. Why does the Emperor's daughter not simply go to her father and ask his permission to marry the man? For once, the answer does not lie in the fact that the young man is a pauper, or a foreigner, or a demon in disguise, or the son of the Emperor's enemy, or a frog. It lies in the Emperor's love of bureaucracy. For of all the prestigious and impenetrable committees in the Empire, surrounded by pretentious working parties and implacable clerks, none is more authoritative or more secretive than the Emperor's Social Committee. At its head is the Social Registrar, and it is his duty to maintain, as his title implies, a Social Register, containing the names of all those families with whom it is thought proper for the Imperial family to consort. The fiction is upheld that this is an unvarying and closed circle of the socially privileged, but in fact it is widely known that the Standing Committee on Imperial Affairs, which answers directly to the Social Registrar, is responsible for discreetly vetting the eligibility of (and sometimes for disposing of the substantial bribes received from) those families who apply for inclusion within the Register. The members of the Imperial family may pay visits to, and correspond and conduct business with, those families who are on the Register, and with no others. Above all, the Imperial family may only marry within the circle of families approved by the Register. It is, as is so often the case, a system that was conceived to deal with a genuine difficulty – in this case, the extreme rivalry of powerful families within a large empire that led to feuding of a bloodthirsty kind, and to challenges to the supremacy of the Emperor himself – which has become a cumbersome and arbitrary machine, attended to only when its regulations stand immovably in the way of common sense and humane decency. But those regulations cannot be ignored, and they exact severe penalties for a breach at any level – and in the case of marriage, or of a liaison that might lead to marriage, they exact the severest penalty of all, the death of both transgressors.

The young man whom the Emperor's daughter loves is, it hardly need be said, not on the Social Register, and that is why their love has to remain a secret. How, then, did they meet? They met because the uncle of the young man introduced his nephew to the Emperor's Entertainments Committee when they were looking for a juggler to entertain the Imperial Court. The young man was a skilful juggler as it happened, and the uncle was ambitious to have his own family included in the Social Register to advance his son's interest as a potential suitor to the Emperor's daughter. Court entertainers, it should be noted, did not themselves require the approval of the Register. How, having met, did they continue their liaison? They continued it at appointed times, when the young man would climb over the wall of the girl's walled garden. He would stand and hold her pale sweet hands, sometimes admiring and petting her bluebird, because she liked him to, sometimes taking apples off the tree and juggling with them for her alone. And how, in the end, were they betrayed (which, of course, they were)? They were betrayed when first one apple, and then another apple, were juggled above the top of the wall into the view of the inquisitive uncle, who peeped over the wall and immediately saw how his own ambitions were being undone by this upstart of a nephew, and took himself off as fast as he could to the Social Registrar.

And how were they saved from death, the two lovers (because you must believe that they were saved)? It was, strange to say, bureaucracy which saved them as well as bureaucracy which condemned them. Because, whilst the various committees of the Empire were processing the uncle's complaint and moving towards an indictment of the unfortunate couple, the Emperor – who was miserably torn between his duty to the law and his love for his child – came up with a plan. By-passing all the committees and all the inspectors, the Emperor arranged to have built in a far-off place in the mountains, with a little stream nearby, a little pagoda – pink like his daughter's cheeks – a secret place where she could retire with her precious bluebird and with a new walled garden, separated from her lover as well as from her father, but at least alive. It was an ingenious plan, and the Emperor, who was good at heart, put all his energy into it, despite the fact that it would mean never seeing his daughter again. At one moment, the Building Inspectorate got hold of the news, and it looked as if all would be lost whilst they carried out their procedures. But, mercifully, the wheels of the legal bureaucracy turned even more slowly than those of the planning bureaucracy, and the pagoda was ready before the girl could be arrested. She and her bluebird went weeping into the mountains.

It is not entirely clear what happened next, or at least not clear how it came about. There was a visit to the little pink pagoda from three men and a young boy who came out of nowhere. Some people believe that the Emperor himself had sent them, others that it was the young man, and still others that they came of their own accord from somewhere entirely unknown. They told the girl how she could be reunited with her lover. She was to dismiss her servants and send them back to the Court. She was to rid herself of every possession. And, by her own efforts, she was to dig a trench around the pink pagoda, as deep as her arm and as wide as her foot, not more, not less. When she had done these things, the three men and the boy would return.

She pleaded with them to have her lover by her, but they refused. The pink pagoda, they said, was to fly to a faraway place where her lover could join her, but two could not fly there together. He would have to make his own way. She pleaded with them to keep her bluebird alone amongst her possessions, but they refused. The calculations had all been very accurately done, they said, and even a bluebird would be too heavy for the pagoda to fly.

The Emperor's daughter was desolate. She said to herself that every successive thing she was asked to do for her own benefit only made things worse, and that this would make her lonely, it would make her hands dirty and rough, and it sounded very dangerous. But still she agreed to try. With weeping eyes she opened the cage of her bluebird and watched it fly off into the mountains. She sent her servants away, and threw out every possession that she had from the pink pagoda. Then she began to dig. The work was hard and she was weak, and she feared she would never finish before the three men and the boy came back. Wiping the tears from her eyes and the perspiration from her forehead, she looked up towards the mountains where her bluebird had flown, and saw the sky black with every kind of bird and the ground darkened with every kind of animal. Leading them all was her own bluebird, who flew about above the pagoda and showed the animals and the birds where to dig and how to set about it. Pretty soon, the trench was finished, and all the animals went away, except for the bluebird who sat on a tree some way off.

After dark, the three men and the boy returned. They each stood at a corner of the trench and, with enormous effort, lifted the piece of ground upon which the pink pagoda stood high into the air, high enough so that the winds caught it and carried it clear of the earth, clear of the mountains, and far away. It all happened so fast that the girl hardly had time to notice, and no time at all to thank her mysterious visitors for what they had done. She was not even sure she wanted to thank them. It was cold flying so high, and she had nothing with which to warm herself. And she thought she was all alone. It was after a little while that she noticed with delight how the bluebird was flying along behind her, following her every time the wind changed direction and the pagoda took a new path. In her excitement she called to the bluebird, and held out her hand. The bluebird landed on her finger, and instantly the weight was too much for the flying pagoda. It came out of the sky at great speed, and came to land in an entirely unexpected place.

Now, there are different ways in which this Game might

end. In the best of them, the young man will be visited by the same three men and the boy who will tell him how to find his beloved in her pagoda. And being brave and very much in love, he will set off across an enormous swamp, across a desert, across a mountain-range, through a dark forest, across a mighty ocean, into a forbidden city, and finally across low-lying marshland and through rough quarries to where the pink pagoda lies. It will be many years and many adventures later, but he will arrive, they will marry and be happy. But in other Games, he will never arrive – he will be lost in a wilderness, set upon by bandits, injured in a fall, or tempted into straying into a luxurious and forbidden city. Perhaps he will be unable to find the pagoda, after its unexpected landing. Or it will not have landed, but crashed, and the Emperor's daughter will have been thrown out of it in the vortex of its swift descent. Perhaps the country in which it lands will itself be plagued by a bureaucracy nearly as excessive and rigid as the Emperor's bureaucracy, and the pagoda will have been impounded by some Aliens Committee, and the girl caught up in a labyrinthine tangle of regulations. The young man may, after all, arrive only to find the pagoda surrounded by armed and uniformed guards who will refuse to tell him anything of the whereabouts of the Emperor's daughter. Or to find it in a state of ruin, uninhabitable, and no news of a young girl at all. Or the vaguest news that she is no longer there, and may have gone in search of somewhere else to live – a big house perhaps, such as she knew when she was growing up. Or, in some ways worst of all, in the delays and anxiety of the intervening years, she may have given her heart to someone else (these things do happen), and require the young man on his honour to leave her to the new life she has chosen.

Any of these things may be. All that can be said is that there is a rumour amongst the people who live in the land near the pink pagoda, about some three, or maybe more, finely made and well-decorated clubs, of the kind that are used in juggling, having been found in the waste ground behind the pagoda. But the clubs in question will have been lost, or sold at auctions, or otherwise dispersed. There will be talk of sightings in and around the gardens of the pink pagoda of an unusual bird, a blue one – though these too will remain unconfirmed, and the experts will not be convinced. There will be a story too, told by the people, about the Emperor of a far-off land and his beautiful daughter, and about a magical flying house that is lifted off the earth by the help of all the animals and all the birds. But they will not think to connect this story with the rumours, and the children who listen to it (who are themselves unusually pale-skinned and pink-cheeked, and whose dark hair invariably hangs in a single lock over their brows) will grow up believing it to be a piece of pure invention, and nothing more.

13

Hide and Seek

Up from the terraces, down from the rooftops, shrieking and banging, the wind was mercilesss towards the old mansion on the hill. Round and round it went, demanding sanctuary. Inside, with the curtains drawn and the door locked, nothing fluttered or was flattened. The grandfather clock in the hallway marked the solemn passage of the seconds, unrattled. The great fire in the drawing-room burned steadily, and its roar of heat outdid the chilly whistling in the flue. The pieces were being put away in the library after a game.

'You realize how improper it is for a guest to beat his host so soundly, and for youth to win against old age?' said one voice.

'It shows that I do not think of you at all as an old man, Sir Henry,' said the other voice. 'And it shows moreover that you have made me feel so comfortably at home that I forgot I was a guest. Thus understood, my little victory is the highest compliment I could pay you.'

The older man smiled, and said, 'You win again.' The younger man inclined his head to accept the compliment. 'But,' said the other, 'tell me in detail what it is you're planning. All I really know is that you came two months ago to work in my library, and now you've come to dig up my grounds. It is an imposition, to be sure! You'll be wanting to move in next.'

'Not quite all your grounds, Sir Henry,' came the reply. 'I want to dig in the area behind your summerhouse, and if it's not inconvenient I'd like to stay in the summerhouse rather than here' – Sir Henry looked up quickly – 'because I will be working by myself, and examining my finds at any hour of the day or night.' It was the summerhouse, the curious pink pagoda at the foot of the hill, that had especially delighted the young archaeologist on his previous visit, and it was both a private indulgence as well as a convenience that made him press his request.

'The pink pagoda,' repeated Sir Henry in a slow voice. 'And to stay there. The rooms would need to be cleared.'

'Only one,' the other interposed.

'Because you see the place has been left unused for a long time, since –' he paused as if to calculate the date. 'For a very long time indeed.' After another pause, Sir Henry sighed and said, 'But I'm sure this can be arranged for you. Yes, I'm sure it can. Now tell me what you're hoping to find, Mr Player.'

Edward Player explained to his host once again how his earlier study of the maps, manuscripts and property records in Sir Henry's possession had confirmed the almost certain existence of the site of a large Roman villa near where the pink pagoda now stood. From the finds that he could make there, he was hoping to add further evidence, another piece or two, to his jigsaw picture of Roman life under the late Empire.

'It's not the objects themselves,' he said with enthusiasm, 'that interest me, so much as the charting of a way of life. Don't you find it extraordinary that this soil here was touched by their ideas, their standards?' It was notorious within the university that Player always spoke of the Romans with this special kind of awe. His archaeological pursuits he conceived of as a supplement to his historical and philological work, but also as a symbolic adventure in its own right: digging through layers of rapacious, ugly, mindless human existence, until the Roman glory, the Roman order, could shine out once more.

'Beautiful Samian pots came up this river and were sold, he continued. 'Splendid jewels, ceramics, coins, clothing.

I will only find tiny fragments of all this, even if I'm lucky, but it will all be evidence of a complete system. Of a marvellously rational and creative civilization, which we have incomprehensibly allowed to slide back into the mud and the slime. Doesn't that excite you, Sir Henry?'

'I'm afraid, Mr Player, that I can't share your enthusiasm for grubbing about in the past,' said Sir Henry in a tired voice. 'History, history. I can see why anyone might rationally refrain from relying on the future. But to suppose that the past is any better seems to me an obvious mistake. The past is only the futility and errors of the present played a million times over. The same game again and again, with the same limited number of moves. Sometimes it manages to be played out to an even more grisly conclusion than in our own times, but that hardly serves to redeem it in my eyes. No, Mr Player, I will tolerate your activities here, and I will find your company most agreeable, but I cannot pretend to sympathize with what you want to do.'

'But in this beautiful house, Sir Henry,' persisted the enthusiast, 'surely you must have some sense of the past?'

'I do not see why I should have my interests or feelings dictated to me by a mere building,' said the other somewhat sharply.

'Is that, do you suppose,' said Edward, 'because you have no heir, and because you are not in the direct line of inheritance yourself?' He spoke without thinking, and regretted as soon as he had spoken touching on matters at once so personal and so tragic. Sir Henry looked up quickly, and suddenly his eyes were those of a tired, old man, and his voice had become deadened.

'I would ask you, Mr Player,' he said, 'whilst you are here, please do not confuse history with gossip. I must now bid you goodnight.'

As he stood up, the gap on the library shelves came once again involuntarily into Edward's mind. On his previous visit Edward had noticed that a number of sizeable volumes were missing from the collection, and that the lack of dust in the empty space showed they had only been removed from the shelves very recently. Sir Henry had been oddly evasive when Edward had enquired about them, and something in his tone of voice had made the connection with what he now said. The missing books began to arouse in Edward's mind something more than a scholar's curiosity. The truth was that the archaeological purposes of his visit were increasingly being overtaken by other factors, the pleasurable prospects of the pagoda, the intriguing character of his melancholy and sceptical host, and the little mystery of the gap on the library shelves. He felt a curious sympathy with the older man, curious because of the disparity in their ages, tastes and situation – the young historian with his busy college life and his young wife expecting their first baby, and the ageing anti-academic widower, who had lived for many years in this large house, with a single housekeeper for company, since the early deaths of his wife and only daughter.

For a few days, whilst the pagoda was made ready for his occupancy, Edward returned home, and was busy preparing his rooms in college for all the new evidence that would accumulate from his researches, and equally busy fussing over his wife with all the delicacy that an excited father-to-be always feels.

It was on the third day after his return that he found the skull. Although the day was perfectly calm, he felt the chill of an earlier wind around his body and heard a distant howling. By the end of the afternoon he had patiently uncovered the skeleton of an adult with an infant's skeleton at its side. He packed the bones in two sacks, instinctively thinking of them as evidence, though he was as yet nowhere near the Roman level. He knew it was important to conceal the sacks in the pagoda, and to tell nobody about his discovery, but he could not have said why. Sir Henry's face at dinner looked more shrunken and yellowing than ever. The trim grey beard gave it a sharpness of outline he had not noticed before. He kept trying to get the light between himself and his host, as if there were a mystery behind his impassive eyes, and as if it could be made to show itself. He excused himself from cigars and port, and returned to share the pink pagoda for the night with two sets of human remains.

The following morning he made his first real discovery. He had dug down into a new trench at right angles to where he had started, and quickly came upon a fragment of flue-tile – he recognized the type almost instantly – sooty black on the inside of its curved surface, and delicately embossed on the outside, once he had scraped away the dirt with his thumbnail. His confidence in the siting of the villa increased, and over lunch he was able to chat happily to Sir Henry about his discovery, about the quality of Roman decoration, and then to find himself ranging over the organization of the Roman household, the complex systems of inheritance and the education of the young.

When he returned to his labours, however, he could no longer suppress his puzzlement at finding Roman remains so near the surface. It became unavoidably obvious that the earth in this area had been turned over at some more recent date. The knowledge of this came on him like a nausea and he began to dig furiously downwards, careless of any normal archaeological caution. He soon began, as he knew he would, to scrape the earth away around the clear outline of a supine skeleton. An adult, large round the pelvis, and just beyond it the bones of a child. With heavy arms he began to transfer the bones to two more sacks, and continued with his routine digging, trying to think. All he could think of was the dustless space in the library from which four or five large volumes had been removed, and all he could decide was that they must somehow be recovered.

'Anything exciting, Mr Player?' said a voice above him. Edward's eyes shot up, the spade sprang from his grasp despite himself, and he saw the figure of Sir Henry leaning over the trench, rising into the sky. The little beard wagged on the skull-shaped head. 'I'm sorry if I alarmed you,' the voice went on. 'You look in need of a rest, Mr Player. Try to remember that Rome wasn't dug in a day.'

'I'm perfectly well,' said Edward feebly, unable to restrain a sideways glance at the two sacks on the floor of the trench. 'There's always work of this kind to be done between the worthwhile finds. It's exactly the same in libraries,' he said, and bit his lip for having mentioned libraries.

'I came down partly out of curiosity, I have to admit,' said Sir Henry, and Edward could only think grimly to himself, Yes, but I wonder when you actually arrived. 'I may express cynicism about your enterprise, Mr Player, but I can't help admiring your devotion to the cause. I begin to see you, if I may put it like this, as the instrument of a greater authority. I refer of course to the university. You are here to bring the light of reason upon our little darkened world.' The voice was curiously strained, almost shouting against the dulling acoustic of the deep earth. 'You may appear to resemble a man digging his own grave, Mr Player, if you'll pardon me for mentioning it. But in fact you are bringing things to light, if not to life.'

Edward could only mumble a response and try to look suitably amused by his host's arch banter, as if he accepted it as mere banter.

'But you don't wish to hear my petty reflections,' said Sir Henry. 'What I really came to tell you was that I have been unexpectedly called to see my lawyer, and will not be home tonight until late. The housekeeper will prepare dinner for you at the usual time. She's a trifle deaf, you may have noticed, and so be prepared to ring for her loud and long. I may see you, if you haven't retired by then, at around ten-thirty.' To all of this purely functional information, Edward listened a great deal more intently than to the heavy-handed ironies of a moment before.

After dinner, and with a reluctant sense of what had to be done, he ascended the main staircase of the house in search of Sir Henry's dressing-room and study. His reputation as an open-minded and frank researcher faced him like an implied criticism of the silent and secretive nature of the present investigation, the way he ensured, for instance, that the housekeeper was at a safe distance before beginning. What he was looking for could not be easily hidden. But two hours brought no results, and he began to think his suspicions had been ill-founded. Perhaps there was no connection between the burials in the grounds and the missing volumes. Perhaps there was, in fact, no need to be suspicious of the skeletons he had found. Mass graves, plague-pits, even formerly consecrated burial grounds – none of these was uncommon, although he knew equally well that none of them tallied with the established history of the area. Perhaps all his information had been wrong from the start. Or perhaps the books had already been destroyed and there was no point in looking. His last, desperate thought was that somehow they might have been returned to the library, and he decided to conclude his stealthy researches there.

As he stepped on to the threshold of the library, the lamp was turned up at the far end of the room, and a weary voice spoke. 'Is this what you are looking for, Mr Player?' The pale face was unmistakable in the creamy glow. Long fingers rested gently on a pile of black-bound books that were unmistakable too, though Edward had never seen them before.

'You are indefatigable in your investigation, Mr Player,' said Sir Henry. 'I think you deserve commendation. For myself, I seem to have got back here a little before time. I'm sorry to have alarmed you for the second time in one day. I trust your meal was satisfactory. You look tired, Mr Player. We should conclude our business as swiftly as possible, and allow you to get some sleep. Let me bring forward, then, what might be described as the second piece of evidence.' Sir Henry bent down behind the desk and brought into view some shapeless bags. 'I must apologize again. I have been guilty of an intrusion upon your privacy nearly as gross as the one you have just committed against mine. I fetched these from the pagoda earlier in the evening. Now that we have everything, as it were, ready, perhaps you would care for a drink and a seat. You do look most awfully tired. Whisky, Mr Player?'

Edward accepted the hospitality that was offered in silence. Like a sleepwalker he moved forward to the vacant seat. He guided his numbed fingers to open the pages of the volume that was slid across the desk towards him. He forced his eyes to read. He paused to turn several of the thick vellum pages and read again at random. For the second time in a week, the cold and screaming sound of a frenzied wind seemed to surround Edward. What was being presented to his eyes forced into his rational mind the piercing end of a wedge whose entirety was a world of horror and unreason. He found himself thinking about the fragment of curved flue-tile he had discovered. It seemed to answer his real purposes in having come to this place, and its little moulded decorative motif seemed to stand for a whole world of order and beauty. But in his mind's eye, he could see only the black and shapeless side of the tile, and though he scraped away at the gathered dirt of the ages he could get no nearer to the embossed image of petals and leaves on the other side. It seemed to have gone for ever.

'But,' said Edward, drinking from his glass, 'all this. All this,' he said. 'I don't understand.'

'You are perhaps beginning to understand,' said the other man gently. 'Let us try to talk like intelligent beings, even if what we are talking about seems to face us with the unintelligible. What we must address ourselves to is the question of compulsion. I want you to understand the fact of compulsion first of all, Mr Player, because without it everything else is indeed incomprehensible, and I believe I am not mistaken in thinking that compulsion is hard for you to grasp. I believe it does not lie within the range of your experiences. As human beings, we blink our eyes involuntarily. Our knee springs up when the doctor's hammer hits it. We breathe. We dream. We accept these things as part of our nature. What I am asking you to accept is that the same human mind, the same human being, is capable of performing complex actions as if by reflex – fully conscious, carefully planned actions as if in a dream. What you have begun to read are the accounts of unhappy men, going back over many generations, who have known such compulsion, have acted upon it, have failed to understand their actions, have felt grave responsibility for what they have done, but have been unable to feel guilt – and who have turned, also as if by compulsion, to writing in one form or another to try to explain what they all knew was by its nature inexplicable. There are letters here, diaries, confessions, stories written out as if the protagonist were indeed a fiction, there is even a piece of verse – not very good, I'm afraid – and they all amount to the same thing. The attempt to exorcise what is not even understood, to expiate what is not even felt to be a crime.

'This house, Mr Player, has descended from generation to generation but never in a direct line. It is a fact that has provoked much public interest, speculation, even suspicion. You yourself had evidently heard some of the gossip before you came here. But it has never been properly explained. The explanation is to be found in the tragic testimony of these pages. Time and again, as I say, my predecessors – I might with justice say, my ancestors – have sought to rid themselves of their compulsion by committing its history to paper. Time and again, they have failed. Each has then hoped to wipe away the stain of compulsion by bequeathing the house to someone outside the immediate family. In many cases, as I shall explain, this has been because there is no direct descendant. I am the nephew of the previous owner. He was the cousin of the owner before that. If I am not mistaken, he was left it by a close friend. And so it has gone on.

'But it seems as if the compulsion lies not in the blood, not in the seed that is passed from one generation to the next, but in the very ground of the place itself. Especially, it seems, in the ground that surrounds the pink pagoda. Who knows, Mr Player, but that the Romans who built your villa here were not acting under the same compulsion, or were indeed its originators? The pagoda itself was built by one of my predecessors in yet another vain attempt to rid the place of evil. You can read the account in here. The idea was to cover over the evil with something beautiful, and so to expunge it. All that has happened is that the pretty little pagoda now stands as a mockery of beauty itself, and that it too has become the scene of frightful crimes, so much so that I have had it locked up for years. On every page of these sad volumes you will read of people who first came here thinking that they were beyond the reach of compulsion, or who ended their days believing that by wisdom or by cunning they could staunch the tide of evil that wells up in this place. They were all miserably mistaken. I inherited this house with the same delusion, and I have to confess, Mr Player, that I welcomed you here because the foolish hope persisted. I thought I recognized in you a kind of decency, even a kind of innocence, which might unwittingly be able to remove this evil from the earth, as it were, to dig it up. I was right about your qualities. But of course I quickly realized how wrong I was about your powers, and I have since sadly watched you become the witness of this stain, rather than its cleanser. All I can hope to do is to make you an honest witness to the whole of the truth.'

At this Sir Henry sat back, almost as if there were nothing more to say. Fear for his own safety had left Edward. A larger fear now gripped him, fear of the truth. In his mind he could see only digging, layer after layer of life and death gone through, the thickness of clay and mud, the way it clung, the futility of searching in all that black density. No thought of the Roman strata came into his mind. For the first time, he began to have a sense of Sir Henry's hatred of the past, his scoffing at Edward's pursuits. He began to feel a profound pity for the man beside him.

'You already know, of course,' Sir Henry began again, speaking matter-of-factly, 'what you have found. The remains of mothers and their children. Generation after generation, going back I do not know how far. Perhaps, as I say, even as far back as your precious Romans. Slaughtered every one of them by the successive occupants of this house, by husbands and by fathers. And buried in the grounds of the pagoda. My own contribution to this history is that I poisoned my wife and my daughter shortly after the latter's fifth birthday. I removed the bodies to the pagoda prior to burial – not to the room you have been using, you will be glad to hear. I made out that my wife had killed the child and then herself in a fit of depression. By my deception, stones were buried in the local churchyard in their stead. It was all carefully planned, as ingenious as any of the stories you may care to read between these covers. And why? Because of something we have spoken of before, though in a lighter vein.

'You, Mr Player, are an historian, you not only know the past, you clearly idealize it. It is a source of strength to you, as perhaps it is to most people. You must try to imagine the opposite situation, when the past – and all its evidences around you – becomes an intolerable burden, an enemy rather than an exemplar. And when the future seems to be no more than a reflection in time of the same ghastly past, spinning out through new generations the old disgusting saga. This loathing for the passage of time fixes itself, Mr Player, on those creatures that will carry you, in a sense, forward into the future. Not out of hatred for them, but for the world of time that they must inhabit. You will do anything in that state of loathing to prevent there being such a possibility. You will even kill. This is the state of mind, as I can best describe it to you, in which my own family was murdered, and it is, I believe, the reason for every killing that has taken place within this house. It is ironic that it should now be associated with the little summerhouse, as if there were a dark side to the idle pleasures of the pink pagoda – a hatred of the passage of time itself, which would rather destroy time's victims than see them sucked into its remorseless void.

'There is no more that I can usefully tell you now, Mr Player,' said Sir Henry wearily. 'You now know the basic facts. I leave it to you to decide what to do. I trust you to decide intelligently. For me, it has been at least a partial release to share these appalling truths with a fellow human being. I think we should now retire to bed.'

The unease that Edward felt at what he had heard spread very wide. It centred, however, on himself and on the role that he had been called to play in all of this – first, a scholar and a would-be exorcist; then a detective; now a confessor, and a what? an informant? Left to himself, during a sleepless night, Edward could not decide what his next move should be. The following morning, however, made the nature of Sir Henry's game much clearer. The housekeeper found his body dangling from a cord in the stairwell. The police were already there when Edward came up to the big house. Instinctively, he first checked the library and saw that the missing volumes had been returned to their place on the shelves, and that Sir Henry's own testimony had been added as the last signature to the last volume. As he came out of the library the police inspector addressed him.

'Mr Player? How well did you know Sir Henry?' he asked.

'You could say,' said Edward, 'that we were on the point of becoming intimates.'

'He had obviously become attached to you, sir,' said the policeman, and silently handed Edward a sheet of paper. After a moment, he added, 'It's a will, sir. It seems that Sir Henry visited his lawyer yesterday evening to alter the terms of his will, before this shocking business occurred.

Edward read through the formal language, whose final words were:

After such bequests have been made, I leave the residue of my estate, the house and all its grounds, to Edward Player, on the condition that he leave the property intact and live there for the remainder of his life with his wife and any children she may bear.

'You're a fortunate man, Mr Player,' said the police officer, 'a very fortunate man.'

14

Consequences

'But when you said a week in the country, I shuddered at the thought of a dank shack, stinking of peat or dung, or whatever it is that may be used to light the recalcitrant stove, and where the stone flags on the floor are so cold in the morning that one would never get out of bed were it not for the prospect of a horse or cow – or a horribly ruddy-faced cowherd – poking a slavering head through the window. But this,' the man said with a broad gesture, 'this is delightful.'

This was a raised verandah with steps down to a stream and a smell of honeysuckle. The chairs were wickerwork and covered in cushions of various tasselled and thickly embroidered fabrics. With the idle stateliness of a sultan taking sherbet, Basil, the man who had spoken, allowed his gesturing arm to accept a cup of tea from his young friend, Jack. Even more of a delight was the room behind them, a curious hexagon sparsely furnished with exquisite lacquered pieces, black and gold against its white walls. There were a few objects – a fan, some fine vases, one with five blue irises that curled their lips back proudly, several handsome books, some painted parchment rolls – that took the eye, but did not overwhelm it. In the centre of the floor, a radiant peacock-blue carpet of oriental design that shimmered in answer to the crystal chandelier. 'Your uncle,' Basil had said, for the house did not belong to the young man, 'is clearly a person of different tastes from my Aunt Cynthia. Her drawing-room is like a pawnbroker's shop. One feels the impulse to duck upon entering, it is so crowded and behung.'

The ceiling of the room was a gentle dome, which echoed the main exterior feature of the house – a steeply sloping, double-coned roof, surmounted by a small cupola. The effect was enchanting, and all the more so for being painted outside in the most delicate pink. 'It was in a state of terrible disrepair,' Jack had told his guest, 'when my uncle found it. But he has restored it bit by bit. He calls it his pink pagoda.'

Jack's uncle was a painter of some note. There was a large canvas in the converted stables beyond the pagoda which Basil had already seen. It showed startled shepherds, awoken by a blaze of light that was taken to be the angelic presence. The drama of light and dark, the many colours in the flaming centre of the painting, and the tension in the postures of the shepherds, expressed in the way their gowns fell across the taut musculature of their bodies – all this had clearly interested the painter more than any sacred significance in the subject. 'It is always wise,' Basil had said, 'to deck out one's true interests in a subject-matter that can only earn the approval of the popular critics.'

Such a remark was typical of Basil. As he himself was fond of saying, wit was his vice, but he was glad to say it was not his only vice. His status within the university was unclear, perhaps non-existent. His effective role was to act as the central force within a group of young men, amongst whom Jack was often to be found, who flitted between Oxford and London, creating ripples of rumour and disbelief wherever they went. Jack had accepted Basil's tutelage with a somewhat distant fascination for his wit, his unfettered principles and his unremitting search for pleasure. He had suggested a week in the country in order to cement the friendship.

'Honestly, Basil,' he now said, putting aside his teacup, 'you are incorrigibly attached to the hours and ways of the city. Of course I agree with you that the pagoda is particularly delightful, but it is not everything. And we shall take every opportunity to discover how the country-side which you affect to despise can be a source of health and refreshment and quiet.'

'Now you make me shudder once more,' Basil said, visibly shuddering. 'For my health I refer to my doctor. That is his province, and I would no more deprive him of it than I would deny my lawyer control over the settlement of my debts. For my refreshment I would much prefer to have oysters and champagne after a night of mediocre opera, than to have to take a long walk before consuming a luncheon whose only distinction is that it was cooked under the shadow of the slaughterhouse. And as for quiet, I do not like quiet. It makes me think I might be alone, and if I am alone any remarks I might wish to make are entirely wasted. No, the only quiet that delights me is the ebbing of conversation, and the sudden pause in the clatter of crockery and silverware, when a particularly malicious story is told about the hostess across the far end of the dinner-table. Or the quiet of the streets at two o'clock in the morning, when the cabs are infrequent and one can only guess at what is going on behind closed curtains from the subdued hubbub that filters into the street.'

'My dear Basil,' laughed Jack, 'as I said, you are incorrigible!' They were interrupted at this point by a young man with a message from the Hall, an invitation to supper. Jack left the messenger briefly with Basil whilst he went off to write a note in reply.

'You will find the Hall more tiresome, I'm afraid, than any country walks,' said Jack, after the messenger had left. 'Lord Harry is a bore who will confirm your worst expectations. There is a daughter, however, Lily, recently returned from France, a rather dowdy cygnet of the squire-archy who has come back as a surprisingly attractive swan.'

'French polish can make even the plainest deal look passable,' said Basil, who always sneered at women. A

ruthless attitude towards women, coupled with an ideal-
ized view of masculine friendship, and of what the group
called Grecian love, was one of the solders of Basil's circle.
As with so much else in that circle, Jack neither excluded
himself from this nor involved himself wholeheartedly.
Rather he stood on the fringes, disinterestedly – indolently,
one might say – enjoying the exotic aroma that came from
the centre.

'All I ask,' said Jack, thinking of Lily, 'is that you be
polite.'

'When have you ever known me otherwise?' said Basil.
'What you are really asking is that tonight I should be
completely dishonest, rather than disguising my honesty
in words that will cause offence only because our hosts
will not be certain that they have understood them. By the
way,' he added, 'who was our charming messenger, and
why do I think I know him?'

'One of my uncle's shepherds,' said Jack. 'The young
one whose arms are raised up on the left. In real life, an
under-gardener at the Hall.'

On the way to the Hall, Basil expanded on his earlier
theme. 'You must understand,' he said, 'that the country-
side is no more than a factory for the production of some
necessities of life. But the reality of life is lived in the cities.
Every ten-shilling farm-labourer knows that the life of the
country is a servitude that does no good to anyone who
lives within it. If he has a spare penny, which is unlikely,
he spends it on a newspaper, or a trinket, or on something he believes to be in fashion, in short on things which
give him a taste – however falsified or watered-down –
of the life of the city. In this he is much closer to reality
than your fanciful child of nature. If we were truly children
of nature, we would be as bored as sheep, and quite as
indistinguishable. The beauty of your uncle's pagoda has
nothing to do with nature. It is beautiful in despite of
nature. It has to do with the fantastical notions that men
begin to have only when they are free of the humdrum

103

demands of nature, and cease to be beasts. It turns a little corner of what would surely otherwise be a puddled farmyard or a heap of brambles into something cosmopolitan, something clever. It claims this acre for the city, and laughs at nature.'

Jack laughed, as he always did, at his friend's expansive paradoxes, and allowed him to give them free rein in the hope that he would be exhausted by the time they arrived at the Hall. In the event, Basil's behaviour towards his hosts was impeccable. He praised what he could of the food, and he refrained from passing comment on the wine. He engaged Lord Harry in a lengthy discussion of poaching practices, and he flattered Miss Lily without requiring her to speak French. When he elected to walk back to the pagoda rather than accompany Jack in the carriage, Jack began to feel that the benefits of the countryside were having a speedy influence on Basil's temperament, and he was pleased. He was pleased, too, with the evident attentions that had been shown him by the daughter of the house.

The following morning, when dressing, he saw a figure dodging between the trees in the early-morning mist, but the figure had disappeared before he could make him out. When he tackled Basil on the subject over breakfast, all Basil would say was that he was 'playing a little game of his own, a rustic dance you might call it, not dissimilar in nature from the measures that were being trod between Jack and Miss Lily'.

'But not, I fancy, as open,' said Jack sharply.

'My dear boy,' said Basil, 'there are palaces and chambers and caskets that should never be opened to the public gaze, lest everyone see the delights therein and rush there in a mass, spoiling it for all. Of such,' he added, producing from his pocket a little silver phial which Jack recognized, 'there are smaller treasures too.' The Poppy was the nickname given to this other thread that bound Basil's circle into a unity. Jack had drunk there on occasion, and he was therefore obliged to accept Basil's rebuke towards his own censoriousness.

During the day, the subject was more than once returned to. The illicit pleasures of the silver phial, as of Basil's own private 'country dance', were all somehow of a piece with the pink pagoda, according to the fantastic phrases that Basil wove into a seeming argument. 'We must think of ourselves as trespassers here,' he said. 'We come without rights, and whilst we are not so childish as to think that the breaking of rules is of itself a pleasure, neither are we so dull as to believe that such pleasures could be had by anyone who respected the mere conventions of the tribe. We climb on the shoulders of the law-breakers in order to gain access to the secret garden.'

Whilst Jack applauded the convolutions of Basil's argument, he did not for a moment accept its conclusions. He did, however, out of friendship and established custom, accept the Poppy when it was offered that evening, sipping where Basil drank plenteously.

Under its influence, Basil became more and more melancholy and vehement as the evening wore on. 'I am the only person I know who truly loves,' he said to Jack, 'because I look at the thing itself, and take no cognisance of the world's opinions or my own future. Other people are always trying to placate the prospective father-in-law as well as trying to woo the bride.'

Later he said, 'Goodness is only laziness. It is just obeying other people's rules, without the courage to make up your own.'

Finally, as Jack helped him upstairs to bed, his bitterness turned in upon itself. On the stairs, he paused to hold Jack by both shoulders, and said, 'I was always trying to be Dionysus, and I think I have succeeded only in being Thersites.' It was then that Jack realized that the whole appearance of fastidious and exotic principles in his friend, the celebrated hauteur and impenetrability, was a façade, an elaborate and much-admired construction that covered up a nonentity. The thinness of its walls was terrifying. How could anyone hope to survive in that! Hazily, Jack vowed that he would no longer play the overawed pupil to Basil's unprincipled master, though he had no clear idea of how to go about this. He would start tomorrow, the pink pagoda would become the setting for a transformation.

During the night, overinflated opiate dreams came to him again and again. The pagoda was magnified into a vast palace, its pale colour heightened into crimsons and livid purples. There was an epiphany like the sunburst in his uncle's painting, but it was an explosion of monstrosity, a thing made up of congealed hair and blood and dirt – the obscene pellet of a vulture, perhaps – rather than anything of wonder and beauty. Basil, Jack, their circle of friends, his uncle, the young gardener from the Hall, Lord Harry, and Lily too, were all there as witnesses, constrained to watch, held by manacles and chains, as the thing descended upon them. Time and again he awoke before it smashed in their faces, and then he would fall asleep and have to repeat the ordeal. Finally he could bear sleeping no longer. He opened the curtain to see if it was light, and was amazed to see in the half-light something disappearing through the trees once more. This time, however, it was a group of figures, four of them, and gone even more quickly than before. He stayed by his window as the grey early-morning light gathered strength, and allowed his brain to toy idly with the puzzle of the figures in the garden.

Before breakfast, he went to Basil's room to suggest a morning walk in the woods, and to make enquiries about the mysterious visitors during the night. Basil lay on the bed as he had left him, but the entire left side of his face had been smashed in, and the matter that had been his flesh and brain and blood-vessels was smeared and spilled across the bedclothes, across Basil's own clothes, and on to the walls and floor of the room. No words came to Jack's

106

lips, no ideas into his head. The richness of colour swam in his eyes, and he held himself to avoid fainting. There was a long-handled spade, of the kind that has an almost heart-shaped blade, lying near the bed, lumpy with old earth, and now crimson up to its handle with blood. Jack moved towards it instinctively, but touched nothing in the room, before walking on to the landing to call huskily to a servant.

The man was caught, the young under-gardener from the Hall. He more or less gave himself up, after a day of almost continuous aimless wandering across the fields. A bag of blood-soaked clothing was found in his family's cottage. He said nothing about any accomplices, despite fierce cross-questioning from the police and later from lawyers. At his trial, Jack too said nothing about the group of figures he had seen in the garden. But he noticed at the back of the courtroom each day three grim-faced older men – the lad's father and two uncles, it was said – who sat with folded arms listening to every word. The trial became something of a national pastime, with some taking sides with the fine gentleman who had been struck down by an almost illiterate peasant youth, and others preferring to believe that something lay behind the young man's assertions that the gentleman had made him do things, beastly things – things which, he stammered, he would never tell, but which were true. Whatever could be said on either side, the conclusion was not in doubt. If Basil deserved punishment, it had already been meted out with spades and hoes and shovels. It remained for the judge to sentence the young man to the rope. The three older men, Jack noticed, were nowhere to be seen as the courtroom emptied.

In this version of the Game, there are no winners. Having begun the Game as Occupant of the Pink Pagoda, albeit temporarily, the Player has even this taken away from him by the end. The Pink Pagoda was locked up for the future; the shepherds and the angel remained unfinished; the Friend was dead; the Boy too; even the Old Men can take no satisfaction from their presumed evasion of justice, since the Boy was all they had between them. The Owner of the Big House closes his doors to the Player, and the Beautiful Woman is forbidden to see him. Home offers no sanctuary under such circumstances. What the World thinks – in the form of family, friends, fellow students – is said behind his back. It makes no difference that he was innocent. To them, his cry, 'But I *did nothing*!' sounds like a confession of idleness and self-centredness. And who is to say that they are not right? It is the Player's duty to play the Game, not by turning his back on the world, but by using every opportunity that the Rules of the Game allow to increase the bounds of delight within the world.

15

Child's Play

Thursday. The summer holidays began at the weekend, and this afternoon, at last, my friend Sam arrived by train from London. After lunch, we waited for Steve to come down from the big house where he lives, and then all three of us went down to meet the others at the boat. Rob and Lucy were already there with their dad, and he showed us for the tenth time all the things we needed to remember about the boat. As soon as he'd gone back to the quarry-pits where he works, the arguments started. First of all, it was Rob and Lucy about whether we should have a girl with us. Steve said Rob was much more the odd one out than Lucy, being older than the rest of us, and besides it was all arranged. Then it was Steve and me, about which of us should take our bikes. I said I had to go on the boat because of the dog, and Steve said I should go by bike, because Sam was my friend. We tossed for it, and I won, which is a good job, because Steve's a lousy navigator, even though he's always looking at maps. Finally, Lucy started arguing with me about whether the dog had to go at all. I said I wasn't going without him, and besides Bodge was more sensible than the lot of them. Sam, who hadn't said a word during all this, looked as if he agreed. But it was only because we were all excited, and it will all be different tomorrow.

Friday. We were up really early this morning, and everyone came to my house. My mum kept asking me the same questions again and again in front of everybody, and she was only satisfied when she'd found out we didn't have any spare batteries for the torch. But eventually we said goodbye to the grown-ups, and then Sam and Steve set off by bike whilst the rest of us went down to the boat. We set sail smoothly, doing all the things that Rob and Lucy's dad had shown us. Once we'd got going, Rob started pretending that he was captain and that Lucy and I were just galley-slaves he'd press-ganged. He and I nearly got into an argument about whether there were press-gangs at the same time as galley-slaves, but Lucy stopped us from quarrelling, and reminded us what a beautiful day it was. Rob stopped his stupid pretence, and we each got on with our jobs, and spent time looking at the pale shapes on the horizon and trailing our hands in the water. Bodge was our figurehead, sometimes barking at the flocks of birds that moved ahead of us.

Sam and Steve were already at the creek when we arrived, even though the last bit of their journey had been right off the road. We ferried them and the bikes across in three trips, and then got the tents up and lit a fire. We were too tired to start exploring today. It just feels good to be on this side of the water, where there aren't any signs of other people or of old campfires. Steve's got the torch out looking at the maps, so I'm doing this before we go to sleep.

Saturday. Our first day of exploring. Steve had worked out a route to a church that was on the map, and we all set off to find it. It was very hot, and Bodge kept going into the shallows at the edge of the creek to cool off. Where the path turned inland towards the church, Bodge suddenly started barking at something on the shoreline. I couldn't see what it was, but Bodge kept barking, so I went to take a look. A little rowing-boat had been jammed into a gully off the edge of the creek and almost covered over with reeds. It seemed an odd thing to do, but we decided that somebody must use the boat to come across the creek, for fishing or something like that. We carried on walking, but the church was nowhere to be found. Steve insisted that we were in the right place according to his map, but even he had begun to give up. Then Lucy said she thought she'd found something. We all followed her towards what looked like a great flat hedge trailing with ivy, but when we'd pushed through the undergrowth it turned out to be the wall of a ruined church, mostly caved in and with bits poking out high above us that looked as if they might drop off. There had obviously been a fire. Steve said it must have happened after the map was made, and Rob said that showed how useless maps were. It was strange inside a space that was not really inside at all. All the sounds were muffled, and it was very cool, which we all liked. It was the kind of place that makes you imagine long ago, and we stayed there quite a time looking around. Sam found a strip of newspaper on the ground, only a few days old. It meant that somebody had been here before us, very recently, which rather broke the spell of the place. We couldn't go on imagining that we were discoverers, and in fact, when we left, we found that there was a much less hidden entrance to the ruins from a turning off the main path. Anyway, Sam folded the bit of newspaper up, and kept it as a kind of souvenir.

Steve suggested a different path back through the wood, and despite Rob wondering out loud whether the wood might have been burned down too, we all agreed that a change of route was a good idea. When we came to it, the wood was fairly heavily fenced with barbed wire. Sam wondered whether we ought to go in, but we all laughed at his town boy's hesitation, and carried on. We were right to do so, because pretty soon we found a lovely quiet pool in a hollow in the middle of the wood, which was just what Bodge and the rest of us needed. We all stripped off for a bathe, even Lucy, and then lay drying off in the broken patches of sunlight that shone through the trees. Finding two magic places in one day made us feel very good. It's only now, since we got back to the camp, and the fire has been put out, that we've begun to think anything at all about the rowing-boat and the newspaper and the other people who seem to be here too.

Sunday. The day began well enough, with sausages over the fire, and more bright sunshine. We all wanted to go back to the pool that we had found, except for Steve, who had his maps out again and said he wanted to explore a different path through the wood that led to an interesting-looking building. Finally, we agreed to go to the pool first and then on to Steve's building. But, when we got to the pool, it was so nice again that the rest of us wanted to stay. Steve quickly got bored and sat on the edge of the pool snapping twigs, until he stood up and said he was going to go exploring by himself. None of us splashing about in the water had the sense to stop him, and he disappeared along a path that went north through the wood, saying he'd come back and find us when he was finished.

It was only when the sky clouded over, and there were even a few drops of rain, that we gave up swimming and noticed how late it was, and that Steve had not come back. 'We shouldn't have let him go off by himself,' said Lucy, 'it's the one thing we promised not to do.' 'It's him who shouldn't have gone,' said Rob. 'Knowing his map-reading, I expect he's got himself lost.' Sam said there was no point in deciding who was to blame, and that we had to work out what to do. 'Either we stay here and wait for him,' he said, 'or we go back to the camp and wait there. Or we could go after him.' We quickly decided to do the last of these. We all said it was the best thing to do, but I think we really meant it was the most exciting – and the warmest, because it was getting really chilly and wet by then.

The path that Steve had followed twisted and turned through the wood. It was raining properly now, and we were only sheltered by the roof of trees. Eventually we could see a misty blur at the end of the path, which was daylight, and as we got closer to the fence we began to see the outline of Steve's interesting building through the trees. When we were clear of the wood, and could see the whole of it from the back, it occurred to me that, at another time, this building would have made a third magical place to add to our list. Most of it was a pink-painted cottage with a neat garden, all looking rather dreary in the cloudy twilight, but one part had a funny umbrella-shaped roof that made it look special, and even rather mysterious. There was no sign of Steve, however, and all the curtains were drawn in the unlit cottage, which suggested that it was all closed up. Lucy said we should at least knock to make sure, but Rob said we'd only make fools of ourselves. 'The most likely thing,' he said, 'is that Steve has worked out a short-cut back to the camp, and completely forgotten about us.' 'Let's go back then,' I said, and everyone was glad to get out of the rain, except Bodge who kept growling and tugging at his lead.

To keep ourselves warm, and to keep our spirits up, Sam and I suggested playing a chasing game we knew, which is good because you can play it and still keep walking. I was running out in front, ahead of the rest of them, when I ran round a corner and smack into the rock-solid body of a man who strode up out of the gloom. I could feel the others skidding to a halt behind me, even Bodge, especially when we all saw the gun that the man was carrying in his hand. 'What the hell is all this?' said the man in a thundering voice. And I began to explain very hurriedly about our game and the pool and the camp. I knew, for some reason, that I mustn't say anything about Steve or about the cottage. He listened to what I had to say, and then said, 'Right, but now you get the hell off this land. This wood is private, and I don't want to catch you here again.' As we were leaving he shouted after us, 'And keep that dratted dog on a lead. My job's to look after the livestock in this wood, not fatten them up for your precious mongrel.'

After we'd been walking for a bit, Sam said, 'You really should have asked him about Steve.' Rob said, 'You must be joking. Suppose he's got something to do with it.' But none of us wanted to take that possibility seriously, not at least until we got back to our camp, and we passed the rest of the time telling more and more far-fetched stories to each other, in which the man was no longer a game-warden but an escaped convict, or an enemy agent, or an alien from another planet in human guise.

Steve wasn't here when we got back, and there was nothing we could do to stop ourselves from feeling very cold and very worried. None of us wanted to eat, and we've decided to go to bed so that we can get up early in the morning and make plans. We've lit a fire in case Steve comes back during the night.

Monday. Steve had still not returned by the morning. Nobody said anything during breakfast, and afterwards we discussed what we should do. Lucy thought we should go straight back to the nearest village across the creek and get help. Rob said we should try to find out what had happened before we started worrying other people. It was possible that Steve had taken shelter somewhere during the night. 'There was a storm, remember,' he said. 'Perhaps he went back to the ruined church.' Sam said that we should split into pairs, two to go off in search of Steve, and the others to go to the village. But the rest of us were certain that we should all stay together. I thought Rob, as the oldest, was more bothered about getting himself into unnecessary trouble than anything else, but I still thought his plan was right. 'We should search till four o'clock,' I said, 'and if we haven't found him by then, we should go to the village, like Lucy says.' This was agreed, and we set off, taking our bikes in case we needed to get anywhere fast. Remembering Bodge's growling of the evening be-

114

fore, I also took Steve's pyjama jacket with me, so that Bodge would have a scent to work on. 'Boy detective!' the others laughed, but nobody disagreed.

After yesterday's experience, we weren't taking any chances with the wood, so we took the path along the creek to the church. Steve wasn't to be found, and there was nothing to suggest he'd been there. We decided to carry on towards the funny pink cottage, hoping that the track past the church would lead there. Rob and Sam rode ahead on the two bikes, and it wasn't long before they came back at top speed, waving their arms wildly, and saying over and over what we could eventually make out as, 'There *is* someone! In the garden, there *is* someone!' We decided to leave the bikes inside the ruined church and continue on foot. Both Rob and Sam were sure they had seen a child in the garden, but they couldn't say whether it had been Steve.

The mystery and anxiety were almost unbearable as we came round a bend in the track, and saw the garden and the cottage as we had seen them yesterday, but from the other side. We waited for ages, and nothing happened. Then, in a moment, the figure of a boy came round the corner followed closely by a man with a gun. Steve and the game-warden from yesterday! I almost cried out. But before I did, they both turned so that we could see their faces. Instinctively, we all dropped down out of sight together as we all saw, with painful certainty, that it was another boy, much younger than Steve, and another man, not the one we had confronted in the wood. But before we had time to take stock of all this, two other men appeared and called the man and the boy back inside the cottage.

As they disappeared from view, Sam began to splutter, 'Hold on! Hold on!' and searching frantically through his pockets, he said, 'That boy! He's the child of somebody!' Lucy and I got the giggles at this, but then Sam produced the piece of newspaper from the ruined church, and held it out. 'That photograph,' he said, pointing, 'I knew I recognized it. He's the son of an important diplomat or something, and he's been kidnapped. Look, it's the same face!' He was undoubtedly right. 'In that case,' said Lucy, and her voice trailed off, so that we were all suddenly thinking about Steve again, and what might have happened.

In excited whispers, we worked out what to do. Sam and Rob would go back to the ruined church and wait with the bikes. If Lucy and I were not back within the hour, they would cycle back to the boat and get help from the village.

It was when Lucy and I began to head gingerly towards the garden of the cottage that I remembered the pyjama jacket. I held it to Bodge's nose, and instantly he started to pull towards the cottage. As far as I was concerned, that settled it, but we still had to be sure. There was a stream between us and the open doors on the verandah. I dislodged a stone as we crossed it, and we froze, wondering whether the voices inside the room would pause at the sound. They didn't, and we continued creeping along the edge of the garden towards the cottage, until the voices became clear. 'We've got to get away today,' said one. 'No chance,' said the other, 'not now, with this extra problem on our hands. We'll just have to delay everything by twenty-four hours.' 'You'll send out a message?' came the reply. 'The usual place?' 'The church? Yes, I'm on my way there now. Are you sure you can both manage? This one,' said the voice, 'is a real little bruiser. My belly's still sore.'

We listened without being able to breathe. There was no doubt who the extra problem was, and it made us grin to hear that he was a bruiser. But more important than that was the fact that one of the men was now on his way to the church, where Rob and Sam would be waiting. We should have guessed from the piece of newspaper that the place was being used by them. It was as if we had unknowingly sent the other two into a trap. There was only one thing to do. I whispered my plan to Lucy, and she nodded agreement, giving my hand a reassuring squeeze as she did so. Then I let Bodge off the lead, whispering 'Home!' in his ear and giving him a shove. Bodge has a curious habit of always racing back the way he's just come if you tell him 'Home', which was exactly what he did now, scampering through the stream and back along towards the track. I lobbed a largeish stone into the stream, and then Lucy and I ducked behind the wall. With the noise, one of the men came on to the verandah, saw the movements in the bushes, and started to chase. At that moment, Lucy and I ran with all our might the other way, towards the front of the house and back to the path we had taken the day before. I heard shouts, and a gun fired, and hoped Bodge would be all right. But then the shouts were coming closer, and I realized that one of the men had seen us as well, and was in pursuit.

Lucy and I dodged under the wire fence into the wood, and down the path. Because we knew where we were going, we had a good start on our pursuer. But still we could hear feet thudding behind us as we went, and I could only see flashing gun-metal every time I turned my head. And then suddenly it seemed as if everything we were running away from was there ahead of us. I let out a scream of pure panic as I fell into the grim-faced body of a man carrying a gun. But when the voice said, 'You again, you little blighters. I thought I told you . . .', then I knew it was the man from yesterday, and I started to jabber out everything that had happened, with Lucy jabbering too, and panting, and pointing desperately behind.

Our words seemed to make little sense to the man, but in no time at all our pursuer came into view, and words were out of the question. Without a thought, the man pushed Lucy and me into the undergrowth off the path, and confronted the other man. They stood there for what seemed like ages, each with his gun levelled at the other, trying to threaten or reason their opponent into sub-

117

mission. I decided to try something out. Hoping I wouldn't be noticed in the tension, I darted between the trees until I was behind our pursuer, and then ran at him along the pathway, flooring him with what was probably the only good rugger-tackle ever in my life. Lucy ran on to the path, and picked up the man's revolver that had fallen to the ground. The game-warden came forward, and told the man to get up very slowly, and not to try any funny games.

As soon as I could, I told the man about Rob and Sam at the church, and the other man who was supposed to be on his way there. We headed that way as quickly as possible. The other two were there unharmed, but very anxious. They'd been alarmed when Bodge had turned up by himself. But when they saw us, with Lucy holding a revolver, our enemy from yesterday with a rifle, and another man shuffling along unwillingly in front of him, they didn't know what to think. We started our hurried explanations, interrupting one another, until the game-warden cut us off and reminded us about Steve and the other boy. He ordered Sam and Rob to go to the track and keep their eyes skinned for cars, in case they tried to make a quick getaway. He took off his belt to secure the other man, and we all set out for the pink cottage.

My trick with the dog had obviously delayed them. They were still only loading up a Land-Rover when we arrived. Two shots were fired, both of them by the game-warden into the front tyres of the Land-Rover, although Rob looked as if he would have loved to try out the revolver he had somehow managed to get off Lucy. The little boy we'd first of all seen in the garden came running up the drive, and then Steve. We all gathered round and began to swap stories with Steve. Lucy noticed the other little boy looking lonely and tried to cheer him up. Then the game-warden had to butt in again, and remind us there were things to be done. The telephone line in the cottage had been cut, so Rob and Sam were to go back to their bikes, and across the river to the nearest phone-box, where they were to call

118

the police. They were to use the concealed rowing-boat at the end of the track, which belonged to the game-warden and not the kidnappers. The three kidnappers themselves were locked in the room where Steve had been held, and Steve and Lucy and I sat with the little boy and the game-warden in the verandah room, feeling suddenly tired and very relieved.

There was a lot of waiting after that, too much really. We tried to think of games to keep the little boy occupied, but none of us could concentrate. Eventually the police arrived in three cars and a van. We were all taken back to the village, where there was more waiting until our parents turned up, and then the parents of the kidnapped boy arrived from London.

Tuesday. The hardest part was trying to persuade our parents to let us have one more night in our tents. But in the end even they had to agree that the chances of another gang of kidnappers appearing in the same area were small, and besides the tents and the boat had to be brought home somehow. We wanted to let the little boy who had been kidnapped join us, but his parents wouldn't agree. Instead, they invited all five of us to join them the following summer on their boat when they went sailing in the Mediterranean.

At lunchtime today the game-warden arrived carrying a massive bone for Bodge, and some equally enormous steaks for the rest of us. 'Better than sausages,' he said, 'and easier than pheasant to cook on a fire.' It turned out that the cottage belonged to his employer, and that it was always left empty over the summer months. 'So you see,' he said, as we all tucked into our feast, 'I'm feeling pretty stupid for not having spotted anything. I'm good enough at catching harmless trespassers in the wood,' he added with a smile, 'but no good when it comes to real criminals. For that, I have to rely on kids!' We all laughed, and agreed.

16

A Homecoming

'Welcome home, Mr Edmund – Captain Hall, I should say. Welcome home.' It was Mrs Fraser by her voice, her precise high Scottish voice, but it had gone paper-thin, and her face too, creased and cracked like old paper. It was not my home, of course, and it would perhaps have been better had I taken the warning and fled the place there and then without once looking back. It was not my home, but as I stepped inside, the very banister-rails seemed to bow over to greet me, and in an instant I could recall every room and every corner in the house, the places where we played our private games, the doorways it was best to walk past on tiptoe. I could remember the occasion when I had first arrived, and had seen nothing of my great-uncle for three days, only to meet him finally by landing at his feet, having ridden down that banister-rail shouting gleefully, 'Your go now, James, your go now!'

Mrs Fraser asked after my journey as we went into the library. She explained that Mr Hall, senior, was resting and I would see him later, that Miss Annabelle had been driven into town, and hoped to be back for dinner. Mrs Fraser would fetch me tea. But before she did, she stood over me and folded her arms to say, 'Well!' – an exclamation, not a question. All I could reply was, 'Well,' and smile with real warmth of feeling. Too much had happened in all that time for there to be questions asked and answered, and Mrs Fraser knew as well as I that such answers as there were would trickle out over the next few days or weeks. It was not answers she wanted, in any case, it was to have the one she called her Edmund, her poor orphan Teddy, back in her sights again, and back home.

'You do look fine!' she said at length, and then, in instruction to herself, firmly said, 'Tea,' and hurried from the room. It was hurrying out to weep, I knew, as much as to fetch refreshment. Because there was more to our speechlessness than just an excess of news. There was also the sudden overwhelming presence of all the ghosts that time had built up between us. We, who had been such little gossips in our way, such natterers, had not talked through the mourning of a host of names. And so there had to be a minute's silence, a minute at least, and a wet eye, before we could resume.

The paper-thin face had lost its tremor when the tea came back in. But for me, the ensuing days built up the roll-call of loss to even greater proportions. Living in the old house became like looking at one of those restored mosaics or frescoes where the areas of bare plaster, to my perverse eyes at least, always seem more significant, more resounding, than the surrounding remnants of conjectured pattern or design. For me, of course, the house had always in a sense been tinged with death. I had come there, at my grandfather's insistence, shortly after my father's death, the father I had never known, except as the stiff portrait of a man in uniform, a man with a gun. It was only later that I came to realize that the true occasion of my adoption into the Hall family had been my mother's hasty re-marriage – not on account of its haste, but on account of it being a marriage into trade. It was later still that I realized how her husband, my step-father, the owner of the local quarries, had been the one to rescue a young widow from her inconsolable grief. From all this, I was protected throughout my boyhood life. I spent my growing years, and when I was older most of my school-holidays, at the house – the place and its people became my home and my family.

And now there were just a few survivors. Of the three

121

old men, as I thought of them, who dominated my childhood, my grandfather had died early on, and now my
great-uncle was dead too. He had been the prop or main-
stay of my early life, taken for granted. When the news of
his death was relayed to me, I remember saying to myself,
almost the words themselves, Now you are alone, Edmund, now you are finally a man. Only my cousin, James's
father, remained, and he was a widower, keeping mostly
to his own rooms. There were other losses too – of the
three other adults who had figured importantly in our
childhood, only Mrs Fraser survived. Digby, the dignified
old butler, who had ruled us, was gone, as was the old
head gardener, Turpin, always Turpin, and only Turnip
behind his back, whose songs and stories and jokes kept us
amused for hours, and never wore thin through repetition.
Even an aunt who had intermittently visited the house,
and had been the closest in blood to my father, was dead,
tragically killed by lightning in an accident that had gutted
the local church. But the greatest gap of all was James
himself, my constant companion, almost my brother. As
the deaths of our contemporaries always do, the news of
his death had put me in mind of my own fragile mortality,
of the number of times I had foolishly touched death's
skirts, only to dart away in time as death turned to catch
the culprit. The beginnings of my determination to return
home date from that time.

The emptiness of what I found began to impinge upon
me that first evening. In the past, the dinner-table, with
my grandfather and later my great-uncle presiding, had
always been a teeming affair, with visitors and friends
adding to the numbers. Now it was sadly shrunken. Apart
from myself, there was only my cousin, Mr Hall, and
Annabelle, a strangely silent young woman who would
have been James's wife, and now stayed on because there
was no one else. Mrs Fraser was in attendance and did her
best to make my return a celebration. But nothing could
disguise the fact that we were a pale and unlaughing group

122

compared to what had been, and that the familiar habits of eternity were now kept up as if for eternity's sake only.

A round of gatherings with the local families to honour my return only made things worse. The more people there were at these well-meaning occasions, the emptier they seemed. Those absences that had, as it were, been built into the structure of my life added themselves to other more recent losses, deaths that at the time had elicited from me only a terse letter of condolence, sometimes my only letter for years. It was as if there were an accrued debt of mourning that had to be paid. For the first time in my life, I found myself missing my father. What was meant to have been a homecoming brought the discovery that my home no longer existed, perhaps had never existed, and that all I had achieved in the intervening years was to build up a set of acquaintances – and a good deal of wealth – in a place which was, for all the vibrancy and fluidity of life there, still a foreign place and a life lived on the surface. After Africa, England inevitably seemed grey, depleted, stodgy. When I decided to return, I would have said that it was exactly this quality of the familiar that I sought. But a few days back in England, in the old house, showed me that there was no profundity to this sense of the familiar either, that it was no more than a mesh of memories and affections for what was gone. The discovery that I belonged nowhere was one I was unprepared for, and I began to wish I had never booked my passage, never returned to the gravel driveway or to the double staircase leading to the main door.

There was, in the grounds of the house, a little summer-house that I remembered from my youth. It was a curious affair, done in the whimsical style that was much in vogue at the turn of the century, and had reputedly been built to house a governess of my great-grandfather's after her retirement. Its fanciful curlicue of a roof had earned it the name of the pagoda, and it had been a favourite haunt of mine when the self-absorption of youth got the better of me, and I wanted to be apart even from James, with his loud enthusiasms and his cracks. Since my departure, it had been lamely restored and freshly painted pink, but it retained a governessy touch in some of its furnishings and in the prints that hung on its walls, and it still existed in that strange half-state between being occupied and being empty which is typical of summertime or holiday places.

With nothing else to do, and with the morose feelings that I have described, I began to go there again. There were still the old volumes of journals whose topical frame of reference had never been known to me, but which it had always been a quiet pleasure to leaf through. Some of the gravures of trial scenes, or of incomprehensible pieces of machinery in the advertisements in these journals, were as well-known to me as any family photographs. And now there were piles of boys' adventure stories as well, that I remembered from the big house, each with its embossed coloured illustration on the front, and boxed games too, with many of the pieces missing, that James and I had played together until they were worn out, or until we knew every conceivable move. Perhaps, in retrospect, it was not the best place for one who was so prone to melancholic nostalgia. But it was what it had always been, a peaceful place, and I fell into the habit of walking down there with the old retriever – another survivor of the old days – and spending more and more of my time sitting on the pagoda's verandah in the sunshine or in one of the high-backed chairs in the pagoda-roofed room inside. It was, above all, more nearly mine than any other place.

The pagoda had been bound up too, in its curious way, with my later career, and even with Africa. For the desire for privacy which began to show itself at about the age of fifteen or sixteen, and which was expressed in my devotion to the place, caused a flurry of concern amongst the adults who ruled my life. My great-uncle, my aunt and my cousin – even Digby, Mrs Fraser and Turpin – were perpetually engaged in little chats about the problem. 'Edmund must

124

find something to do,' 'Edmund must not be allowed to brood,' 'Edmund must have an aim in life' – these were the whisperings I could hear about me, and frankly they made me long for the summerhouse all the more.

The vicious circle was broken only when I announced on my nineteenth birthday that I was leaving university to seek a commission in the army, in my father's old regiment. The intake of breath was audible, and seemed to last for days. My great-uncle called me to his study more than once. I was taken aside by my aunt, by Mrs Fraser – even old Turpin was put up to it. 'You wanted me to make a choice in life, you wanted me to stop mooning,' I would say with unnecessary petulance, but genuinely surprised by their reaction. 'What could be more of an indication of my good intentions than this?' They would say guarded things about what was good for the father not necessarily being good for the son, about having my own life to lead and it being no sign of maturity to carry another's banner – meaning my father's – for them, and about carrying hero-worship too far (this from my aunt, and I became sufficiently heated on that occasion to storm out of the house and spend the rest of my holidays with friends in Cornwall).

I was convinced that I only wanted to join the army for the sake of adventure, and to break a self-centredness in myself that I did not love. One never really knows why one does things at that age. My father's life, as a soldier, the heroism of his young death in the Zulu wars, these had been instilled into me throughout my childhood. As I became more stubborn in my intention, and it became clear that I would be posted upon receiving my commission to South Africa, where the rebellion of the Boers was being put down, I admitted to an interest in my father's associations with the place, and to an agreeable sense of family continuity in the scheme. But I insisted that I was in no way motivated by a conscious desire to emulate my father, and I tried to allay their fears by saying cheerily that I

125

certainly did not intend to emulate him to the point of death. This was on my farewell visit to the house, a cheerless occasion by any previous standards, and made even more empty by James's absence on a climbing holiday in Scotland (during which he presumably exacerbated the condition which was to kill him seven years later). I made it my business whilst there to take leave of the pagoda, because of the fond memories I would retain, and because it at least would not look back at me as I bade farewell as if I were beyond hope or recall.

To South Africa I went. I saw the rebellion to its ragged conclusion. I took a kind of root in the thin soil of the interior. I farmed; twice I thought of marrying, but each time the idea of fixing myself to this foreign land prevented me; I hardly thought about my adopted family and home, or about the pagoda; I became rich. I also became frustrated by degrees, until the time came when I knew I either had to leave once and for all, or commit myself to die there. I left; I docked in Southampton; I took the train to London, which seemed grey and spineless after the new prosperity of the South African towns; I could not wait to get out of the city and see the old house. And now I found myself nowhere, lost between past and present, death and life, England and abroad, youth and the onset of middle-age – with the only thing I wanted to call my home a flimsy unlived-in folly of a cottage, with its bogus touches of the exotic and its dusty piles of old reading matter and useless games.

I realize that as I approach the climax of these events, there is no way at all of preparing for it by any normal means. I can only really draw up a tally of what happened – and even that has to be a tally of what happened over a period of twenty years rather than of six weeks, since the six weeks I spent at the house after my return were as uneventful as any period of six weeks could conceivably be, and seem in recollection truly to have been spent sitting in the summerhouse turning over old books and older emotions. I can point to things that did not happen. I did not talk to James's father or to Annabelle, or even to Mrs Fraser, about the past that weighed so heavily on me. I did not do so, because I sensed that it must weigh on them as well, and I did not wish to add to that weight, and because it was somehow more important for all of us to keep up the pretence that my return to the house meant a restoration of the old days, when it clearly meant no such thing. I can point to one thing that did happen. The old retriever died, my one companion at the summerhouse. Rationally speaking, I should have marvelled at a life that had, by any normal measure, been extended by five or more years. But I was not rational, and privately the death of the dog seemed to be just one death too many.

All of this adds to the tally, but it does nothing to explain the cause of what happened next, or even to make clear how entirely unprepared I was for any kind of crisis. It is true that I had asked myself on occasion during that languorous six weeks if I was undergoing a nervous break-down. But the very act of putting the idea into words was enough for me to shrug it off. The term had nothing to do with me. I associated it with women, or with the kind of young men I avoided at university. It did not relate to a man who had been brought up to think of himself as self-reliant, ordered, rational and ambitious. Accordingly, the warning that lay in the question went unheeded in the conspiracy of idleness and complacency from which I was suffering, and this made what followed even more disturbing.

What followed was this: I was found – found, mark you, for I have no recollection to this day of any of the events leading up to this moment – found by Annabelle in the pagoda-room, sitting by a table upon which were laid out (as if for a game of Pelmanism, to use Annabelle's phrase) my loaded revolver, a lethal-looking knife, a bottle of medicine from my army days, which is deadly in sufficient quantities, a full bottle of whisky, and a length of rope.

127

The panoply of suicide was there displayed, and I was saying softly to myself over and over, 'It's so peaceful here, so peaceful here.' It was my voice which had alerted Annabelle.

There is no saying what might have happened if quiet, young Annabelie had not intervened. Perhaps nothing. Needless to say, I was taken to the house, I was attended by doctors, I was pampered. I am told that I became attached exclusively to Annabelle, and was tetchy and ungrateful towards everyone else. My gratitude for their forbearance towards me is unbounded, as for the fact that the idea was never entertained of transferring me to a sanatorium.

The first thing I can remember occurred, I am told, on the sixth day after I had been found. Annabelle came to me in a state of obvious agitation. She had been told, she said, to tell me something. The doctor had decided that I was strong enough, and that my future improvement might depend upon my now being put into a position of possibly enormous stress and pain – but that, rather in the way that a painful blow on the head can, under some circumstances, restore a blind man's sight, so this painful relation might bring relief and illumination immeasurably greater than the immediate pain. I do not know how such things happen, or what loops and folds there are in the fabric of time, but at that moment I said, 'My father!' Annabelle quietened me, but everything she went on to say confirmed my premonition. In what she told me, it was as if my rootlessness and my melancholy were themselves being given a home – they were being put in the story to which they belonged. Simply put, she told me that my father had not died in Africa. He had been severely wounded in the circumstances that I had known as the circumstances of his death, and as heroically as I had ever been told. But he had been brought home to convalesce when he was well enough, and he had stayed at the big house with his young wife and his father. Physically his condition improved rapidly.

128

The wife, after all, was later left as the mother of a son. But the shock of the injury or the terror of war had taken a deep hold on his mind. He became morose and solitary. Doctors said he was in need of activity, and when he was physically fit enough he should speedily be allowed to work again. But he had become only more morose and more solitary, spending increasing amounts of time in the rooms of the pagoda-cottage, reading or just sitting, and refusing any interference or any company. He simply said that he found it a pleasant and peaceful place, and it had indeed always been a favourite spot of his since boyhood. After several weeks of this, and without any previous sign of violent behaviour, he had shot himself through the skull in the pagoda-room of the cottage with his regimental pistol.

All this had been kept from the young orphan. It had been at first the grandfather's, and then the great-uncle's insistence, that no boy should grow up believing his father to be a coward or a madman. The history was therefore changed, and in time it became the family history for the deceivers nearly as much as for the deceived. It was my mother's inability to bear this habit of deceit that, along with everything else, led to her estrangement from the family, and to the distance that was maintained between us throughout my childhood. It had been revisited in an indirect way in the crisis of my youth. It was being revisited now, and in full, only at the insistence of my doctor.

This is no more than an interim report. It is two months since Annabelle related to me what was also a revelation to her. I know that a door swung open as she spoke, but it is not yet clear whether that door leads out into glorious sunlight or into an even darker room. I am hopeful. Indeed, I can say more: I can say that Annabelle and I are hopeful. But there are things that are hard to bear. The conspiracy of kindly silence, which means that my life to date has been lived in untruth, or not truly lived at all, is one of them. And I do not know whether this is worse, or whether it is the dread realization that I must build up my life from fresh foundations, that, at my age, I must give birth to a new father, a new mother, a new past altogether, and expunge the old heroes and the old villains even from my dreams.

17

A Game of Catch

Convey to your imaginations, if you can, the image of a woman of legendary wealth, beauty and talent. She of the long neck has risen, after a scholastic career that brought her a number of O-levels and a pleasant sojourn in the Girls' Sixth, followed by a spell of early professional experience tending the infants at Miss Hambleton's nursery group in South Ken., to the coveted heights of Pictures Editor on one of our thicker women's journals. Daily, from ten till three-thirty or later, she pores over glossy prints of angular beauties posed against backgrounds suggestive of the Caribbean or Alps, and makes decisions – this one or that one – with the discreet advice of her underpaid graduate assistant. Often she lunches with distinguished names at one of her favourite bistros, and the momentous indiscretions or vital agreements that are arrived at in a haze of champagne and brandy are left to be reconstructed by sub-editors or lawyers the morning after. Frequently she leaves work early on a Friday to prepare for the ordeal of being the admired focus of everyone's attention somewhere in the Home Counties or the Cotswolds. She is Algeria Titt, one of the Hampshire Titts, Algeria on acount of being born in the year of de Gaulle's return to power, and her father's witticism on the occasion of her birth to the effect that '*Algérie n'est pas Françoise.*' Françoise, of course, is Lady Françoise Sappe, the MP's wife, Algeria's sister.

Imagine to yourself too, if you are able, a young man of no particular abilities, of clean, though unremarkable, appearance, but of infinite *jouissance*. He is Danvers Pellett, known to his close chums and intermittent chagrin as Dan. His career has had neither the pep, bounce or zap of Algeria's. Its high point was probably the fifth-form cross-country which he won with the aid of a friendly local milkman's float. His pass degree in Divinity was an act of charity. He has been the member of a losing professional bridge-partnership for some years. Much of his inheritance was invested in a scheme to market ice-creams with savoury flavours – MeetFreezees, the Cornet that Can Be a Picnic, in Roast Beef, Bar B-Q Chicken or Salmon Mousse flavours. It was somebody else's idea, and Danvers's money. You still occasionally come across the product in outlying village stores, but nobody buys it much – certainly not twice. Danvers is the kind of person who is given to peeing out of upstairs windows at parties as a bet, and who still subscribes to the *Beano*, though without any of the affectation that might make it seem like a smart eccentricity. Imagine, then, the manner in which Miss Algeria Titt strikes such a young man. He had seen her first when an aunt's book on succulents was being launched, or lunched, at a Foyle's do, and he was the good aunt's escort. Algeria had struck him as a creature of fabulous dimensions. It was mainly something to do with the neck. He had heard her laugh across the crowded room. Not a word had passed between them. She had not been struck by him at all, or even noticed his presence. But his every waking thought thereafter was devoted to the discovery of the means of meeting her, and of smiting her with such charms as he could muster. He began to fall expensively behind in the games of chance with which his waking thoughts were more normally occupied. But never mind, he said to himself, here is a rising star to which my wagon deserves to be hitched, a real thoroughbred filly and no mistake.

And then it happened, all without him doing anything. He was invited (albeit in a rather no-offence-if-you-can't-manage-it-old-boy kind of way) to a weekend party being given by the Posterns for their daughter. The Hon. Phyllis Postern had been at school with Algeria. In fact, Algeria was reputed to have introduced a system of fagging into her school just as it was beginning to die out in the boys' schools, and Phyllis had been the great Titt's adoring slave, rumoured to clip her mistress's toenails for her in the bath. Lady Postern was best known for weeping profusely on the shoulders of younger married men at functions, which had led to the remark of Danvers's friend, the wit Dribble, who said, 'Is this the face that laundered a thousand shirts?' Lord Postern is rarely seen in public these days, on account of what is politely known as a condition. The other guests were to be a nondescript gaggle of shooting fellows, Claude Upjohn, John Goodfellow and people like that – all green wellies and loud laughs. Myrtle Bunch, known as Budgie from her habit of listening to you with her head cocked on one side, was to make up the female party. Danvers could not understand why he had been invited. He did not shoot. His dancing also suffered from a poor sense of direction. His last party, the one with the joke cushion, had not been a success. He dreamt that the delectable Titt herself had contrived it, and so vowed to be on his best behaviour, and read *The Times* each morning in the week before the party to improve his conversation – though by the end of the week this had whittled itself down to scanning the Announcements to guess which of them were coded messages from Soviet spies. He insisted to his manservant that the lavender suit should be packed, in the face of much protest and over-watered whisky, and gave him firm orders to remove any party tricks from the suitcase that might find their way there by the week's end.

The day came. A train, a cab, another train, and then a car sent down from the Hall for the guests. Having arrived, there was time to kill before dressing for the evening, so Danvers went for a wander. He began by taking deep breaths of country air on the steps overlooking the river, but this soon bored him. He tried calling the deer in the park to him as if they were cats, but they only glared and scattered. He could not help being jaunty of step and smiling of face, and had to rein himself on occasion, saying to himself as he went, 'Steady, Dan boy, steady.' It was in this state that he ran across the little pink pagoda at the bottom of the slope, and remembered having heard about it before. It had a story attached to it, but he couldn't remember what. A tennis ball fell from nowhere at his feet, and as he stooped to pick it up, thinking to throw it back gamesomely to whichever boy or girl wanted him to play, he found his wrist the sudden centre of interest for a small bunch of fur with teeth. It was the teeth he really noticed, for having begun to tear into the sleeve of his jacket, they shifted to gain a better purchase by embedding themselves in his forearm. He had that slow apprehension, familiar to those in pain, that turns an objective awareness – that arm there is being bitten by that little dog – into a subjective sensation of agony. 'Ow, ow! I say!' he said. 'Get off! Get off, you little brute! Ow!' These words were interrupted by a tinkling, which said, 'Get down, bad boy! Let go, naughty Fleck! Let go, I say! The gentleman will throw your ball for you if you stop holding on to him.' 'Hold on to' seemed a trifle understated in Danvers's watering eyes, but he was in no position to engage in argument. He shook his arm, and eventually the hateful Fleck did indeed tumble to the ground, in protection of its own lethal dentistry rather than in obedience to its mistress's command. At this, the mistress rushed towards the furry fiend and picked it up to caress it for having taken such a fall. By degrees, the animal-lover and the agonized man took a civilized notice of one another.

'Hullo, Myrtle,' said Danvers. 'I'm Dan Pellett. We met at the Doberrys'.'

'Oh yes,' said the little voice. 'I remember.' She proffered a dog-free hand, and Danvers put out his gouged and tattered arm.

'Look,' said Myrtle, 'you've torn your sleeve. How did you do that?'

Upon returning to the house, Danvers took leave of Myrtle and Fleck in the hallway and went in search of a drink. His manservant found him a while later sitting by the clothes that had been laid out for dinner, absent-mindedly licking his wounded arm.

At dinner, the neck, with Algeria's lovely head balanced delicately upon it, was all that Danvers could see. His bandaged wrist made eating somewhat toilsome, and he had little appetite for food whenever the neck swayed beguilingly in his direction. Conversational gambits came to him with a surprising ease after the initial hesitations before drinks were served. Recollections of a Foyle's literary luncheon; the care and maintenance of cacti; the use of personal columns in newspapers by foreign spies; a day in the life of a magazine journalist; how they probably do the speech balloons in the *Beano* – Danvers heard himself moving with a catlike grace from one subject to the next, mixing topics designed to flatter the object of his adoration with those designed to impress her with the breadth of his own erudition. Several of the wit Dribble's lesser-known remarks were passed off as his own. But the conversational high point was undoubtedly when, by some miracle of recollection, almost the whole of the relevant section of *My Mauve Book of British Engineers* came back to him, and he was able to speak at length about the life and major achievements of Isambard Kingdom Brunel. There was no doubt that this one scored. Algeria looked at him in wonder and astonishment, the neck barely swaying. Over dessert, the *coup de grâce* – a deft mention of the fascinating pink pagoda in the grounds – was rather spoiled when the bandaged hand became inextricably entwined with an otherwise impeccably behaved spoon, and in attempting to wipe some chocolate roulade off Algeria's bared shoulder, he unhappily mistook the tablecloth for a napkin and spilled, among other things, a flower vase into Lady

135

Postern's bosom. Servants rushed about uncertainly with cloths. Danvers was saved from the worst of his embarrassment by having to re-tie his bandage single-handedly, a time-consuming exploit, as anyone who has ever attempted it will testify. But when he resumed his conversation, he found the glorious Algeria engaged with one of the shooting cronies on her right, and he was forced to spend the remaining time talking to the deaf Lord Postern about policy in Ireland.

The next phase of the plan was to follow up the hints of the dinner-table with a note. For this, Danvers felt it wise to draw his manservant into his confidence, for he always floundered a little at anything in the vicinity of the literary.

'How would you put it,' he began, 'if you were wanting to encourage a young lady to meet you, not exactly in secret, but away from the gaze of the madding crowd and whatnot, without putting the wind up her, eh?'

'Alluring yet not alarming, sir?' enquired the manservant.

'That's it,' said Danvers. 'The very thing.'

'And the young lady,' said the manservant, pausing to clear his throat, 'does she reciprocate any of this sentiment of attachment you have towards her, sir?'

'You mean, does she think I'm all right?' said Danvers. 'Actually, I rather think she does.'

'It is an advantage, sir.'

'Well, then,' said Danvers, 'how would you fix it?'

'I would dispense with names, sir,' said the manservant confidentially. 'That is certain. I would address her in heightened epithets that would suggest that mere baptismal nomenclature was beneath the level of your passion.'

'Would you really?' said Danvers, doing his best to follow. 'You mean "Secret and Adored" or "Oh Alluring One"? That kind of thing?'

'That kind of thing precisely, sir.'

'Right then,' said Danvers, all enthusiasm now. 'How

about "Secret and Adored" on the envelope, and "Oh Alluring One" at the start of the letter?'

'Admirable, sir,' said the manservant. And so it went on, phrase by intensified phrase, heightened epithets surpassing one another in their elevation, until the passionate style of the *billet-doux* was likely to squeeze out any clarity in the instructions contained therein to meet at the pink pagoda the following afternoon, weather permitting, and in the billiard-room otherwise. But Danvers liked the tone, and inscribed 'Secret and Adored' on the front with a flourish.

'Now, be a good chap and deliver it, will you?' he said to his manservant.

'To whom, sir?' enquired the manservant.

'Oh you stony-hearted clod,' began Danvers, for whom the language of the note was still simmering away. 'Are the gentler passions of the heart entirely foreign to your kind? Does not the meeting of eyes and the sighing of breaths make itself obvious to you? To Miss Titt, of course, with the beautiful neck.'

'Very well, sir,' said the manservant, and left the room.

The morning passed slowly. Danvers played draughts with one of the younger brothers, but the boy became bored at always winning and left Danvers by himself. For a while he played alone, but this became boring too. He twice went upstairs to re-check his clothes for the afternoon. He sat and listened to the shooting in the game wood until its rhythms fell into those of a familiar dance tune. So that Phyllis and Algeria found him at one point fox-trotting by himself in the sun-lounge with a cushion for a partner.

'Not shooting?' Phyllis asked.

'Too busy practising his dance steps,' said Algeria with a wry smile.

'Can't,' said Danvers with a confiding grin. 'Not this afternoon anyway. Got an appointment.' He managed to suppress a wink.

137

'Oh,' said Phyllis and Algeria together, and turned away giggling. Oh cool one, thought Danvers to himself, oh icy cool and lovely lady, and then found himself humming the advertising jingle from the MeetFreezees campaign and dancing to that tune, as the gunfire had momentarily fallen off.

Over luncheon Claude Upjohn held the table with an account of the morning's sport, which brought him round by degrees to his brother's attempt on Everest. Every conversation brought Claude round to his brother and Everest. Danvers, at one point, picked up the thread in a desultory way and brought it round to the Orient in general and then to pagodas in particular. He looked at Algeria as he spoke, but no flame ignited her lambent eyes. Oh icy lady, he thought to himself again. Only Budgie Bunch responded with, 'Oh yes. I take my little Fleck down there to play ball.'

The time came for Danvers to put on the lavender suit, choose the tie, and stroll, as if aimlessly, down the slope towards the place of assignation. There was no one there when he arrived. He adjusted his pocket-handkerchief, tossed a pebble or two into the stream, and then occupied himself by circumambulating the pagoda. The language of the note was still glowing in his memory, and he shivered with excitement as he remembered the phrase about the majestic marble column of your capital neck.

'In that most secret corner,' he pronounced to himself in a whisper, 'where our troths can be openly plighted,' and came round the corner to run bang smack into the squat, smiling figure of Budgie.

'Oh I say,' said Danvers, glancing instinctively to the ground for the dog.

'Hullo,' said Budgie with a demure glance at the same ground.

'Hullo,' said Danvers with a sudden shiver of misapprehension.

'I've come,' said Budgie huskily.

138

'Yes,' said Danvers slowly. 'So I can see.'

'Hold me,' said Budgie suddenly unabashed, 'hold me as you said you would.'

'I?' began Danvers, but the words stuck in his throat. What was it? The intoxicating language of the love-letter? The absence of the little dog? The magic of the pagoda? Or something about Myrtle Bunch that Danvers was now seeing for the first time, a blushing in her cheeks, a strength in her short arms, a fineness in the hair he found himself suddenly nuzzling? Danvers did not pause to ask. He held her, as she had said he had said he would, and pretty soon he kissed her, and she him. The sensation was not disagreeable. His fingers sought out her stubby neck to stroke, and events moved with a swiftness which surprised both participants. In his newfound happiness, Danvers made to leap across the stream, slipped, and fell into the shallow water. There was to be no arguing with his manservant's insistence, therefore, that it could not be the lavender suit for the evening. No more need be said about the pink pagoda. Suffice to say that the Hall that evening became the setting for an impromptu engagement party. Lady Postern wept a good deal. Congratulations were voiced in a way that made the private remarks between Claude and Algeria and Phyllis and John seem irrelevant as well as unappetizing.

After they had returned home, it occurred to Danvers to ask his manservant how he had known where to deliver the love-note.

'But sir,' he answered, 'don't you recall? You gave me precise instructions, which I naturally followed in every detail. You told me to deliver the note to the misfit with the beast called Fleck. Is there anything wrong?' he added.

'Oh, not at all,' Danvers answered, looking a little as if there might be. 'In fact, absolutely not at all,' he continued, recovering confidence. 'You've done what you always do, old friend. Like the *deus ex* whatsit in a Greek play, you descended at the psychological moment and booted me niftily from catastrophe into funsville. Rather well done!'

'I'm glad to have given satisfaction, sir,' said the man-servant, beaming, or rather gleaming, from ear to ear. The manservant's name, by the way, was Jove.

18

Major Playfair's Motives

Whenever she glimpsed a figure in gaudy silks passing through the garden of the ridiculous pagoda, or saw a dingy face staring out of one of the windows, Lady Court was reminded of the appalling Major Playfair and of all his affronts.

From the moment of his return from India, he had refused to fit in. His appearances at the annual fête, the flower show, the hunt ball and the Mayday garden party were reluctant and brief. His subscriptions to the accepted local charities were miserly. His attendance at church was, by any standards, lax. His own home was a shabby little cottage near the station, far inferior to what was called for by his standing in the community. The same could be said for his personal appearance. He still had the military bearing, all right, and a dashing way with sports jackets and brightly coloured waistcoats. But beyond that he did not take pains, he did not take pains. And when it came to bridge, or any of their harmless village amusements, he simply would not play.

All of this was a vexation to Lady Court. It was *her* bridge evenings up at the big house, *her* hunt ball and *her* garden party, that he slighted. To all intents and purposes, it might just as well have been thought of as her fête, her flower show, her charities and her church. What rasped and rankled beneath it all, of course, was that it was *her* he slighted. And yet she could not simply ignore him. Not for her own sake, to be sure, but for the sake of her late husband (they had been in the army together), and that of his relations who were friends of hers (for he was, despite appearances, well-connected), she had to remain sociable, and even occasionally offer hospitality. Besides, it could have been such a bonus having masculine companionship of the right sort in the narrow sphere of her existence. If it had been of the right sort. As it was, he did himself no good by this queer way of carrying on, either amongst Lady Court's circle or down in the village. Amongst the villagers, Lady Court knew, there were whispers. She had once had to see to it herself that a rumour of his dishonourable discharge from the Indian army was promptly squashed. That was too much. The stories of excessive gambling or of excessive drinking were, to her mind, evidence of the narrow obsessions of the villagers rather than of any plausible profligacy on the Major's part. They were too absurd for words, given the visible rectitude of his habits. He was quiet in his ways. The big old Morris rarely left the drive. There were no visitors to speak of. Nothing noteworthy in his mail beyond the odd letter from India (which was only to be expected) and a parcel or two on his birthday. The woman who cleaned for him twice a week reported nothing unusual beyond the absence of a television set. Even his refuse was unexceptional.

'I wonder what he thinks he's up to,' said Lady Court to her resident companion, Miss Prout. 'Sometimes I think it must be a deliberate snub to me. That his return here, and his whole way of carrying on, must be designed as an attack on me, and on the memory of dear Henry.' She would say the last with a little whimper in her voice, as if it were on the cards that she was going to weep, so that Miss Prout would automatically look up from her crochet. But she did not weep. She pursed her lips and sniffed, and settled into looking cross.

Occasionally he would come to tea, accompanying the late vicar's widow, Mrs Venables. He was always punctual and always polite. But he invariably came inadequately dressed – a cardigan, or frayed cuffs, or open sandals –

and, in conversation, he simply would not open out. Whatever interested enquiries might be made, however delicately or subtly put, he would respond in mono-syllables or not at all, so that an afternoon could pass with nothing revealed about his past or present life, his family, or his experiences in India. Mrs Venables, whose brother had been a missionary in the sub-continent, would some-times trail exotic place-names in his path, in the way that one might lure a puppy along with chocolate drops, but he was never tempted. He sat, looking affably wooden, accepting scones and refusing small-talk. Usually, he left as early as he decently could, plucking from his back pocket a fob watch that had long since parted company with its chain, and making as if to dash, without even the elementary social unction of a feigned appointment.

Once he had gone, the three elderly ladies sat back in habitual indignation.

'Well!' said one, willingly conceding by her tone of voice that she was noticing only the very smallest of his failings, and could easily be out-matched by either of the others, 'did you notice the darning on his sleeve?'

'What about the state of his heels?' said another. 'I don't think I've ever seen anything more disgusting.'

'And his tie,' said the third, usually Miss Prout, intent over her needle, but picking up the rhythm of the litany all the same. 'Which was pattern and which was stain?'

'Not a word about your new loose-covers,' said Mrs Venables.

'Didn't ask after your health,' said Miss Prout, 'when he must have heard about your leg on the grapevine.'

'Never so much as a mention of my dear Henry,' said Lady Court with a sigh of inward suffering. 'Not that there ever is, or ever will be. To whom he owes *everything*,' she added with emphasis, as if 'everything' were a debt outstanding that might have been left discreetly on the hall-table.

After almost a decade of this attrition – a sedate kind of

143

warfare in which Major Playfair had been unvanquished simply by being unaware, it appeared, that any kind of battle was going on – Lady Court received a message which seemed to announce a new level of hostilities. Some little while before, her accountant had impressed upon her the urgent need to realize some capital. Without thinking anything of it, she had agreed to the sale of a piece of land on the estate, adjacent to the game wood and occupied only by a rather ramshackle fishing hut and some equally dilapidated outbuildings. The merits of the land, both from her own point of view as vendor and from that of any prospective purchaser, were that it was reasonably self-contained, with its own road access, and interfered in no way with the prospects or the estate of the big house. All these considerations were transformed when she now heard that the land had been bought, and the buyer was Major Playfair.

Lady Court's first reaction was to put down the telephone with great gentleness of movement and to watch the blood return to her whitened knuckles. Almost immediately she rang her solicitor back, and screamed, 'Stop the sale!' It required many guineas' worth of patient explanation to make her realize that the property had been sold on her instructions and paid for with cash, and that it could neither be reclaimed nor bought back, unless the purchaser wished to reconsider, which he did not.

'What's he think he's playing at?' said Lady Court to Miss Prout, who happened to be in earshot. 'What's his little game? Tell me that.' She spoke with a vehemence unusual even for her, and Miss Prout felt obliged to give some sort of answer.

'Perhaps he means to build a house on it,' she ventured.

'Don't be ridiculous,' Lady Court retorted. 'What does he want with a house? He's got a house.' And then with added conviction, 'And if he can suddenly afford to start buying up land, then why doesn't he buy himself a decent house and have done with it, if that's what he's after?

144

What have you got to say to that?' But Miss Prout had nothing to say, and subsided into further crocheting. She had long ago come to terms with the fact that 'companionship', in Lady Court's lexicon, included being at the receiving end of salvoes such as this, and she had learnt to live through such moments with her little honour intact.

Nothing else could be spoken about in Lady Court's presence for days but the iniquitous purchase of the horrid piece of land by the ghastly Major Playfair. Mrs Venables, who rather inclined to believe that the news did indeed confirm her ladyship's worst suspicions of the strange man's intentions, nevertheless did her best out loud to soothe her friend.

'He can't live there as it is,' she said, 'it's worse even than the hovel he's in now. And he's obviously not thinking of building on it right away, or he'd have tried to get permission.'

'Permission!' said Lady Court, her eyes gleaming. 'Of course, he can't build on it without permission. And will he get permission? Over my dead body!'

And so things stood for nearly two years. Major Playfair occasionally visited his plot in the Morris, at which times Lady Court would discover reasons for visiting the corner of her grounds that overlooked the track down to the fishing hut. But nothing else happened. Until Mrs Venables appeared one day with a copy of the local newspaper, opened at the page that listed new planning applications. She was unwilling to be the bearer of such bad tidings – and experienced disagreeable sensations, akin to those of Cleopatra's eunuchs on a bad day, as she went up the drive – but she knew it was the duty of a friend. When she got to the house, Miss Prout opened the door, and made the face of one who lived in troubled times. It was clear that the news had already arrived. Lady Court, at that moment, stormed across the hall, the official letter shaking in her fist, and shouted, 'He'll never get away with it! I'll fight him to the death!'

145

As the ensuing months made plain, she would indeed have fought it to the point of debt, if not of death, had not her accountant intervened, and an official at the hearing leaned across the top of his desk, and said with authority and assuaging deference, 'I'm truly sorry, milady, but this is a perfectly regular application that has been dealt with in a perfectly regular way, and there *are* no further channels of appeal.' Major Playfair had not even deigned to appear at the hearing, and this seemed to incense Lady Court more than anything, as if the mere sight of her fury would have been enough to stop him in his tracks.

'What I'd still like to know,' she said, once the three ladies were assembled back at the big house, 'is what that coward imagines he's doing. Look at it!' she commanded. Miss Prout raised her eyes. 'Look at it! It's completely ludicrous.' What she held up before them was her one consolation prize from the committee, a blueprint of the proposed structure, which she had obtained only after fierce argument. It showed in front and side elevation how the former fishing hut was to be transformed, not into a decent dwelling (which would have been bad enough), but into an oriental fancy with a pagoda-roof and prettified windows.

'It's not manly at all,' said Miss Prout with a shudder.

'The East must have turned his brain,' said Mrs Venables mournfully, and then with the full authority of her brother the missionary, she added, 'It does happen, you know. There are cases.'

'It can be a sign of perversion, or of madness, or of anything you like, for all I care,' said Lady Court. 'All I know is that it's an attack, a blatant attack on me.'

Progress on the building was slow. There were delays with the roof, delays before the carpenters could move in. For some time it stood only half-painted, in a pink which only increased Lady Court's perplexity. There was clear evidence of financial difficulties. Lady Court was in triumph with every delay, and in despair with every resumption of work.

'It is odious,' she said, 'odious to watch this man, who claims now to be some sort of landowner, who has been a guest in my house – who knew my dear Henry – to watch him carry on like this. He is unworthy. He is obviously incapable of any kind of dignity.'

'At least we can begin to understand now why he's always lived like a pauper,' said Mrs Venables. 'This must be costing him his life's savings. And more.'

'It's all of a very high quality,' said Miss Prout thoughtfully, and ducked her head down in case this observation brought on another jealous attack from her employer.

But what she said was true. The old fishing hut was not merely being given an ornamental façade. It was being transformed inside and out into a kind of opulent miniature palace. Every imaginable luxury had been acquired. When the work was in hand, there were deliveries almost weekly from London: fine carpets, hand-made furniture, splendid crystal. The garden, too, was the object of meticulous attention. Soon it would all be finished, in the face of Lady Court's firmest predictions and deepest wishes.

Even then, things once again stood still. Major Playfair did not move in, nor did anyone else. Lady Court was almost beside herself with impatience, inquisitiveness and the old hostility. It was bad enough to have seen the outrage take place at all, but for it not to come to any kind of conclusion – not to have anyone living there as a focus for her outrage – was beyond reason.

And then, quite suddenly, Major Playfair died. There had been no warning, save that he seemed to have lived without much domestic heating through the previous winter. He collapsed in the village street, and died before the ambulance got to the hospital. Lady Court's reactions were entirely proper. She led the village in mourning. She said nothing untoward, even amongst her intimates. Her most private thoughts, too, were not unmixed. Grief, of course,

147

was out of the question. It was not grief she had felt when her own husband had been killed, only the keenest irritation at all the trouble, and a flurry of anxiety for her own impending loneliness. Now she felt irritation at this further turn of the screw in the saga of the dratted fishing hut, and she felt a little the absence of the Major, if only as a lively topic of conversation. She did not allow herself to feel victorious, partly because it would have been unseemly, and partly because she suspected it to be premature.

In this, she was right. Even as the Major's coffin was being trundled down the road to the churchyard, so the first trunks were arriving at the pagoda (this was already its nickname in the village). They had come from abroad. The P & O markings were clearly visible. The funeral congregation was alive with speculation. Stony-faced, Lady Court presided at the obsequies, and then led her little entourage back to the big house for tea and hypotheses.

A few days later everybody's questions were answered. A most beautiful young woman, an Indian girl, arrived at the doorway of the pink pagoda, and went inside. She could not have been much more than twenty, was unaccompanied, and did not re-appear for days, except to visit the churchyard, once she had heard the news of Major Playfair's sudden death.

'Well!' said Mrs Venables. Miss Prout chorused, 'Well!'

'Well may you say well,' said Lady Court. 'So that was it, all along.' Her lips pursed in contempt. The conversation that day at the big house was surprisingly subdued. Disparagement of their neighbours was one thing, almost their stock-in-trade. But this sense of communal shame was a burden too shocking to be borne.

The villagers were less inhibited. 'What do you reckon to that coloured girl up at the pagoda?' said Frank that lunchtime in the village inn. 'Do you think it's his woman, the sly old goat?'

148

'Can't be,' said Chuffy. 'Think about it. He's been back here these dozen years or more. That girl can't be more than around twenty by the look of her.'

'They do that,' said young Phil, with knowledgeable relish. 'They do that over there. Marry them off when they're only seven or eight. Little girls and grown men.'

'Not in the army they don't,' said Chuffy.

Then old Wilf spoke up from his corner, waiting his turn as always, and then holding forth with oracular authority. 'It's his daughter,' he said. 'Stands out a mile. It's all been done for the sake of a bastard daughter.'

What was unknown to them all in their murmurings, or whenever any of them, from the big house or from the village, caught sight of the girl living in the pagoda, was what had happened a little more than twenty years before, in one of the northern provinces of India. There had been trouble, religious trouble, in the town where Major Playfair was stationed. A temple had been broken into. A nervous Major Playfair had pursued the intruder into the temple's inner rooms. The man was carrying a gun. There had been shooting. A fire was started when some lamps had fallen against an awning. It quickly began to spread amongst the screens and into the timbers of the roof. Playfair had been shot in the shoulder, and could do nothing. Suddenly, out of nowhere, his servant had appeared, and risking unimaginable defilements, as well as the flames, he had sought to put out the fire and to find the intruder. He knew as clearly as Playfair the wider risks of letting a temple burn down, and of allowing even a petty criminal to be found dead in such circumstances. He managed to drag the intruder from the flames, and keep him in his sights until help came. Nothing could be done, however, to contain the fire, and the temple itself was virtually destroyed. In the process, the servant himself was severely burned. Nobody had known how seriously until he collapsed, and a stretcher-bearer had tried to peel the clothing away from his seared flesh.

149

It was an event when, a week later, Playfair visited the man in the natives' hospital. The man's wife, with a baby daughter in her arms, moved deferentially aside when he arrived. Everybody in the ward was straining to listen. There was nothing Playfair could say. He had wanted to express a sense of how the man had acted to save not only lives and reputations, but also the peaceful well-being of a town. In the event, he found himself making light of his own injuries compared to the servant's, and of repeatedly calling the man 'my friend'. He wanted to give the man his hand, to touch him as a sign of friendship, but he was afraid of causing him actual pain, as well as being hampered by his people's reticence towards the natives. Finally, he blurted out something about 'whatever I can do, absolutely anything, it will be done' – and left in a hurry, flushed and annoyed at his own incompetence.

The following week, when he returned, the wife, once again, moved aside, and the man sat up slowly and deliberately, with evident pain. He then began to speak, also slowly and deliberately, and in his delicate, strange accents he uttered a carefully worked-out speech, as if in direct reply to Playfair's words of the week before.

'Mr Playfair, sir,' he began. 'There is something you can do for me, if it is truly your wish. My wife and my little girl will be alone. I am going to die.' Playfair made the embarrassed, clucking noises with which such remarks were habitually treated amongst his kind, but he was brushed aside. 'I am going to die. England is a beautiful country from everything I hear. India too is a beautiful country. But it is not such a good place for a girl to be in all alone. The women in England have freedom. They have education. They have dignity. I would like this for my daughter. Mr Playfair, I know it is a great deal to ask, but I would like somehow for my girl to live in England when she is a woman. I would like for you to arrange this.'

The man stopped speaking. Slowly he sank down into

150

the bed again, and looked patiently at Playfair, as the soldier wrestled with a reply.

'But are you sure it would be for the best?' said Playfair at last.

'I am sure,' the man said. Playfair turned to look at the baby girl, and at the mother who smiled shyly and bowed her head.

'And your wife?' said Playfair. 'What about your wife?'

'Let the girl grow up with her mother,' the man said, perfectly prepared for this objection. 'And then, when she is grown-up, let her come to England. Let them both come, if necessary. You can arrange all this.'

There was no more to be said. Playfair felt the oddity of the situation, but he knew that there was no arguing with the man, no saying it was all nonsense, or that it might be difficult to manage. He felt too the force of his promise, of his indebtedness to the man, and of the creation of a kind of bond between them – a bond sealed by the man's impending death, and which Playfair was already power-less to resist.

The servant died shortly afterwards. Playfair visited the widow and her daughter. Arrangements were made for the girl to be educated at an English school. From a distance, he would oversee her upbringing. But he would not interfere, there was no question of a formal adoption. And when the time came, if it was still wished, the girl and her mother would come to England. It was wished, it had been the sacred wish of the father, and it would now become the sacred wish of the mother and her child.

When Playfair resigned his commission and returned to England, his little pension and small private income were carefully husbanded. Some was sent to India to pay for the girl's schooling and her upbringing. Some was saved against the time when a house would be needed for the girl and her mother. A little – as little as possible – was reserved for Major Playfair himself. In time, the project became his whole concern, his life. He had neither the time nor the resources to live the life that was expected of him in the village that was his chosen home. Instead, he devoted himself to the life of someone else – someone with whom he had only the most fortuitous of connections, someone he hardly knew – and to bringing about a transformation in that life that would be as complete and perfect as possible. To this end he devoted all his imagination, all his talent, all his time, and all the love that had found no other outlet in his life. It became his obsession. He did not stop to consider the rightness of it, or otherwise. He hardly considered the girl's position at all. For all purposes, she was still the mindless, staring baby in the hospital ward, an object of other people's pleasure and protectiveness. It did not occur to him to think whether she might wish to have no part in this at all, or whether (as was, in fact, the case) he had become for her a kind of magic figure, the focus of her young life, and of all her dreams.

The land was bought, the house was slowly built – lavishly built, a palace for an exotic princess. And as it neared completion, the news came that the mother had died. Hurriedly, a one-way ticket was sent to bring the girl to England, and her journey was quickly begun. It was when she disembarked at Naples, her first taste of Europe, that the telegram announcing the Major's death had been sent. But she had missed it by hours. She came to the village, with its curious houses and its other inhabitants, all so vividly described in his letters, to find that the godfather of her new life was no more than a gravestone. He had intended the pagoda to be a debt magnificently honoured, a promise lavishly kept, a gift, a transformation. He did not know that it would become a place of mourning, a prison, a lonely outpost within which the girl was left to live, and from which she could not venture without meeting the hostility and the contempt of those amongst whom she lived, and by whom she was treated as an intruder and a disgrace.

19

Murder in the Dark

There was no doubting it this time. That last stretch of flooded road had finally stopped the car. Augustus Palindrome looked at his watch, and sat back in his seat to relax. Half past eleven. It would take his driver perhaps another five minutes to admit defeat, and then they could set about something useful. The routine was always the same. Suggett would always spend these extra fruitless minutes with his head under the bonnet, even after Palindrome had made his judgement perfectly clear. At the back of it, Palindrome guessed, lay a belief on Suggett's part that if ever his master decided to exchange the old machine for a more reliable model the analogy might extend to the driver. Well, damn it, thought Palindrome, let him have his five minutes then, and good luck to him. He sat further back in his seat and meditated upon the essentially untrusting nature of the servant class.

Shortly, Suggett's waterproofs clattered at the window and a streaming, steaming face spoke. 'I'm awfully sorry, sir, but she's not going to start. I think we'll have to wait until daylight.' This was the signal for Palindrome to spring into action. In a single movement he issued from the car, barked 'torch' at his companion, and climbed on to the roof of the car, cutting through the surrounding darkness with his torchbeam, and apparently sniffing the air like a pointer. He then addressed his driver rapidly. 'You'll have noticed these brick and flint walls for the last mile or so. Stands to reason there must be an entrance to an estate quite soon. There seem to be lights over yonder. Come on.' And in another single movement, he was straining to guide the car through the puddled lane, with Suggett pushing from behind. There was then a cry of, 'Ahoy there! What did I say? Look at these! Rather fine birdies, don't you think? I wonder whose?' Two stone eagles glowered at them from the entrance to a driveway, but at that moment Suggett was unable to summon up a substantial interest in eighteenth-century stonework and his only reply was an almost inaudible grumph from the depths of an over-exerted body.

Three-quarters of an hour brought an immeasurable improvement to his condition. Dry bathrobes and good brandy were provided, and Suggett sank into self-satisfied dozing as his master talked amiably and knowledgeably about the internal politics of the Farmers' Union. Their host was Sir Henry Vestibule. The name of Lord Stoat, dredged up from somewhere inside Palindrome's capacious memory, seemed to have done the trick, and quelled any initial hesitancy about letting these two complete strangers into the house. The bottle had been opened in honour of the guests. The storm was discussed, and the loss of the telephones at some earlier point during the night. Sir Henry's chauffeur had been sent into the village to make enquiries, but it looked as if he too had been marooned by the storm. Eventually it was time for bed. The houseboy was called, and a note for extra breakfasts was sent to the butler who had already retired for the night. 'You'll find yourselves joined,' said their host by way of explanation, 'by Mr Harold Lobby. A business associate you could call him. See you in the morning.'

Palindrome acquainted Suggett with some further information about their whereabouts as the driver unpacked what was needed for the night. A sad tale, according to Palindrome, in which Sir Henry, a splendid old fellow, had allowed himself to be sucked into the schemes of a vastly younger, very beautiful wife. It had been a second marriage; the first had ended tragically with the sudden

154

death in the Far East of the highly esteemed bride. 'I have little doubt,' said Palindrome with distaste, 'but that we shall find this Harold Lobby – whose business interests, if my information is correct, are in mining or something similar – to be a thirty-year-old man-about-town who knows his cocktails and wears pale suits. I didn't realize things had got to the point where the present Lady Vestibule flaunts her attachments under Sir Henry's very nose. We shall leave in the morning.'

But in the morning, whilst Suggett was helping himself to more kedgeree, the grey-haired chauffeur returned in a state of some agitation. The village church had been burned down during the night – 'Lightning, I suppose,' the butler had been quick to say – and what was worse, a body had been found there in the morning, burned to a cinder. Nobody could say who the body was, and nobody had been able to make contact with the police or the fire-brigade in the town. The roads were still flooded, and the chauffeur had walked back from his sister's where he had spent the night. 'Nobody knows what to do with the dead man in the church,' the chauffeur said, 'though there's little enough to be done with him, the Lord knows.'

'You're sure it *is* a man?' said Palindrome.

'It's not certain, sir,' replied the chauffeur. 'I've seen it myself, and I couldn't even have said for sure that it was a human body, sir.'

'Ghastly business,' said Sir Henry, 'ghastly business. The village'll miss its old church, you know. To say nothing of this mysterious body.'

'If it's all the same to you, sir,' said Palindrome, 'I think I'll go down to the village after breakfast and take a look.'

'As you please,' said his host, 'though it sounds as if there'll be little scope for your sleuthing down there.' It was the first indication since his arrival that anyone had heard of the minor celebrity that had accrued around Palindrome's reputation as an amateur detective in the years since he solved the bizarre Kilcoil Wines affair.

There was a knot of people around the church when Palindrome and Suggett arrived, some of them helpers, some of them onlookers, none of them really sure what to do. There were trails of smoke still rising from the jagged piles that had caved in from the church roof during the blaze. Palindrome moved about inside and out, for all the world as if he were just another antiquarian church visitor, oblivious of the circumstances. Suggett went to the spot where a protective group of villagers was gathered around the corpse. One look was enough. It could have been a charred log except for the forking of the legs and the narrowing of the neck. There was a blackened vacuity where the face should be. Palindrome came and glanced, and then beckoned Suggett to follow him through a narrow doorway in the north aisle that gave historic access to the squire's family coming from the big house. 'It's a wheelbarrow we're looking for, probably in the bushes there,' Palindrome said curtly, and moved in amongst the thick undergrowth of the wood that bounded this edge of Sir Henry's estate. Suggett found the wooden barrow a while later in an overgrown ditch. As they hauled it into the light, they both saw, glinting absurdly in the light, the painted arms of the Vestibules.

'A single fairly deep wheel-mark in the mud outside the church,' said Palindrome over luncheon in answer to the question. 'It stood to reason that the body must have come from somewhere unless it had been killed in the church. And it looks as if it came from here, Sir Henry.'

'Now, hold on, Palindrome,' said the old man. 'You're making some very large assumptions here. For a start you're talking as if you're sure it's murder.'

'He's right,' said Harold Lobby. It was the first time that Palindrome had met the other house guest or the lady of the house, Lady Violet. 'There's a score of other possibilities.'

'I'm well aware of all the possibilities,' said Palindrome. 'But the probabilities nevertheless remain that when you

156

find a dead body that has had half its face smashed in, it is the result of deliberate, brutal violence rather than of a piece of falling masonry; that when you find that body in a perfectly regular supine position in the middle of the floor rather than in an angular heap in a corner somewhere, it has been put there and not fallen there; that when you find a wheelbarrow discarded near the church without showing any signs of having been there long, it is the vehicle that was used to bring the body to the church; and that when you find the Vestibule crest on the said barrow the body was most likely to have been brought from here. Probabilities only, I agree, but pretty good ones all the same, wouldn't you say?'

'I think,' said the sweetly smiling Lady Violet, who had been silent until then, 'that we should let Mr Palindrome treat this as a proper investigation in the absence of the police. And I think we should all agree to be questioned, the staff as well.'

'Shouldn't Palindrome be a suspect, though?' said Lobby roughly. 'Arriving as he did out of nowhere, I'd have thought he was a prime suspect.'

'Mr Lobby,' said Palindrome with elegant patience, 'your open mind does you credit. But I think my alibis are obvious, a complete ignorance of the area and a lack of clothes until this morning.'

With this objection removed, and with Sir Henry's permission, Palindrome occupied the library for the afternoon, interviewing Sir Henry himself, Lobby, Lady Violet, Hoskins the elderly butler, Carter the chauffeur, Vic the almost retired gardener and Jem the young houseboy who had been in attendance the previous evening.

Lobby was testy when asked about his movements the night before. Lady Violet, more candid and cool, revealed why. They both began by saying, when asked, 'I was in my room from about eleven-thirty for the rest of the night.' 'But were you,' Palindrome then asked, 'alone?' And what Lobby had denied, Lady Violet admitted. Lobby had been a visitor in her room from eleven-thirty until about two in the morning, when he had returned to his own room. The only other information that came from this first survey of recollections was that the gardener remembered being awoken in his cottage by a sudden clatter, which he realized now might have been the wheelbarrow being removed. This was at about three-thirty.

After tea, Palindrome and Suggett made a tour of the grounds, walking down towards the wood and the path to the church. At a distance from the main house, and near the pathway, they found a second cottage, pale pink in colour, and partly built to resemble an exotic temple. The door was locked, and from what could be seen through the window, the cottage appeared to be in an unused but tidy state. As they walked around it, Palindrome suddenly crouched down over a drain-cover and appeared to be peering into its depths. Suggett knew better than to ask questions at such a time.

Upon enquiry, they discovered from Sir Henry that the cottage had been a guest-quarters in its time, but that now it was not in great demand. 'Lady Violet has the key,' he said, 'but I don't know what use she makes of the place.' From a slight hesitation in his voice, Palindrome inferred that Sir Henry would rather *not* know what use she made of it, and in any case her 'use' of it had evidently passed nowadays to the main house.

After dinner, when the murder was deliberately not discussed, Palindrome took Lobby to one side. 'You are a gallant man,' he said. Lobby raised his eyebrows in enquiry. 'You would prefer to protect a lady rather than have an alibi. Lady Violet has told me everything.'

After a pause, Lobby said hastily, 'So I suppose one lie immediately makes me the suspect. I know you don't approve of me, Mr Palindrome.'

'Nonsense, nonsense,' said Palindrome. 'All I want to know is that, since your evidence has changed in one part,

158

do you wish to change it in any other? Specifically, did you notice anything suspicious at two o'clock?'

'As a matter of fact, Palindrome,' said Lobby, 'I did. There is a landing window just outside Violet's, her ladyship's, bedroom, and as I went past I noticed a figure walking away from the house towards the wood.'

'At two o'clock? You are quite sure.'

'Perfectly sure,' said Lobby, and went to pour himself a drink.

It was Palindrome's habit to think aloud in Suggett's presence. This time he said, 'Lobby could, of course, be lying, to cover himself. But if he were, he'd be better to lie about it being three-thirty that he saw this figure in the grounds. And if he's telling the truth, then we have an hour and a half between Lobby's mysterious figure and the noise of the wheelbarrow, whereas the wheelbarrow and the fire in the church tie together nicely. An hour and a half to kill, if you'll excuse the expression. That's an odd thing. But the oddest of all,' at this point Suggett looked up in expectation. 'Oddest of all is the butler who goes to bed before his master. Now that's something you'd never do, eh Suggett?'

'Certainly not, sir,' said Suggett, both a little affronted at the suggestion and puzzled at the sudden shift of the conversation towards matters of etiquette. 'Do you mean, sir, that you think the butler did it?' Palindrome merely smiled.

In the morning, he spoke to the butler again, who confirmed that it was indeed unusual for his master to let him retire first. 'But he said he felt like a quiet drink,' Hoskins went on. 'I rather think the presence of other guests,' meaning Harold Lobby, and others of his kind, 'upsets his lordship more than he shows. Still, Jem was about, I wasn't worried.'

'And Jem left you a note about the extra breakfasts needed for the morning?'

'Not a note, sir,' said Hoskins. 'He told me about that first thing.'

159

'I see,' said Palindrome. 'Tell me, Hoskins, how long have you worked here?'

'Many years, sir,' said the butler. 'I came immediately after Sir Henry's marriage, sir. His first marriage, that is. There was a large staff in those days, a dozen or fifteen at least. Only three of us left now.'

'And Jem? How long's he been here?'

The butler's lips tightened. 'Two years, sir,' he said. 'About that. Her ladyship's idea. Someone for the horses, I think she said,' and he coughed.

Palindrome next sought out Jem, the houseboy. He asked him if he enjoyed working at the house, if he didn't ever get lonely. 'A good-looking young fellow like you. What do you do in your spare time?'

'Oh I'm all right, sir,' said Jem blushing. 'Fact is, I'm engaged. Peggy in the village and I, we're hoping to get set up soon enough. Saving like mad we are.'

When Palindrome asked him about the note, Jem looked blank. Then he remembered receiving it, and how he had thought not to bother Mr Hoskins with it, since he knew he'd see him early in the morning anyway.

Before lunch, Palindrome went for a walk in the grounds alone. He had already suggested to Sir Henry that they should all meet in the drawing-room of the pink cottage in the afternoon, Sir Henry and Lady Violet, Mr Lobby, the three elderly staff and young Jem. 'Why down at that old place?' Sir Henry had asked crossly. 'And do we have to have the servants there as well?'

'Everyone should be there,' had been the reply. 'And I fancy that the cottage has some interesting associations.'

The group assembled uneasily in the sparsely furnished room. Sir Henry and Lady Violet, who had actually dressed for the occasion, took two of the available chairs. At first, Lobby sat down, and then decided to remain standing. The four domestic staff held back against the walls, unaccustomed to sharing a space with their employers in this way.

160

Suggett had already said to Palindrome on the way in, 'You know who it is, don't you? It's that houseboy, isn't it, some sordid little business getting out of hand?' Again Palindrome only smiled.

Then he began. 'One curious thing about this business,' he said, standing in front of the elegant fireplace, 'is that by rights almost any one of you ought to be the victim in this case. There are enough jealousies, suspicions and rivalries here, above and below stairs, to set off half a dozen murders. But in fact the murder victim is someone else, an unknown someone else. Someone whose identity the murderer went to great lengths to obliterate. To smash a victim's head in is not unheard of in passionate crimes. But to transport the victim from the scene of the crime to another place in order to burn it seems to me more like a carefully thought-out plan of concealment than an act of frenzy.

'Speaking of the scene of the crime,' Palindrome went on, 'I believe that this is it. I believe that the murder was committed in this cottage, probably in this room, and then the body taken to the church for its curious cremation. There were too many people in the main house to risk committing a murder there, and the night was too foul to imagine our careful planner committing a murder out of doors. Besides, the interior of this cottage is somehow too tidy and clean for a building that is supposed to be out of use. The drains smell of disinfectant. No, I am as reasonably certain as I can be that the murder was carried out here, and the cottage then very thoroughly cleaned.

'But if our murderer was so careful, why did he – or she – leave the house at two in the morning, assuming that the figure in the grounds seen by Mr Lobby was the figure of the murderer, and then come back again at half past three to fetch a wheelbarrow which the murderer must have known would be needed? At one point I began to think that Mr Lobby had seen the victim and not the murderer. But I discounted that on the grounds that the

161

victim seems unlikely to have come from the house, since, as I have already said, the victim is not one of us. We shall have to worry about where the victim came from later.

'My conclusion was that the murderer required assistance in the commission of this crime, and that the person who fetched the wheelbarrow was not the same person as the one who came down here – if I am right that this is where they came – at two o'clock. Perhaps the person who committed the murder was in some way too weak to carry out this complex plan of concealment which entailed wheeling the corpse all the way from here to the church. This would give the murderer time enough to carry out the deed, clean up carefully, and wait until a pre-arranged time when the accomplice would arrive.

'The obvious candidates for such an arrangement, you will excuse me for saying so, are you, milady,' he looked at Lady Violet, who glanced up with a curious smile, 'and your friend, Mr Lobby.' Lobby came forward, and for a moment it looked as if he was about to strike Palindrome. 'But,' said Palindrome with an emphasis that stopped Lobby in his tracks, 'despite the fact that Lady Violet has the key and you, sir, have the strength to carry out this arrangement, it is unthinkable that you would testify against your own partner in the crime by telling me that you saw someone, whom you knew to be the murderess, in the grounds at two o'clock. Are there any other candidates for strong man? That was the next question I asked myself. And the answer was obviously, yes. There was another pair of hands, attached in fact to yet another pair of arms with which her ladyship was more than usually intimate. It was you, Jem, wasn't it, who fetched the wheelbarrow, and carried straw down here, and then helped to take the straw and the body down to the church?' Palindrome glared at the pale young man, who said only, 'But, but. You can't make out. You mustn't. I –', and then fell silent.

Palindrome impassively continued, 'That much I think

162

we must take as established. Young Jem was persuaded to help in the crime. It was he who took the barrow, and probably he who accompanied the murderer to the church. But are we prepared to accept that Jem was willing to put himself into this extraordinary predicament for the sake of what – of love? Are we required to imagine Lady Violet on bended knee, saying to her handsome young houseboy, "For the sake of the love we bear one another, help me commit a murder"? It seems implausible. It seems an insufficient and unrealistic motive for Jem, who, after all, is happily engaged to a pretty young girl in the village, and knows that he has no serious future either as a houseboy or as the fancy-man of a rich woman. But what if Jem didn't know he was involved in murder, not at least to begin with? What if the pressure placed upon him affected his own real interests at their heart? What if somebody had begun by saying, "You just be my messenger boy, and if you don't I'll put an end to you and sweet young Peggy by spilling the beans about you and her ladyship. And if you do, I'll reward you generously"?

'This seems inherently more probable. It also raises the important side-issue of a messenger boy. For, if the murder was to be carried out at two o'clock according to an efficient plan, it was obviously essential to have the intended victim on the spot at such a time. Now, two o'clock is a queer time to arrange a meeting without arousing suspicions. So perhaps the meeting had originally been arranged for a somewhat more civilized time, say midnight, and hastily had to be re-arranged. At that point, certainly, a messenger would be needed.

'Admittedly all this is speculation, but it occurs to me that there was an occurrence on the night in question of exactly the unpredictable kind that might force such a re-arrangement. I have to thank you, Mr Lobby, for putting me in mind of this when you reminded me how odd was my arrival on that night. It was then I began to think of some of the odd things that had followed on from my arrival. A note was sent, but only a mundane note about extra breakfasts for uninvited guests. Except that such a note never arrived. The butler had been sent to bed. The chauffeur had been sent into the village on a somewhat pointless mission. The gardener, the only other resident staff member, in any case lived outside the main house. Everyone was away or asleep except his lordship and Jem. His lordship was supposed to be having a quiet drink, but three-quarters of an hour after this was supposed to have happened the bottle still remained unopened. It was generously opened only after my arrival. And then the note was sent. Would it make sense if the message about breakfast was only ever intended to be carried by word of mouth, and the handwritten message that was passed was in fact intended to be taken down here saying, "Unavoidably detained at midnight. Will see you at two o'clock", or words to that effect?'

Palindrome was interrupted by a low growling noise from his right. 'You know, then. You know everything,' said Sir Henry. He looked up and around the room, blinking a little as if at the daylight.

'I know this much, Sir Henry, that the note was sent as I have just suggested, and that the drink was unopened because you had never expected to have to open it. You had sent Hoskins to bed, and Carter into the village, because you needed a clear space of time in which to sort out the final arrangements with your accomplice, Jem. You were the one who was feeble enough to need an extra pair of hands to carry out your intentions. And yes, certainly, you were the one who came down here at two o'clock and killed your victim, probably shooting him or her with your gun, and then beating the skull in until you were satisfied.

'What I found hard to understand at first was why you had chosen Jem. Certainly, it was easier for him than for someone else to obtain the key to the cottage. And certainly you had a hold over him – blackmail and bribery, in the way I have already described – that didn't apply to the

164

others. But why select a newcomer, when you had three devoted older servants to choose from? This was the question that I needed to ponder this lunchtime when I went for a walk. And the conclusion I came to was that the newness of Jem was precisely his attraction, and the oldness of the others was precisely what debarred them. Jem, I decided, must have been the only one who could pass messages to the intended victim without himself becoming suspicious. And then I remembered how important it was for the victim to be disfigured and unrecognizable. Clearly the victim was someone who would not be recognized by Jem, but would be immediately recognizable to Hoskins and the others. Someone from your past, Sir Henry. My strong guess would be your first –'

'Wife,' said Sir Henry in a blank voice. 'Yes, you are right. My first wife.'

'Returned from the dead,' said Palindrome. 'To haunt you, and to drive you to murder.' It was an unusually histrionic flourish for Palindrome to allow himself.

Bit by bit the story came out. The first Lady Vestibule had not died abroad. Nor had she been the paragon of popular reputation. On the contrary she had been defiantly unfaithful to her husband from the moment of their marriage, and had finally absconded with another man in Singapore. 'A dreadful man,' Sir Henry had bitterly said. 'A powerful merchant. Dreadfully rich, with a real pagoda on his estate, a real one!' The laughter had been hollow. Their liaison had seemed to be final, and to save himself and his family any scandal Sir Henry had contrived the story of her brief and fatal illness. He had come home, and then, after many years, he had married Lady Violet. 'This time,' Sir Henry said, 'it was someone I truly loved. If only you had known how much. If only you had known.' For the first time, as he spoke, his wife looked at him, if not with affection, at least with pity.

Abandoned by her merchant lover, and perhaps by a succession of others, the first Lady Vestibule had returned to England to claim her marital rights. She had then heard of Sir Henry's re-marriage, and realized that she would be better to operate by stealth than in the open. She had seen that Sir Henry was wide open to blackmail on account of his bigamy, and she began by demanding somewhere to live. In desperation, Sir Henry had allowed her to stay in the cottage. Jem had looked after her, sworn to silence by Sir Henry's own blackmail, and believing that the woman was Sir Henry's mistress, a belief that seemed in complete conformity with the general habits of the household. All along Sir Henry had known that the only thing to do was to rid himself irrevocably of the woman, ensuring if he did so that she would remain unrecognizable to the world. The storm had seemed to present the perfect opportunity. The church was chosen because it removed the corpse from the estate, and because its ancient fabric was easily combustible. Everything was well in hand, until the un-expected arrival of Palindrome.

When the story was finished, Palindrome looked about him, and said, 'We have six people here who are in no way party to this crime. I have played at being detective for the last two days. No harm will come, I think, if the remaining six of you play at being a jury. You have heard my version of the evidence. You have heard a confession from Sir Henry, and what amounts to a confession from Jem. The question before you is, whether knowing everything you now know, you believe that the corpse should be identified. There is no doubt, in law, what your answer should be. But you might prefer to believe that the law, in all its rigour, ought for the moment to be in abeyance, like the telephone lines. You might prefer to take into consideration questions of weakness, and fear, and even of fidelity. You will have to weigh grave crimes against the present affections that motivated them. Sir Henry, Jem – I suggest we leave the room. Suggett – you be foreman of the jury. The choice is between the dreadful truth and a conspiracy to perjure yourselves. The telephone lines will be up again, by my guess, before dinnertime. You'd better have made your decision by then. And soon after then, Suggett, perhaps you would be good enough to overhaul the car for our return home.'

20

Single Combat

What is now happening? The curtains are being moved at the big house. It is more than a hand lifting them aside; arms are lifting them down, there is a clatter of rings, dust rises, heavy drapes are folded that have not been shifted in years. Fresh paint is applied to the paling on the driveway, fresh plaster to the cracked cornices. There is a noise of hammers and saws. New wallpapers are carefully matched to new fabrics. And what is this? A fleet of vans arrives to take away stacks of furnishings and crockery, valued books and silverware, brasses, vases, paintings. Store-rooms will be filled; auction houses will be busy. And now another fleet of vans arrives with new beds, singles and doubles, new wardrobes and chairs, plush seating for the old library, low glass-topped tables for the hall. Wiring and plumbing have been ripped out and renewed. A handsome desk in mahogany veneer stands across one corner of the entrance-hall, and judicious lighting picks out the fancy mouldings on the ceiling and in the alcoves around the fireplace. What had been the front drawing-room becomes a lavish bar. What had been the upstairs gallery becomes a dance floor, easily converted for exhibitions or conferences. Staff are fired and retired; new staff from the surrounding villages are fitted out in new smart styles, discreet enough to blend in with the atmosphere, but clear enough to mark them out for the convenience of patrons. Capital is moving in where before there had only been family and class. Capital is renewing the stonework on the crumbling balustrade, expanding the gravelled area in front to make more room for cars, and converting the garages that had once been stables into a games-room, with table-tennis, pool and video games. Capital – bold Capital – at last paints signs around the newly turfed entrances, buys advertising space in the press, and announces the location of a new and luxuriously appointed country house hotel.

The end is about to begin. A consortium had been formed. There was only a daughter left. The estate was in the hands of trustees. The estate could not be managed at current prices, and fell into disrepair. The estate was put up for auction, and Mr Harvey Frontage, on behalf of the consortium, won the bidding handsomely. For years, he had been accumulating the necessary backing to convert the Piece into a Hotel.

Mr Frontage does his rounds, pausing vigilantly but unobtrusively in every room, checking the menu with his chef, smiling at the girls and making them feel relaxed, chatting with the shooters in the bar, who are being some-what noisy, and making sure that no offence is caused to other guests. Tomorrow Mr Frontage will host a meeting of Scandinavian colleagues who are studying the success of enterprises like his own. Yesterday he was pleased to do the honours at the opening of an Antiques Fair. Today is quiet, relatively speaking, leaving Mr Frontage free to enquire after his customers' well-being and to check on those few details which the staff will always let slip if someone fails periodically to remind them. Details are Mr Frontage's obsession. It's the details, he tells his staff, that make our customers come back, and make them recom-mend us to their friends. It's the details, he tells his fellow investors, that have to be paid for, and if we scrimp on those we can say goodbye to the rest of our profits altogether. One of the details, he tells the girl behind the bar, as he takes a last drink before retiring, is that you serve a whisky in a whisky glass and not in a tumbler.

But Mr Frontage, well satisfied though he has every

right to be, also has an enemy, an enemy close at hand. Not any of his business rivals or former associates who are suspicious of his methods and jealous of his success. Nor his former bank manager, who lost Mr Frontage's business after an argument over £2-worth of charges. Not his ex-wife, nor the local journalist who is unaccountably obsessed with exposing him. Not even the girl behind the bar who is less cheery tonight than usual, on account of being made to look a fool, and after such a long day of it too. This enemy is an elegant, crinkly lady of eighty-four years of age, whose sharp mind is devoted to cheating Mr Harvey Frontage – the gravel merchant, she calls him, remembering where his money first came from – out of what he secretly most desires.

Elizabeth Main-Portle, the middle daughter of three born to the late Sir Herbert Main-Portle, who had all survived their three brothers by many years, is the last link with the big house as it was. Unmarried, she will remain that last link. Like so many unmarried daughters, she had been the one to stay on at the big house after her mother's death. She had never really been away, therefore, except for a time when she joined one of her married brothers in India, to nurse his wife after the birth of their first child when she was ill and unable to cope. She had nursed her father, too, through his last long illness. But because she had kept her own health she had never lost touch with the big house herself, nor with its grounds. Every day she would walk in some corner of it, or through some of the rooms that were no longer used, so that the whole of it remained as fresh to her as it had been sixty or seventy years before. For as long as there was a family willing to be entertained, she had presided at Christmasses and christening parties. In short, she had become wedded to the place, perhaps for want of anyone or anything else, and because she had known no other world.

When the big house was put up for auction it was stipulated that she was to be given the little pink pagoda within the grounds as a dwelling place for the rest of her life, and that this property would revert to the new owners only upon her death. Anyone else would have loved the little summerhouse. Elizabeth made it pretty, if a little cluttered, with her things. But she hated the place, and felt like a prisoner within its walls. Partly she hated it simply because it meant the loss of the big house, and partly because she felt it was absurd to use this little summerhouse as a permanent dwelling – an absurd way to live, and a preposterous waste of money (not that the money for the conversion had been hers, her lawyers had seen to that). But she also hated it because of a memory that was hers alone, a secret she never shared, and an image in her mind that she could still hardly dare to look upon directly, or even clearly decipher any more. In an upstairs room of the pink pagoda, one August evening during her childhood, one of the gardeners had come to her with a knife, and made her promise silence, or ever afterwards fear his wrath. Those had been his words, this at least she did remember, like out of a storybook – fear my wrath. She had been only eight or nine at the time, and he held the knife with one hand whilst busying with the other at his belt. Whether he had finally put the knife down to help him with the job she could not remember; nor whether he had made her touch him, or only look; nor whether his hands had touched her to take her knickers down, or whether she had had to do it herself. Why she did not scream, or whether it was true that at the time it had all seemed quietly exciting in a conspiratorial way – because he was one of the friendlier gardeners, always ready to give the children a ride in his wheelbarrow – and even comical, with the strange faces and noises he made, and the queer cucumber of a thing that did not accord with anything her brothers had spoken of or that she had ever seen; all these were questions to which the answers were now closed off for ever.

The moment remained, however, the strange words he

had spoken, and the vivid sense of disgust she felt at the greenish urn water she had splashed over her dress to make the stain disappear. This, and the fear that somehow he would speak of it to someone, for it all seemed to be her fault. When a week passed and it was clear he would not tell, the fear began to drain away, and things returned to normal. Not that she would ever play in the pink pagoda after that, or accept wheelbarrow rides again.

As she grew older, she became better able to understand something of what had happened, and both the moment and her feelings about the moment became distant from what they had been, or were replaced. The event became nothing, or perhaps it became the kernel around which everything else took shape, so that the whole of Elizabeth's life became a business of repeatedly re-burying or re-visiting it by stealth. In her own mind, however, she was disinclined to give the incident the weight it might necessarily appear to have to an outsider, and when the question of the hatred of her new home was raised she said only this, with a sweep of her thin arm, 'It's so – cramped.'

The source of energy upon which she survives is not so much her hatred or ingratitude. It is, on the contrary, her knowledge of the special regard in which the pink pagoda is held by Mr Harvey Frontage. It had all come out in their one, chilly conversation, in the early days of the sale, when she had entertained him to a meagre tea in the drawing-room of the big house, and nearly swamped him with her vivid memories of the times there had been, and made it clear that she regarded him as an intruder, a destroyer. She had been polite though. He had tried to tell her about his private regard for the place, about how he had grown up in the locality, a railwayman's son with a cousin of his mother's who had been a kitchen maid at the big house. Elizabeth had bitten her lip to prevent herself from asking who this was – she knew that was what he wanted. He told her how the big house had loomed large in his childhood imagination, and hinted, in an embarrassed

172

way, at the time that he and his friends had come into the park from the end by the river, young trespassers, no more than nine years old or thereabouts – and how they had discovered the pink pagoda quite unexpectedly, and how delightfully mysterious and grand it had then seemed. 'Grander in our eyes than the house itself, because it was extra, you see, superfluous. And the big house was really too big for us to take in,' he said. He told her how he had set his heart on it even then, as a place for him to aim at, and had never forgotten it, even when the War, and later his work, had taken him away. The pink pagoda was his particular delight in the whole property, it was to be his crowning personal reward for all he had achieved. He would have it as his own private cottage when it became free – 'When I am dead, you mean,' Elizabeth had coldly corrected him. It gave her no sense of sympathy for his ambitions, this little tale. On the contrary, she held it to herself as her sole advantage over the odious man, the fact that she knew his secret and he did not know hers. It made it easier for her to bear living in the cramped quarters of the place, and it gave her life a purpose, that of denying Mr Frontage his dearest wish.

For three years she nursed her project, satisfying herself with strange little acts that seemed to her to be the height of malevolence directed against the gravel merchant and his trespass. She would go up to the big house when she knew Frontage was away, and perch on a bar-stool drinking gin and bitters. Patrons would find themselves sitting next to a frail old lady who would suddenly begin to weep, and when they sought to comfort her she would moan, with a broad stretch of her skinny arm, about how magnificent the balls had been that they had held in these same rooms, or about the lovely mare she used to ride across the park, or about the family party assembled on the steps in readiness to drive to the old king's coronation. Those she accosted in this way would feel, not the anguish she had intended, but a quiet sympathy for the dotty old woman and a vicarious sense of pride in how it had all been.

On other occasions, she would go at night from the pink pagoda up to the big house and press herself up against the curtained windows of the ground-floor bedrooms or the lounges, listening to the dulled murmur of conversation and laughing silently at her own wickedness. She had kept for herself a set of keys to one of the side-doors of the big house, and she would let herself in and wander down the broad corridors she knew so well, and curl her nose up at the ugly metal room numbers on the ugly new doors. Her old pleasure in the familiar shapes of the big house gratified her. But she was gratified far more by imagining the complaints that would be made the following morning to a puzzled management about the hotel being haunted, or about a mysterious figure that had been seen in the grounds.

There would be one or two guests who would vow never to return because of her little games. But not enough to satisfy her real desires for revenge. The dangers were twofold, that she would begin to enjoy these diversions for their own sake (they were the only occasions left to her for putting on her best clothes), and that she would die before her great plan was fulfilled. She had in mind a device which, at a single stroke, would put Mr Frontage's public reputation in an unpleasant light, and deny him his private ambition. She relished the silent symmetry of their two childhood secrets, his dream and her nightmare, and perceived it as a race to the finish between them.

With great care, and over a long enough period of time to avoid raising suspicions, she put her plan into effect. And then one night she locked the front door of the pink pagoda and drew the curtains; she left all connecting doors and one or two upstairs windows open, and went around the house depositing small piles of newspapers, and soaking each pile liberally from one of the dozen cans she had assiduously collected; and then – like the faithful wife upon the death of her beloved spouse – she set fire to herself, and the pink pagoda became, as she had intended, the pyre upon which her widow's funeral rites would be concluded. The charred body was found the next morning; in a mysterious way, she had finally won.

21

Trumps

It is well known amongst those who pursue the Game that the greatest secrets both of knowledge and pleasure are to be found in the Pink Pagoda. It is widely believed that, amongst these secrets, the Pink Pagoda conceals the secret of the perfect means of entering its own envied domain. They say that this was written out in gold-leaf on a deerhide scroll, and was placed in ancient times in a jar of jade whose lid is studded with precious stones. Very well, you may say, let us take the Pink Pagoda by storm, unlock all its secrets, and since these will no longer be of any use to us, let us destroy the scroll and sell the jar for as much as it will obtain – or even dispose of it to the obsequious curator of some museum, where we will immediately be named amongst its benefactors.

Unfortunately, it is not so easy. The Pink Pagoda has ways of repelling even the most determined intruder, or of keeping him at bay. The Victorian antiquary, Sir Henry Porch, was amongst the first to discover this. Having entered by force of arms, in the first room he came to he found himself surrounded by fancies beyond his own imagining, tableaux of delight which had never figured even in his most alluring dreams. There were negro women on snakeskin sheets; a real-life Shiva serving opiate treats; golden boys with feathered lashes, wearing only gold cuirasses; and a maiden girl with a smile of pearl, whose hair was a curtain, parted behind, revealing tattooed scenes of a forbidden kind. There was no likelihood of Porch passing through such a room without pausing, and once he had tasted any of the delights that were offered to him there, he was stuck fast, transfixed by the sticky web of endlessly novel pleasures that were available to him, and less and less capable of releasing himself. Indolence, and the variously drugged foods that were his only diet, deformed a hitherto active body and mind, and he died some months after his arrival, without ever having gained access to any further rooms. His wife never recovered the body, and she announced to the world that he was missing, presumed dead, on an expedition to recover certain Coptic breviaries from a monastery in the desert. His memory, even amongst the few who have guessed the truth, is still honoured.

A more recent victim of the Pink Pagoda's resistance to the would-be intruder was Mr Harry Lobby, Jr., the wealthy industrialist and adventurer, whose fortune, you may recall, was made in the scheme to sell hardcore to the Gobi Highway Corporation. His attempt on the Pink Pagoda was thwarted, not by any egregious sensual pleasures – there were few that a man of Lobby's tastes and wealth had not experienced in the world outside the Pagoda – but by a small bespectacled man in a dark suit.

The man appeared in the first room that Lobby came to, and simply asked him with a gentle confidential seriousness if, all things considered, the overland route would not have been the better alternative. Lobby only looked up once, turned away from the Pink Pagoda, and locked himself in his top-floor office, having instructed his secretaries to fetch him various files and to keep open all available telephone and telex lines as a matter of priority. Through the night Lobby worked, calling colleagues from across the world out of their beds in order to check figures and to be reminded of contractual details. It was the one business decision of his career that he remained doubtful over, and whilst his fortune had been made through that contract, it was the only time in his career that he had resisted his own instincts and succumbed instead to the cautious and conventional thinking of his associates. The argument was between transferring the entire exploration, excavation and transportation business to the site of the projected highway, and using clinker from his own domestic quarries transported in a vast overland fleet of trucks. The overland route, as the bespectacled enquirer had obviously known, was fraught with detailed difficulties concerning complex currency fluctuations and the effects of various national transport regulations. But, if these problems could have been overcome, the advantages were enormous, in that the scheme left Lobby with all the newly developed plant and sites in his own hands once the contract was complete, and even with an international route established that could be re-organized to fit new developments.

In the end, Lobby had fallen in with the obvious solution. The pressure of time became overwhelming. But the overland route had never lost its attractions for him, and it needed only one word to re-awaken the old obsessions. All other work was put aside. He ignored all his colleagues' attempts to dissuade him from pursuing it further, and requisitioned more staff and more computer time for the project. It went on like this for nearly three weeks, until his fellow directors saw that a thriving business was being put at risk by its founder's misguided activities. They removed him from his own board, locked him out of his own offices, and within six months he had been committed to a private clinic where he is still receiving treatment.

But perhaps these stories, and the others like them that one hears, are as far-fetched as they sound. Perhaps, in fact, the Pink Pagoda has one means, and one means only, of securing the defeat of any intending trespasser. And this is that when you arrive there, stepping in through the french windows from the verandah or finding the front door invitingly ajar, the first room you come to is occupied by a group of people. Upon inspection, it is clear that they are intent upon their own Game of the Pink

178

Pagoda. The dice rattles, the cards are shuffled, the pieces are laid out. Moves are made, counter-moves are plotted, all eyes are firmly fixed on the Board. Nothing you say or do distracts their attention from the Game. When they have finished and a winner has been declared, it is usually the winner – momentarily wreathed in smiles – who suggests another round. The pack is cut, the Pieces are put back in their places, and they are off again. If the secret weapon of the Pink Pagoda is its ability to discover the weak point in any Player, and lure him away from the real point of the Game by playing on that weakness, then there is one weakness that is shared by all Players of the Game: their obsession with competition itself. So that even in the longed-for heart of the Pagoda itself, the Players cannot resist the chance of a game.

The new arrival is thrown by this into a state which some may prefer to call epistemological confusion, but which generally feels more like a profound sadness. After all, the Player has just risked everything to get there, invested time and money in the expedition, abandoned his family and all the satisfactions of Home, and finally arrived with a clear sense of the rewards of victory and a sober estimate of the options that are open to him in the event of failure. The question that springs to his lips is not, Why are they, the evident winners of the Game, content to spend their time in endless play, when they could be tasting all the fruits of victory? – so much as, Can it be worth it, after all, if this is what winning means? And, in dejection and exhaustion, he will depart from the Pink Pagoda, wondering how he came to devote his life to such a pointless expertise. Or he will wait until the moment is ripe, and try to squeeze himself on to one of the benches where the Game is being played. Either way, he is defeated.

And perhaps, indeed, the jade jar and the deerhide scroll about which so much is spoken in such awed terms by devotees of the Game, perhaps these too are a fabrication. Perhaps there is no secret about the Pink Pagoda at all, either about how to enter it or about what is to be found there. Perhaps it is truly open to all and always has been, and that is its only secret – the one that those who play are incapable of discovering. They, the few, are also the determined, and they must have some veil of mystery, some aura of hidden riches, surrounding the Pink Pagoda, to justify them in their obsession, and make their playing of the Game seem comprehensible. So that it is those who have made most of the Game's fabulous dimensions who are most vulnerable to the Pink Pagoda's means of exclusion. Whereas the thousands who cross its threshold in a year, never having heard of all this, and who walk through it only because it is their quickest way from where they work to the bus-stop, or who have used its gardens to walk their dogs in for as long as they can remember – they are impervious to defeat. In the terms of the Game, they are constantly winning because they have never counted themselves as Players. Years ago, it is said, one of them clumsily brushed a jar from a shelf in one of the inner rooms and broke its lid. Before it could be put back, the wind picked up a dusty rag that had fallen from inside and blew it through a window, where a dog found it some time later in the bushes and chewed it up. This may have been a different jar from the one of which we have spoken, and its contents may indeed have been worthless. Or perhaps this story too was untrue. Or, conceivably, at that moment, the secret of all secrets was finally destroyed.

22

A Shattered Peace

Miss Paroxysm sang, tra-la-la, tra-la-lee, as she pushed down into the moist grey hole her thumbs had made. She trilled, she hummed, tra-la-la, standing at her treadle, intent upon the lump. Thrilled by it all, her senses spinning with the wheel, she felt the good ooze upon her fingers, she treadled, she tra-la-leed. But try as she might, the waters still trickling into every groove, the inert shiny mass would not come into shape. Full of mirth at her failures, still tra-la-leeing, still trying, singing her song again, throwing again, Miss Paroxysm would press down the soft centre with her delighted fingers, and watch, tra-la-la, as the floppy grey lips rose and spread and trembled at their topmost. She would laugh with glee at the toppling. But no pot would come of it.

In the next room there was the sound of snapping wicker, indistinguishable almost from the audible 'tsk' on Miss Terry's lips. Bent haggish over her work, tongue between teeth, she dropped each broken strand with a whisper on to the accruing pile beside her. The others in Beginner's Basketry pursued, in silent endeavour, their simpler baskets. She had been instructed, 'Oh do try something basic, dear Miss Terry, don't be ambitious' – but she had so wanted this kind with a lid as a present for Virginia to give her mother. A younger sister who is devoted to patchwork is a godsend to the basket-maker.

'Grand,' said the warden, standing on the verandah. 'Isn't it grand?' he repeated, addressing himself half to the

181

garden and half to the beautiful Directress of Studies who stood beside him.

'Yes,' said young Miss Fulbright, turning from the garden to the warden, 'yes it is.' And provided that you ignored the obtrusive line of laundry flapping beyond the trees where the gipsies were, it was indeed a pleasant prospect. The well-stocked garden, the clear stream, the thickly wooded slope and a view towards open parkland beyond the little bridge at the far end of the garden – all made magnificent in the late summer sunlight.

'I must say,' said the warden, 'it's a pleasure to have them all back. It's the fortnight I always look forward to most, you know.' Miss Fulbright smiled. 'I see our three old ladies are here again,' said the warden with a laugh.

Miss Fulbright laughed too, through pretty teeth. 'Oh yes, Miss Terry and her crew. Where would we be without them? And this time a girl as well, a niece of Miss Terry's. Have you met her?'

But any answer was interrupted by a curious loud wailing that broke forcibly into the intensified summer silence. 'Prayer-time again, I suppose,' said the warden, nodding conspiratorially towards the Hall. But it wasn't a call to prayer, as was seen a moment later when the pale and fleshy body of a nearly naked woman came running from behind some shrubs, screaming and stumbling on a pair of high-heeled sandals. Apart from these, she wore only a pink dressing-gown which floated on the airstream, clear of the flailing arms which tried to grab it around her exposed body, and which failed every time they let go to catch hold of one end of the flying tie-cord.

'Whoops,' said the warden, making a move. 'Trouble in Advanced Life, I see.' He began to walk in haste towards the bushes, though not at a run. As she passed him, his eyes settled furtively on the pair of enormous nipples that capped her jogging breasts. Deep pink, almost purple, and outspread like flower petals seeking the sunlight – 'Pink on her diddies, pink dressing-gown, silly pink shoes,' the warden thought, 'pink bloody everything, like the pagoda.' Behind him he heard her collapse in a heap of execration and tears upon the Directress of Studies. 'Oh Mith Fulbwight!' the silly voice was panting, 'it was dweadful, a thlimy fwog! Unbeawable!'

Miss Paroxysm looked down when the wailing first began to see a naked figure running through the grounds. The next thing she saw was the sturdy figure of Mrs Bounce – for Mrs Bounce had opted for Advanced Life, and Advanced Life had elected to use the shrubbery – preceding by a pace the thin, stiff figure of a girl, dragging her towards the pagoda. On their way they were joined by the warden, and it was then that Miss Paroxysm left her pot to go next-door to warn Miss Terry of the crisis that was about to break.

Sheena, the model, was still missing at dinnertime. Virginia, the culprit, was still silent, hacking steadily at a chop, with those eyes of hers brightly staring in the way that disturbed Miss Paroxysm. Miss Terry kept saying, 'I'm sure she thought it was a prince,' in a loud cooing voice. 'Didn't you, Ginny love? I'm sure she did. You know the imagination of the girl.' But Mrs Bounce was having none of this, and saying equally loudly that the girl needed to be kept on a tighter leash. 'It was all very well,' she would insist, 'but it was only the good work of Miss Fulbright that had stopped Sheena from packing her bags and taking off. And where would that have left our group, I ask you? No, the girl must not be allowed to ride rough-shod, she must be kept on a tighter leash.' She would tell Miss Terry, 'as a friend', that other people were saying that it was Virginia who should leave if anyone was going to. And whilst Miss Paroxysm had much sympathy with these sentiments, she was also glad that Miss Fulbright had sensibly ordered the Advanced Life group to work indoors from now on, since this would minimize the chances of frogs being dropped on the unsuspecting laps of life models from behind trees. Yet she couldn't help admiring her friend's goodness of heart in taking a difficult child off her sister's hands for a spell. The difficult child was still munching in silence when Miss Terry cooed, 'It was a compliment to Sheena really, to think of her as the princess. Like in the stories, you know. Just a girlish game.'

Most probably, it was on account of all this fluster that Miss Paroxysm turned pale when, at the start of the evening session, the Directress of Studies had approached her and said, 'I think perhaps you should try transferring to modelling tomorrow.'

'I, Miss Fulbright?' she had said with a quiver. 'I really don't think I could, Miss Fulbright. I really think I oughtn't. I've had no experience whatever of that kind of thing, none at all. I'm sure there must be someone more suitable.' But when it turned out that all that was meant was clay-modelling, because of the problems that Miss Paroxysm had been having with throwing, she began to calm down noticeably. By bedtime, she was so enthused that she lay awake for a good while thinking what she might do.

In the morning she had it. 'A celebration,' she said to Miss Fulbright – she had caught her in the garden-room even before breakfast was served. 'A tribute to you and to this place. It will have everything in it, and I shall make a gift of it to the Trust when I have finished as a way of saying thank you for everything that has been done for me here for the last five years.'

'That sounds marvellous,' said Miss Fulbright in the unnatural cheery voice that came to her when dealing with students before breakfast. But what she thought was, 'Is it really five years?' – thinking back over the time that the Trust had sponsored this Arts and Crafts school ('in an idyllic country setting,' as the brochure said), and that Miss Terry and her friends had been coming, always the first to book, never improving by a jot.

'A little landscape,' Miss Paroxysm was still saying, 'with the pagoda at the centre. The dear pagoda! And all around it, everything we do, perhaps made a little comic, a little

184

heightened perhaps. But only by way of celebration. What do you think? I shall call it simply Fantasy.'

'I think it sounds lovely, Miss Paroxysm,' said Miss Fulbright. 'You'd better make some preliminary sketches.'

'Oh no, Miss Fulbright!' said Miss Paroxysm, gasping as if in pain. 'I must grab myself whilst the thing is still fresh. Oh I can only work with the feeling of the moment! I was almost going to ask your permission to skip breakfast.'

But, in the event, it was after breakfast that Miss Paroxysm began work. She and Miss Terry bade farewell to Mrs Bounce at the breakfast-table, who was inclined to be late for her morning session, since it was to be indoors and since Sheena had not been prevailed upon to emerge until lunchtime, and they were having to make do with a man from the group who refused even to take off his tie – not that Mrs Bounce wished him to take off more, as he was old and scrawny and would remind her of her late husband during his last illness. Miss Terry departed for Beginner's Basketry at the door, and Miss Paroxysm entered her own beloved den with its clayey odour, springy of step and cheery of song.

She worked through the day, pinching the scraps of clay between her fingers, taking each of the texturing instruments in turn, and on the point time and again of hugging herself in delight at her own inventiveness. There was a strange noise of gongs and chanting up at the Hall, but she had heard it before and had to confess to finding it quite restful. At one moment it was answered by a blasting noise of rock music – it seemed to be coming from behind the trees where the washing was – but this lasted for too short a time to disturb her. So that she noticed nothing of the slow build-up of events during the heat of day, and was oblivious to all the talk about it in the evening, desirous only of getting back to her modelling after dinner in the hope of getting the thing fired overnight.

What Miss Paroxysm missed first of all was the arrival of a delegation from the Hall. There were three men, tall

185

and tanned, each wearing a full-length white robe wrapped around one shoulder, and each with hair cropped down almost to a shadow. They carried staves, and their spokesman asked in a soft voice if they could pass through the pagoda's garden because they wished 'to address some words in friendship to the travellers in the woods'. The gipsies, it seemed, had been disturbing the activities up at the Hall, not just by the loud music which had been heard in the pagoda, but by physical intrusions on the part of some of the young men which had led to the abandonment of some of their outdoor sessions. The warden had predicted that the gipsies would be the cause of trouble before long, and he suggested to the group that they fetch the police. 'We have our ways,' the representative had said, 'and they are ways of peace and understanding, not of force. All we ask is for the travellers to leave us in peace, as we leave them, and to understand that we, in a way, are travellers too.'

'Fat lot of good that'll do you,' the warden had muttered, but Miss Fulbright and he had let them through. Everyone in Basketry was peering out of the window as the white-robed figures advanced across the lawn. Mrs Bounce came rushing out of Advanced Life for permission to ask one of them to sit for them – 'It doesn't matter which,' she said, all enthusiasm. 'They're all so fine.' Only Miss Paroxysm, it seemed, was uninvolved.

A word of explanation is in order. After the death of Lord Narthex, the estate had been broken up. The pagoda had come into the possession of the Trust, and a successful series of residential courses had been held there since. The Hall had lain vacant for a time, but it had recently been acquired on behalf of the Pilgrims of Peace. This organization used it as its headquarters. Its elders – the men in white robes – lived there, and ran a hostelry, as it was called, for 'visiting pilgrims' who wished to sample the mixture of vegetarian cuisine, meditation classes, communal massage, spiritual therapy and the eclectic, though mild-mannered, rituals that were on offer there. The Pilgrims and the Trust had fallen out when the former had tried to use a picture of the pagoda as part of their publicity material. But now all was peace between them, despite jibes like the warden's about prayer-time at the Hall. The gipsies were much more recent neighbours, and it was no surprise to anyone who had observed them that the elders came back a short while later thanking Miss Fulbright and the warden for their co-operation, but smiling and holding their hands out with the palms upwards when asked what they had achieved.

Sheena would only work after lunch if she was allowed to pose in the shrubbery once more. Everyone except Miss Fulbright was pleased, and the Directress of Studies had to relent in order to avoid a full-scale rebellion. The hot afternoon wore on, pencils scratching in the shrubbery, bees still buzzing, Miss Terry's strands of wicker breaking with the same regularity, and Miss Paroxysm humming tunelessly over her burgeoning landscape. There was a monotony of regular breathing as people concentrated on their work, the girl Virginia apparently chastened by yesterday's experience and silently wandering from group to group, picking up a grass-stalk here, a soft ball of clay there, or a strand of wicker from Miss Terry's pile of waste – although the strange dark eyes were still staring in a way that Miss Paroxysm would not have liked, if Miss Paroxysm had been in a position to notice.

All this quiet normality was suddenly shattered – all of it except Miss Paroxysm's concentration – by a monstrous roar of one, two, three motor bikes whipping through the trees at the bottom of the garden and sweeping across the lawn in different directions. One of the bikes discovered the shrubbery, and there were whoops of aggressive joy, followed by wails of terror, as Sheena came forth once more from the bushes, once more white and naked, pursued to the verandah by the three motorcyclists like three stampeding bulls. Mrs Bounce hammered out of the shrubbery

187

waving a fist and shouting, 'You bastards! You bastards!' There was a bang as one of the motor bikes backfired. The warden, who had come running out, went running back in, shouting, 'They've got shooters! Run for cover, they've got shooters!' For a moment, Mrs Bounce believed him and asked herself, Would there be a death? A death, she thought, was just what her painting needed, a shot in the arm. Get rid of all the flaccidity her teacher had pointed out to her only yesterday. When, to her surprise, it was the warden himself who reappeared on the verandah with a battered rifle, and adopted as if by reflex a kneeling posture on the wooden floor. He would undoubtedly have fired, had Miss Fulbright not emerged at that moment from the shadows, shouting, 'Stop! For heaven's sake stop!' Her intervention, as it happened, was unnecessary, because the cyclists had already broken off their fun and all that could be heard was a shattering roar disappearing through the trees.

It was much later they noticed that Virginia was missing. Genuinely missing – not hiding, as they had first thought. And not like Sheena who, in her anxiety, had packed her bags and booked herself into the hostelry of the Pilgrims of Peace for a week's massage and therapy. Virginia was nowhere to be seen, and no one could remember seeing her since the visitation of the motorcycling gipsies. They telephoned the hostelry to check if, by chance, she had followed the handsome elders back to their refuge, but of course she hadn't. Miss Terry was adamant about not contacting the police, since this would inevitably mean involving the mother, and that would be 'such an unkindness'. It was not the first time Virginia had wandered off – 'such a strange young thing, but so intense!' – and the chances were that she would be back before nightfall. It was at nightfall, after she had deposited her model in the kiln, that Miss Paroxysm became aware of what had been going on. Much was discussed, the reasons why the gipsies' tempers might have become heated after the visit by the Pilgrims, and the places where a young girl of imagination might conceivably have gone. But the conclusion remained, even at bedtime, that Virginia was not there, and Miss Terry pleaded with the warden and the Directress of Studies to leave things as they were until the morning.

Miss Paroxysm was up before anyone in the morning, and in the chill, lucid air which promised another bright and breezeless day – a day stolen from the onset of autumn – her excitement was almost unbearable as she walked towards the outhouse where the kilns were, to inspect her model. She lifted it out delicately. Everything was perfect, the little pagoda at the heart of its world, with figures and trees and even the stream put in – everything in its place and in proportions that were a trifle out of true, in keeping with the festive gift she wanted it to be. She held it in her hands looking over it with dancing eyes, and humming her tra-la-la beneath her breath, when behind her on the gravel there was an engine's roar, a great burst across the driveway, a moment's pause, and then another burst as the motor bike shot out of sight. She dropped her model in the shock, and turned towards the lawn to see the figure of a small girl roll over and rise to her feet from where she had been dumped. 'Virginia!' Miss Paroxysm cried, and it was in fact at that moment that the Fantasy went crashing to the ground. 'Virginia! You!'

The eyes that now looked at the strange eyes of the girl – stranger now in this morning light, brighter and more staring than ever before – knew as they moved forwards to meet the girl that a moment before they had seen her sitting in triumph on the back of the motor bike, tight up against the bearded, leather-jacketed ruffian who was the rider, hands firmly held around his waist. Why did she instinctively think 'in triumph' as she recollected the sight? Why did she now approach the girl thinking that there was more than a stare and a brightness about her eyes, that there was – after her night with the gipsies, and the

189

destruction of Miss Paroxysm's Fantasy – a shine, a smile, about her face that was the smile of victory? The elderly spinster took the child by the hand and crossed the gravel with her slowly to go into the pink pagoda, where the explanations might begin, and they might attempt to put together the fragments of what had happened. As they walked inside, the first of the autumn leaves were beginning to fall.

23

The Oriental Connection

I came because I was asked. No other reason counts for much in my line of business. And I stayed despite the fact that I was asked to leave. Which was not minding my business. I should have known better.

The name is Punter. You've probably never heard of Punter and Fairbrother, Investigators. Fairbrother was my late partner. I keep his name on the door out of a sense of attachment. I'm attached to his former clients. But this investigation involved someone right out of the blue, out of the navy-blue, in fact. Admiral Vestibule was an old boyhood hero of mine, on account of stories they told about the Pacific War. And when he called up about some jewels that had gone missing I had a real taste to visit the big mansion on the hill and look the old boy over. Call it sentiment if you like, but there was a hefty fee in it as well. Jewels are not normally my line of business. The chances of getting them back are too remote for my taste. But when he told me on the phone about them being the property of his late wife, there was something touching in his voice that made me take him on. That and my own bit of nostalgia. And the fee. I should have stuck to my principles.

The Admiral had kept up his shipping connections after the war, but on the trading side, and he now ran a healthy business importing furniture and carpets and antiques, that sort of thing. There was evidence of it everywhere in the house. Enough bamboo to feed a tribe of pandas for a year. There was also fancy tea at teatime, which I've always had a fondness for. And if you stayed around long enough listening to his memoirs, there was malt whisky, ditto.

The second visit produced an even better reason for going. Gloria, his daughter, was there, all there. She had the kind of looks that make your teeth go cold. And though she clearly thought the Admiral was out of his depth on the subject of criminal investigations, and that I was making easy money out of an old man who liked to talk, still we got on fine. Personally, I'd have been quite happy fighting the Civil War all over again with a girl who could smile like that, rather than agreeing on everything with a dozen others.

She was there the third time too, decorating the sofa. But the fourth time she was there by herself, telling me that the Admiral was unwell and giving me the message to drop the whole investigation. With that, she gave me an envelope containing my last payment plus a little bit more. Now, I've been suspicious of a little bit more ever since I was a boy, when the store-keeper put some extra candy in my packet, and I found out afterwards he'd sold my mother a bum sewing-machine the day before. I peeled off the extra and handed it back. She smiled her smile, saying something about honour that made it sound like a dirty word. I made the usual clumsy pitch before I left about seeing her again. But all I got was the smile like a boot in the teeth.

I decided to take a look over the Admiral's property. It was all done up very fancy, a garden in the French style, one in the Tudor style, another in the English style. At the bottom of the slope there was the Japanese garden I'd heard about, with the little rose-coloured pagoda the Admiral had had built. Cute, I suppose, if you like something between a doll's house and a temple in your back yard. I was looking at the view, and beginning to wonder what the guy was doing who was hefting crates into the pagoda from a van parked up against the front door – those big crates with stencilled lettering you get on ships, too big usually for one guy to manage – when any idea I might have had of offering to help was cut short by the butt-end of a gun being brought down out of nowhere on the back of my skull.

It could have been centuries later when I opened my eyes. All I saw was the ceiling caving in on me and then floating up out of reach. This was no fun, so I turned on my side. The room had movable walls as well, so I shut my eyes. Next time I opened them there was a movable man by my side, the guy with the crates, and better looking at a distance. The room had pink walls and white lacy blinds which somehow made the traction engine revving over in the back of my head hurt even more. I must have slept, and when I woke up there were voices. A second guy came in. You could tell by the way he looked me over, with a smile of approval on his skinny lips, that he was the gun-butt champ. He called me by my name, but I took no notice. All I could notice was that one of the voices outside belonged to Gloria.

'What are you doing with her?' I said.

'Who's her?'

'Miss Vestibule,' I said. 'What are you doing with her? You lay a finger –'

'Miss Vestibule, Miss Vestibule,' said skinny-lips mimicking. 'Don't you worry about Gloria, pal. Let's worry about you.'

Whether we talked or not I don't remember. I remember noticing the way my arms were tied and my feet, and I remember the traction engine blotting out most things. I felt like a turkey with a hangover. Anyway, I must have slept some more, because when I woke up only guy number one was there. I had a kind of picture of Gloria in danger in my head, and it must have been this which moved my muscles. I got the guy to come over, and then swung against him with the full weight of my trussed-up legs. By chance, he fell against the edge of the bed and smashed himself much worse than I could have managed.

It gave me time to shuffle towards his gun and grab it off the floor, so that when he came round I could invite him to take a walk backwards into the closet, looking fierce – holding the gun like a bunch of flowers between my two soft fists, though he wasn't about to know that. I felt pretty silly locking the closet with the key in my mouth, and I could easily have gone back to sleep laughing if it hadn't been for the picture of Gloria in my head. I broke a glass, listened for footsteps, and when they didn't come started slicing through the ropes on my hands and feet.

There were voices somewhere downstairs, one of them Gloria's, though she sounded none too harassed. I kept on tiptoe, even though the place was coated with overgrown carpets. Finally, I came alongside the room where the voices were. There was my blonde angel sitting at a desk, with a mile of leg in front of her, puffing at a cigarette, and talking things over with the gunman. She wasn't exactly relaxed, more like keeping herself deliberately cool. But she certainly wasn't getting a rough time either. It sounded like the kind of conversation you might expect between a bank clerk and a regular defaulter. The defaulter was Gloria, and payment was due no later than Friday. The bank clerk was the other guy, and the item of security that was going to be called into play if the cash didn't show was a set of pictures that the bank clerk had and which he might be about to print.

'Sometimes I wish you'd just print the wretched things,' Gloria said at one point, 'and get the whole thing over.'

'Sure,' said the bank clerk. 'I know how you feel. But think of your father. After all, it's not costing you the earth.'

I began to have a rough sketch of a racket that was different from what I'd first expected, but still a racket. My first thought was to go to the Admiral. But I could imagine what sort of pictures were in trade, and I thought twice about this. I also had a hunch that Gloria's financial difficulties might be the explanation behind the jewels, and I

194

didn't feel like shopping Gloria to her father on two counts.

My second thought was to go to the docks. There was a name, or part of a name, that even my addled head could remember. Ahara, it had said on the side of the crates that were being brought into the pagoda. Perhaps Ahara would give me a clue to the kind of racket we were up against. It didn't take long to turn up a ship that had docked two days before from Hong Kong, Yokahama, Hawaii – the Eastern route. It gave me a pretty good idea what the cargo was likely to be, and how Gloria had got herself involved. The pricey white powder that's been in fashion lately is a dangerous business though, and I didn't like the idea of my angel being involved. Particularly not when I discovered that the *Sakahara* – which was the full name of the vessel – was a ship in her father's fleet, which seemed to mean that not only was Miss Gloria buying the stuff off the market and helping to buy it wholesale with the dough she laid out to her blackmailers, but it looked as if she was fingering the ships that brought it in, on account of her special connections with the trade.

The deeper Gloria was involved in this game, the more danger I reckoned her to be in. My next move was to go back to the pagoda. The quiet way this time, under cover of the trees in the Admiral's bird reserve. But the place had been cleaned out completely. No Gloria, no gunman, no crates, not even butt-ends. Even my would-be jailer had gone, though not in a healthy state as I guessed from the three splintered bullet holes in the closet door.

I decided to tackle the main house via the front door, and was glad beyond words when it was Gloria who slammed the door in my face, saying, 'Get out' through clenched teeth and a thickness of timber. At least she was safe. I said to the woodwork, 'Look, I know about the pagoda. I know about the jewels. I'm beginning to know about the *Sakahara*' – and slowly the door opened again. 'You'd better come in,' she said grudgingly. Not her pleasantest manner, but at least it was an invitation.

'Is your father upstairs? Is he well enough to talk?'

'He's gone out.' I should have realized, of course, but there hadn't been time to see, that the stuff about the old man's illness was a phoney. It didn't matter for now. I began to talk. She listened. Then she talked and I listened. She hadn't known about me being in the pagoda, she said. She'd only gone down there to explain why they had to wait for the money. She talked about the jewels, though you could tell she didn't like to. She liked talking about the pictures even less. It was because of the jewels she'd had to try to get rid of me. Had told her father I'd made a pass at her, or something, and he'd agreed to my dismissal. 'I'll take you up on the scheme one day, honey,' I said.

It was when I came to the *Sakahara* that I'd got it all wrong. She knew nothing about it. All she knew was that she'd let them use the pagoda for a while to keep them sweet. She'd gone there just as she'd gone to other places before to get her stuff, but where it came from she'd no idea. What had happened after I'd left was that Sammy, the man with the gun, had gone upstairs. She'd heard a yell followed by three bangs. Sammy had been shaking when he came downstairs. Almost immediately another car had arrived, and a man had come to tell them they had to clear out fast. There'd been a change of plan. I asked her who the man was. She said she didn't know, though she'd seen him once or twice at big functions. A rich-looking guy with black hair and chunky cufflinks. I should have realized. Punter's First Law of Investigation reads: If you come across something that stinks and it's within a sixty-mile radius of the office, then the chances are that Harry Portico's behind it. Harry Portico's behind most things in this county, most of the dubious things. He's a man (if you're loose with language) who scares people. He scares me. In my case, it's specific. It was Harry Portico who bumped off my partner, Fairbrother. Lured him out to a little monastery on the edge of the desert to get the pay-off in a kidnap deal, locked him in the monastery

196

chapel there, and then set the building alight. Did half the crematorium's job for him, did Portico. There's talk of other bodies dumped over at the quarries, which are the legitimate side of his business. Plenty of other bodies. I don't like Portico. And the rule is that if Portico decides not to like you, your best move is to be somewhere else.

If it was Portico who had come to the pagoda, and it obviously was, then the only odd thing was that it sounded as if Portico wasn't quite in charge. Portico ran Sammy, but somebody else must be running Portico to get him into a panic like that where he was obeying orders to clear out as much as they were. I took Gloria back to my apartment to get her out of the way of trouble. She seemed keen on the idea. Then I took off to the ugly slab of concrete on the bay which is Portico's house. The kind of thing they call modern. A thug bursting out of a butler's get-up answered the door and told me Portico wasn't in, that there'd been a call and he'd gone to the pits.

I went to the pits after him. If I was in a hurry it was because there was a picture beginning to take shape in my head which made me feel uncomfortable, although I couldn't have said what it added up to. The big mesh gates were locked, so I left my car on the road and monkey-climbed over them and started walking towards the cluster of huts on the far side of the first quarry-pit. I had not got very far when there was a shout from one of the huts, a door flung open and someone came lurching into the open, bending low and running. Portico appeared in the doorway and levelled an automatic across the open space. My arm reached inside my pocket and Portico slumped in the doorway just as his gun went off. I ran towards the figure between us, and had to bring him down in a friendly tackle to stop him from plunging over the edge of the pit. Portico's gunshot had caught his leg and there wasn't much strength in the man. But still we had to roll around a bit on the ground before he made out that I wasn't

Portico. And at that moment I was able to make him out as the Admiral.

I checked that my one shot had done to Portico what it was meant to do, and went into the site hut to telephone for an ambulance. I also called my apartment and told Gloria to meet us at the hospital inside an hour. I didn't say much else, only that Portico was dead and she was quite safe to come out. The Admiral's story came out between breaths when I got back to him. It was the Admiral who was the top end of the racket whose bottom end included Gloria. It was he who financed the operation and had the shipping lines at his disposal. When he'd found out about Gloria's involvement he'd tried to use me and the jewel theft to shake her off, to frighten her into stopping. And it was only after the news about me and the pagoda had got through to him that he found out about the pictures and about Portico's bit of blackmail on the side. For the father of a daughter who'd got herself involved over the years in some pretty fancy amusements, including taking her vest off at parties, it was a bit late to do the paternal care routine. But he'd gone wild with Portico, demanded the return of the negatives, and Portico had played for time by saying he could collect them from the quarries in the afternoon. When he'd gone, of course, Portico had roughed him up a good deal, and that was the point at which I'd showed up.

I had wanted to get this story out of him before I did any telephoning the police. It was pretty much the story that had begun to take shape as I'd been driving to the quarries. But now I heard it I rather wished I'd left it to the cops to untangle. I had started with some boyhood fantasies about a brave old seafarer, and been taken in by a stately house, a beautiful daughter, the laid-out gardens and the neat little pagoda. But none of that counted for much now. I stood in the wasteland of the quarries feeling like a kid who had opened the lid of a cookie jar and found it full of a heap of crawling worms.

24

Space Invaders

It was all a question of what we were going to tell Control. Out-of-control was no part of a professional pilot's word-pack. But then the root of the problem was that we seemed to be unable to contact Control, and we were pretty sure that Control had lost contact with us. In that case, perhaps we were actually out-of-Control after all, out of reach.

I looked at Bland, my co-pilot. He was still dazed from the last attack, and it was taking all he had to sit there in front of the screens and monitor directional coefficients without shaking. But he had stopped weeping.

A glance at the panel reminded me of my earlier fears that one of our internal feedpipes had an energy leakage. I made a mental note to check accident screening. But what if the leakage was central, central enough to affect our exchange-terminal with Control? If that was the case, then there was nothing to stop it affecting accident screening too, and we might never pinpoint the leaking feedpipe or find out whether it was something that had happened internally to us, or something that had happened directly to Control.

That was the thought I kept coming back to. Almost exhilarating. Because if you tried to figure out where we were, where we were heading, what we were, or whether it mattered what or where we were, with our link to Control Base probably broken, you always ended up with a zero every time. And what kind of message could be punched out to Control Base if Control Base did not exist? What measurements could be used, what data of any kind, or what functioning programmes? And who could you inform that the basis of the problem was that nothing seemed to be getting through either way? Then the answer was suddenly plain: we must go on operating as if Control did exist, as if it might, and as if somehow it was still getting our messages – with whatever time lag and however indirectly or imperfectly – and as if the confirm signal was still coming through, even though it wasn't. We'd create a new confirm signal and operate it ourselves. Then we'd be sure to carry on as normal. We'd perform our duties, update our reports and re-programme our functions as if, one day at the end of many timespans, we would still have to account for ourselves to Control. Provided we did that, we could survive, even as we were now, hurtling to nowhere in an unknown starzone, possibly in a forbidden planet group, wounded in an unidentifiable part of our system, and with a failed mission to explain. We would still effectively be within Control's grasp. We would not be alone.

I was going to tell Bland about my idea when Bland's tiny voice said suddenly, 'They're back again.' I glanced down at the scanner, and he was right. There were four tiny blips in formation, and heading straight for us.

'OK, Bland, you only have to do one thing,' I said firmly. 'Keep us on twenty-twenty, and I can do the rest. Do that, Bland, and we'll be all right. Fail, and we're gone.' I should have kept the last remark to myself, because when I turned to look there were tears of hysteria rolling down Bland's face, one hanging on to the end of his nose. But his eyes were fixed on the co-ordinates, and his fists were white with gripping the navigational lever. He was doing the job I asked.

It was clear that this attack was going to be different. The others had been an official patrol, and they had kept to the usual manoeuvre of closing in on us in a group, but of leaving it to one man to do the job once his homing controls were locked in. There had been the one hit, we didn't know where, perhaps no more than a glance from his electro-radiation jammer. But those bastards can do a mile of damage if they're correctly aimed and get into your information store. It was only a sudden burst of acceleration that got us out of anything worse that time. This crowd, however, were tailing us in a persistent group, breaking all the rules. They seemed to be in it just for the fun, ordinary idle holiday shooters, banging anything out of the sky that looked alien and they could clap their scanners on.

There was only one way to deal with it. I ordered Bland to reverse the ratios and keep it steady. And then I prayed that the seekers in our system would function, and that they hadn't got fouled up along with the memory. What I was going to try to do was simply to force my way in amongst them, blazing on all guns at once. And then at the appropriate moment – which I would have to calculate down to a nanosecond if I wasn't to lose speed – I would blast on my interference-spread, and assuming that they were equipped with the normal anti-interference missiles and that I had got the calculations right, they would automatically blast each other out of the sky whilst we jumped clear. It was worth a try.

We turned, and I had eye-contact for the first time. It's so rare to have eye-contact with a target these days that a shock of regret went through me. It wasn't that I could see anybody – any machine-users, as the official log language would have it – inside the craft at that distance or speed, but I could see the four machines, actually see them rather than seeing four blips on a screen, three older tarnished models and one brand-new one, only a youngster. This was what confused my emotions. It wasn't the knowledge that these were people like us, or at least perhaps not entirely unlike us, that bothered me. They were dangerous hotheads in space-use terms and the skies would be well rid of them. Rather it was the probability that these people, these machine-users, whom I was about to blast out of the skies, were the last contact with any other being that we might ever have.

Fortunately, my systems were by now locked on, otherwise I might have changed my mind. Either it would work and we would be safe whilst they were destroyed, or it would fail and it would be us who would disintegrate in ten seconds' time. We went through them. The coding for the interference-spread went up at exactly the right moment, and we were past them. I glanced across and saw Bland involuntarily duck at the moment of impact. But, of course, our cabin was environmentally sealed, so we heard nothing. In fact, throughout the encounter, the sound environment had automatically changed to Beethoven's Sixth, which is standard for battle situations. And we knew we were safe when there was a brief burst of the victory song, followed by a return to film themes of the forties, which was pre-set as one of Bland's favourite tapes.

In the quiet that followed, I explained my idea for dealing with the apparent break in our link to Control. I didn't spell out the possibility that it was Control that had gone dead rather than us, since I could see he was only just beginning to come out of the state of shock that had followed from all the recent disasters. He liked the idea, and we agreed on a suitable signal and programmed it in immediately, so that every time we put ourselves in touch with Control we would automatically get the new confirm signal in response. After this, Bland cheered up considerably, and began to use the line in a completely frivolous way that was normally considered to be a serious breach of discipline. He sent birthday greetings to an aunt, he indicated several votes on the last referendum game we had been sent, and he asked Control if they had heard the joke about the pilot who went on a mission with his dog but forgot to take his orgone-intensifier. Every time the bogus confirm signal came back to him, Bland was delighted, and made even more outrageous demands on air time just for the pleasure of being able to create a sense of contact. After all the days of silence we had been through, it was an understandable response to want to play games.

A day passed like this, until we began to get magnetic readings that suggested a planet group. Bland said we should go and explore, and there seemed no reason not to. We re-set our coefficients and headed for the centre of the group. Fortunately it was a single-sun system which made navigation much safer, but nothing came in from systems recognition data, which could have been explained by the ship's faulty memory, but which equally seemed quite plausible given where we thought we were. There were four satellites, one of enormous size and three of more moderate size. Pretty soon we began to get individual read-outs on the planets, and even some rather blurred visuals. The big one had a very high gravity reading, and this spelled trouble for the system in the medium future. It's a common enough phenomenon whereby the force of a single large planet on others can pull the entire system into new alignments, and even destabilize the sun itself. In the case of the nearest of the smaller planets this had already happened. It had been dragged into an orbit too close to the sun and was already a pitiful burned-out affair, hardly worth calling a planet, a ruin of what had been. The second one had a thin atmosphere and the visuals were already showing it as massively cratered and pitted across its entire surface. The other was farther off, and we'd been able to see it in direct vision as a pinprick of pink light for some while. The sensor was unable to make out whether the colour was atmospheric or surface, but the place had a reasonable surface temperature and signs of water. We both agreed that this was the one for closer inspection, and Bland re-set everything for an exploratory orbit.

It was then that he made his suggestion. 'Why don't we go down and stretch our legs?' he said, as if it were the most normal thing in the cosmos. 'It looks nice.' He knew what he was saying, by the nervous smile with which he

203

said it, but it was also clear that he was perfectly serious. He must have known that it was against every rule in the book, and that I would have been entitled to arrest him on the spot for an almost unthinkable breach of the Vanguard Pilots' Code. This was drawn up partly to protect the rights of Colonizer Pilots, but also for our own protection, since our radio-active power sources could easily be impaired inside any atmosphere.

I said as much to Bland, and he heard me out. Then he said, 'But it's all OK if Control says so, isn't it?' And then Bland did what I should have guessed he'd do. He leant over to the verbal processor and punched out, 'Control, tourist permission requested to land on orbited planet, confirm message if permission granted.' We waited a moment, and the invented confirm signal obediently flashed up on the screen.

'That's all we need,' said Bland, 'isn't it?' And he proceeded to cut off all the piloting equipment and go into navigational phase. With extreme delicacy – for Bland had always been a supreme landing pilot, and it was astonishing to the rest of us that he had asked for a posting with Vanguard Mission – he took us down through layer after layer of atmosphere, and brought us to land so gently that I did not realize it had happened. We did the standard tests for toxins and stability, and an elementary visual scan. Everything was perfect, there was the need for only the most minimal head apparatus before we could get out.

I followed Bland down tentatively. The surface, when we reached it, was a crumbly mineral substance, more like one of our machine-made fillers than soil. But it was evidently organic from the stunted trees that were around, only as high as shrubs and with large floppy leaves. There were also massive flowers, these as high as elms on stalks of an extraordinary height and thinness. From the tops of these flowers there came showers of floating things that could have been seeds, but might equally have been butterflies or birds. There was a stream running near where the craft had landed. And there was no evidence whatever of the presence of other machine-users. What was more impressive than anything else was that all these things were uniformly pink – the ground, the trees, the flowers and the flower stems, the seeds or butterflies, or whatever they were, even the water in the stream was a transparent pink. It was no atmospheric effect, but the whole of everything that we could see. The sky was pink reflecting the pink ground, and through the pink atmosphere the sun shone pink, and lit us and our ship, like everything else, as we looked at one another, with its uniform pink glow.

We have been in this place for a notional month now. I say notional, because the pink moon changes every notional day and the pink sun every notional hour, so that time here goes faster and never settles. There is a constant flux between the bright pinkness of midday and the duller pink, almost purple, of nighttime, so that we are forever living in a sunset glow. Bland, who has really taken over since initiating our desertion, says that we are free to stay here, free. Certainly, nothing constrains us to leave. Every probe we make confirms the edibility of the pink crops, the drinkability of the pinkish water. The climate is gentle. A warm pink rain fell yesterday from small pink clouds. Pink dew sits in the petals of pink flowers after every hurried dawn.

Bland has a dream about there being a single inhabitant of this planet, a pink woman in a flowing pink robe with pink hair falling about her shoulders. He says he is determined to search her out. I tell him that the dream only signifies his real desire to get away from here and to return home. I am worried that he is becoming overwhelmed by the pinkness all around. He tells me not to be so narrow-minded, and to join him when he sets off on his journey of exploration, dreaming my own dreams. But my dreams are only dreams of home, of green grass and red flowers, brown earth and a blue sky, of apples and oranges in a yellow dish, a black cat, grey metal, of blue eyes and of foaming white water. Yet when I look at our craft I see that these will always now remain only as dreams. For the craft now stands there, embedded deep in the crumbly pink ground so that it has become immovable. It begins to look like a curious pink tower with some kind of steeply sloping roof – a pink feature of the pink landscape – rather than what it is. As my hopes of escape become fainter, so I find by way of recompense that I am beginning to distinguish between the different tones of pink on the planet, so that what was at first only distinguishable by shape and distance is increasingly definable in terms of colour. Soon perhaps I shall have a native's refinement of perception, and be able to detect a rainbow of shades within the single spectrum of pinkness. When this happens Bland and I have already agreed that we will set out to utilize our spare time in constructing a new vocabulary of colour for the planet. We cannot decide, however, whether we should base that vocabulary on the old colour words, borrowed from colours we will almost certainly in time have forgotten, or invent entirely new ones for the purpose.

Meanwhile, these old words are being punched out daily into interstellar blackness. I wonder if Control will ever read them? Or if anyone else will ever pick them up on this particular frequency? And if they do, I wonder if their translation bank will be able to cope with our alien language?

25

Stalemate

. . . and I, alone on that path, totally uncertain in the glare, unsure of my way, should I go forward or back, which was forward, which back, till the voice came to me again, the same voice only louder and this time in my right ear, saying, Go forward, the way you go is forward, that'll get you there in no time, so that I took a pace forward, and then a few more, oh nothing rash at first, but gaining in confidence, thinking, despite the November fog and blinding low sunlight below the level of the fog, that I could go on like this quite contentedly for as long as it took, were it not for the bad leg, and then remembered quite suddenly that before, when the voice had spoken before, the words had been in my other, my less bad, ear, so that I had not had to strain so hard to catch them, but that they had said roughly the same thing, which meant what, which meant that this voice, only friend I have in the world, save the swans creaking painfully upriver on the waterline, always on their last flight I like to think, save them and the one old sore place in my cheek my tongue always searches out for company, was sending me back along the way I had already come, and perhaps would do it again shortly at the end of the coming stretch, perhaps had been doing it already many times over, for the fun of it, so that here I was in a tract of land, visibility down to twenty yards or less, marching back and forth like a fool, like a fucking soldier boy, in the same space, with nothing to guard, getting nowhere, and all because of my infinite capacity for trust, which has always been

my downfall, that and my optimism, unless perhaps I had
been mistaken about which ear and when it was, and the
voice really was my ally, and the instructions worthy of
my trust, my infinite trust, or unless the first time had
been a mistake and this was the correction, not that it
made much difference, not that it made in point of fact
any difference, since if left to myself would I know which
way to go, if left to myself would I care, and because it
had been this same voice which had got me going in the
first place, saying, Seek out the pink pagoda, and I like a
bloody fool had sought, then I might as well heed the same
voice's later instructions, stood to reason, it doesn't pay to
be selective about things like that, even if it did mean that
by obeying the latter I had no hope of achieving the former,
because the voice enjoyed a little joke now and again, at
somebody else's expense, or maybe something grander,
enjoyed a paradox to toy with, and I, the poor sod stuck
in the paradox, going left to right, right to left, up and
down the path, carving my furrow, boustrophedon they
call it in some circles, well it had to be somebody, so what
could I do, leave a sign, I thought, that's what, leave a
token to establish my presence, which, if it were there
upon my return, would confirm that this was indeed my
return, endless recurrence, so I dropped my hat, just like
that, last I ever saw of it, of course, which at first restored
my confidence, now we're getting somewhere said I to
myself, until the nagging doubts began to grow, that
perhaps the voice had allowed for this one, and had removed the hat surreptitiously, or perhaps a stranger had
appropriated it, though this was unlikely, since there had
been no one else in view since the outset, might merely
have been a famished bull, it does happen, or perhaps the
voice has a band of willing helpers, all of them trying not
to giggle in the fog in case I discerned their presence, so
that in short even my device of the hat rendered itself
useless in time, as devices will, and answered nothing for
certain, and I was thrown back once more on my inner

resources alone, having to decide totally without foun-
dation, whether I was getting nearer all the time, or
whether I was being made an arsehole of, and would be
better taking it easy on a rock somewhere, or just standing
stock still, or perhaps progressing by deciding to do precisely the opposite of whatever the voice said, forward
when it said back, backwards when it said forward, which
would be a kind of freedom, I suppose, and warmer than
standing still, though the logic of it would demand that I
should disobey the first instruction too, which was the one
that brought me here, though it was bit late for that, and
finally settled, a little half-heartedly, on the option of
ignoring the voice altogether, just doing what I pleased,
which had some of the same problems attached to it, since
searching for the pink pagoda was no longer among the
things which pleased me, if it ever had been, and it was
clear that all this was worse by far than the shithole I was
in before, before I'd succumbed to the voice's power, but
there was no chance of return, not that kind of return, the
shithole had undoubtedly been taken over by some other
worthy creature in my absence, no, there was only this,
only this endless up and down until the fog lifted, of which
there was no sign, that and the voice I was trying to
ignore, though how could I tell I was ignoring it if I didn't
sometimes listen, these and the swans and the sore place,
and I, alone on that path, totally uncertain . . .

26

Solitaire

One day, what you always knew would happen, happens. Surly-faced and unannounced from the edges of your vision, as if one of the trees had turned human, the Man with the Gun is in your path. You have long since had your stories ready: I was trying to find my dog. My great-aunt used to come here as a girl. It was the main road I was looking for. But when the moment comes you say none of these things. As a rule, at this point in the Game, preparation counts for nothing. You say, Oh my gosh, no, really, I'm most awfully sorry, yes of course I will. And a second later you are a worm, a beetle on its back, blurting out from the long grass, No, no, don't do it, I beg you, please don't – though you can perfectly well see that the man's rifle is slung loosely at his side and probably not even loaded. Such surrender, however, is not in the least uncommon in the Game, and is probably a direct result of the intensified state of yearning and panic which the Game does as much to induce as to control.

On this occasion, however, the man does more than merely look at you with contempt as you dust your hands off against the seat of your pants, trying to regain some composure with a faint smile or a collusive glance at the sky, at the ground, at your dog. He passes over the few stern words about private property, or the danger from shooting, or the request to put your dog on a lead, followed by a snarl of abuse. Instead, he jerks his gun at you idly, not as a threat but as a clear instruction to turn and continue along the path in front of him.

In this manner, you find yourself getting closer to the Pink Pagoda than ever before, crossing the boundary fence, where before you have always stopped at the bridge, and actually stepping out across the level lawn. Twice, three times, you look over your shoulder to see if this is what he really means, and each time he silently jerks the rifle towards you in confirmation. There is something, however, about the severe expression on his face which makes you begin to doubt. The fear grows that it may all be a plot, conceived by the others, that they are doing this only to force you into a position of trespass where they can punish you, perhaps have him shoot you down there and then from behind, no questions asked, at the very moment that you are about to reach the idolized pink walls, step in through the pink doorway in a single stride that has been rehearsed and re-rehearsed so many times in your imagination. You want to turn to your captor and say all this to him, that it is no good like this, that the Rules expressly disqualify anyone who reaches the Pink Pagoda under compulsion. But you do not turn, because you could not bear either his scorn, or the certainty that all this is happening only as you fear, to give the advantage to the other Players. Instead you move with the greatest caution, as if a gentle stroll across twenty yards of well-mown lawn were a clamber up a scree-covered slope, or through dense undergrowth never before breached, and all because of your uncertainty and the fear that the ensuing moments may be your last. You imagine yourself escaping, but nothing would induce you to run towards the stream and across it into the impenetrable thickets of the Game Wood, zigzagging to avoid the gunfire, both because you are afraid of what would happen, and above all because the Pink Pagoda – now you are in its force-field – is beginning to exert its own attraction upon you, drawing you forward as much as the gun impels.

In an instant it is all changed. Gun, man and sunlight are all melted away, and it is a dark night, moonless, with the snow thick on the ground like a strange, protective padding to the surroundings of the Pink Pagoda. You are still making your way towards the desired walls, which are now almost drained of colour, and your feet are dragging now because of the depth of the snow, and not only because of your fear or your deliberations. A glance over your shoulder confirms the absence of the Man with the Gun, and a single irrefutable line of footprints, deep shadows in the shadowed snow, plot your solitary progress across the lawn. Even without him, however, there is still a thrill of fear, the knowledge of trespass, of danger, as well as of the imminent achievement of a lifelong goal, and all increased by the darkness and the cold. And then the true chill descends upon you, when you remember what had happened. This was pursuit, but it was not the old pursuit. You had heard her moving about in the darkness, felt the emptiness beside you, listened for the closing of the door, and then rushed to dress yourself and follow. Outside you had noted how each sound was altered by the all-pervasive snow, how the entire Board was somehow held together by it, how it deadened everything, blurred edges, dulled movement. You kept your distance behind her, pausing when she paused to light a cigarette or re-tie her scarf. Her footsteps were ahead of yours in the freshly fallen snow, and you fancied to yourself, as if in a childish game, the idea of obliterating each of them in turn, as if this would somehow put an end to her wandering and make everything once again all right.

As you follow, your heart is a dreadful amalgam of pity, desire and anger all at once – the lover, the hunter and the spy. The jealous mind is an unsteady mind, grim and tender turn and turn about, grim with confirmed certainties that it will go out of its way to procure, spiteful with loathing, and just as suddenly overwhelmed with a softening love that wants only to run forward and protect. At first, it had seemed obvious where she was going, but now it is suddenly vacantly unclear. You lose her at the point where five ways meet. There are no footsteps to follow, none to obliterate. Probably it is your loneliness at that point makes you choose the one pathway you have never followed before and prevents you from turning towards Home, a hunger for someone or something to hold on to that you know can now not be satisfied in the known world, least of all in the warm room from which you started. In this version of the Game, it must be understood, Home and the Quarries, the place you live and the place you work, are the only realities; you and she are the only Players, and all the other Pieces have been taken off the Board – or, at least, have been reduced to a collection of china ornaments that she keeps on her dressing-table: a typical stately home in ivy-painted grey, a chunky village church which is stained with ash from its graveyard having been used as an ash-tray, a clump of squat trees representing a forest with a squirrel and a pheasant modelled on the base, and with pride of place given to a delicate porcelain pagoda with an ornamental roof painted all over in a hideous pink. So it is more than surprise or relief you feel when you find that the pathway you have chosen leads to the Pink Pagoda – it is a feeling of the complete providential overturning of your condition, a sense of the solace for which you had always yearned being at hand, a sense of dreams coming true.

So now you find yourself on the snow-covered lawn, everything curiously checkered by darkness and by snow, with the snow bringing silence to the gravel path and softening all the boundaries between one part and another so that even trespass seems easy. Despite the darkness you know every detail of the Pink Pagoda, every corner and moulding and joint, as if you have always loved it. Your walking round it is like a process of delighted recollection, where in fact it is nothing of the kind. At the far side of the verandah, when you turn the corner, a window spills a yellow glare of light across the snow, invading its blue shadow. Your movement is reduced to a ghostlike creeping with this sudden added prospect of the presence of other people, people who you feel sure are ones you have never seen before except as shadows or as figures disappearing through the grounds. Who will they be, these special inhabitants of a special place, and how will they ease your solitude?

You might have guessed. The hunger for knowledge which is the root of jealousy, preferring knowledge of the worst kind to any sort of doubt, and paying the price of its search for the certainty of love by uncovering a loveless world – the hunger for knowledge is intimate with the desire for a tangible beauty that motivates all play in the Game of the Pink Pagoda. Perhaps, in fact, these two are indistinguishable at some vanishing-point of the emotions beyond the limits of the Game. It was no longer clear which of them had brought you here. It was only clear, as you stepped into the edge of that rectangle of light spilling from the curtainless window, that what met your eyes were her eyes staring back, staring blind in the blindness of orgasm, staring unseeing out into the darkness, in an inward intensity of feeling that was hers alone, hers and his in that single moment, leaving you forever in the permanence of that moment on the outside, cold and clothed against the cold, whilst they, and they only, are warm and golden, glowingly naked, each against the other, her breast against the firmness of his chest, her full lips to his, her soft thighs open to his shuddering, time and again, the Beautiful Woman and the Friend. It is her, it is him. They do not see you, seeing nothing, only their own intense joined-together loveliness, as for a moment they uncouple, unembrace, and then begin to touch again, her hand guiding his hand down, down gliding, idling, idolizing. And you are alone in your own bed, alone and wakeful, the space beside you empty of her warmth, the sheets gone cold, and in your fist, unexplained, the china miniature of the pink pagoda, snapped in two by the anxious pressure of your hand.

214

A Note on the Origins of the Game

This boy kneeling on the sands with his back to you is in all essentials the same as that group of men who have been clearing the land these last few months. They are now ready to build. The boy drags the sand together with cupped hands and makes a mound. He smoothes the surface with his palms and digs with one finger a place for a door. Only he knows what is buried inside. He presses a spiral shell into the top of the dome as a marker. And then he stands up to look down on his work. In the act of standing he knows that he too is a prominence on the surface of the earth, he too has an axis that points into the depths and into the heights beyond reach. He says: I am a building, a tower now, I look down on the world and know its business. Saying this, he may merely smile and pass on to another game, or he may feel his power to be such that he will kick at the shell-capped dome and watch sand scattering in rays along the beach. Whatever he does will be done in the knowledge that tides will come, are even now coming, which will leave his tower as a smear on the beach with a shell somewhere inside it, and that the attrition of the sea will open up even his buried treasure and waste it, and he will become a small boy once more.

The men in the clearing·get busy. The stages of their work are well known to them: first a space free from roots or large stones, then the digging down. Only then can you begin to build. It is part of their habit: building is first of all destruction. Over the next month they are busy in the pit, piling up earth which will be taken away to rebuild walls down in the valley, or left for ramps. Everything is useful. The tallest trees have already been stripped and lie

215

in carefully sorted piles for struts or pillars. Even the scrub is kept for firewood in the winter months to come. The largest stones are looked over to see if they might be good for grinding grain, or for making into steps.

There is no day, therefore, when you can say that at last they are ready to build. The only beginning is when they have gone down so far that they must start building upwards. Or is it before that, when the first man wields an axe-blade to bring the first sapling down? Or when four men come to pace out the site and mark its extent with their marker-stones? Or when the old man had his first dream of the hillside topped by a tower, and began to speak about how it would be when the tower was so much part of the hillside that no one could remember it naked? Or even before that, when as a boy he would squat unthinkingly, solemnly, for hours by the river patting mounds of river sand into the shapes of houses? Or when there were first people in the valley living in fear of the hillsides, who knew what it was like – the fear and the power thrilling together – when one of them climbed to the brow of the hill in safety, and shouted and waved to the rest, sharing his victory with them?

There does not come a day when you can say that at last they have begun. But one day the piles and struts begin to stand above the rim of the pit, and it is as if the forest had sprung up again in the clearing, but a bare and patterned forest that shows the will of men and the victories of men over the wild places. And after that, well, it is not plain sailing. There are days when the winds bring things crashing down, bring men down too, and days when they stand in hopeless groups, their skin shining in the fierce heat of summer or in the fires that are their only comfort in the winter, and the hours stretch out in argument or planning – and nothing gets done. But from the valley it is more or less a steady story, day by day, tier by tier, this pier lashed to this post, this wall building up and around and spelling out this window. So it is the

216

people of the valley who keep the tower alive, knowing nothing, and the men feed off their hopeful ignorance night after night when they come back down, just as they themselves begin to feed off the strength of the tower when they look up from their hoeing or their kilns and ovens.

The old man whose idea gave birth to the tower is now so old that he cannot leave his bed and he will never reach the tower when it is finished. But still he looks searchingly into the eyes of the younger men, and seems to give them the strength of his dream surviving in an enfeebled body, and also the duty of it – an idea entrusted to them as a precious corpse is passed on from generation to generation.

So there will come a day when the terraces are high enough for a man to see over the tree-tops and into the farther valley, though his victory shout will nearly be lost in the slap of wind that meets you at that height. One by one they climb up to see for themselves, balancing on sticks of wood that yield under their feet, and barely able to open their eyes against the ferocity of the wind. Soon afterwards it is time to stop the building and to take the delicately ornamented cupola that stands in readiness, so huge upon the ground, so almost lost after they have hoisted it to the roof-top where it will stand, higher than any terrace, higher than any man can reach – with a carved hand and carved eye on each of its six sides, saying to the valley, I can see further, strike further, than anyone; I can stand here always even when you are not watching with me. It will take the day to lift it up, hands pushing out from every terrace to keep it from being knocked. Hard it is, the hardest day of all in some ways because of the breathless anxiety of seeing it safe, and there will be a pause of concern when it is in place that it is not really large enough, that they might as well have done without it. But, because it is the tower-man that stands atop the man-tower, the human-inhuman guardian of the tower, carrying the idea that the old man had to the very heights

217

of the tower on the summit of the hill – because of this, when it is finished, it will be said that the tower is finished and the people in the valley will cheer and greet the builders when they come home at night, and all their doubts will be lost. There will be dancing and drinking and many comic stories about the times the building nearly failed, about the quarrels along the way, and the obscene names the men have called the tower in moments of doubt will now become its proud nicknames amongst the people.

And so the building will be finished and the tower's life will begin. There will come a day soon after it is finished when four men will lead the people in procession from the valley up the hillside to the tower, carrying between them on a litter the body of the old man who was the tower's father, the father of his people. They will pause to rest many times, but they will not yield their places of honour to anyone, because they are carrying their father back to his tower, they are carrying him home. Outside there is already a fire prepared, music and dancing. The smoke rises higher than the tower but it does not stay. The body is laid in the fire and the fire consumes it as the people sing. The fire is doused with water-jugs and the four men scrape the ashes into a special pot. The pot is carried through the dancing lines of people, through the entrance to the tower and into the chamber that has been in preparation all these years, ever since the man first said, I have an idea. Now the idea is entrusted to the tower. The room is opened up and the special chamber that will be opened only once, and the ash-pot is sealed inside the chamber and left. The men pause to look over the brightly painted pictures on the walls telling the story of the tower, and then they return to the feasting. The body gives its life to the tower, and the tower gives the body a lasting place on the hillside. The tower that is the people's guardian, standing over the fields and the crops they plant, over the warriors and the women in childbirth, now stands over the father of the people. So that when the people look up to the hillside they no longer see a wooded mountain filled with the imminence of danger. They see only the tower and the guardians of the tower on its terraces giving them safety. They see the tower-man with his ever-ready hand and his far-seeing eye. And they see the old man planted in the tower like a seed of its life and of theirs. And so, seeing only the tower when they look up towards the ridge of jagged green above them, their eyes focus in a smile of praise.

In time, when the tower has taken root over many generations, the smile becomes automatic. The inner room holds new chambers, having within them the ash-pots of the old man's sons, and of his sons' sons. The procession to the tower has become an annual feast and a way of celebrating any special day. For the rest of the year, the people have learnt to accept their safety now that the neighbouring valleys can see the tower-man. The strength that comes from its priceless hidden pots is now beyond doubt. The guards still keep watch during daylight from the topmost terraces of the tower, but guard-duty is now an envied assignment amongst the young farmers of the valley, a day away from serious work, smoking or playing games. The seclusion of the tower makes it a place for lovers to meet, for old men and children with their nurses to go for a walk. The older children play games around its walls and race up and down the stairs. Gossips sit and make marriage plans, and stories are told about all the years of lives that have been lived with the tower in mind, the days of playing or flirting or resting that have been spent there. Everyone from childhood onwards will slow their pace and fall silent automatically as they pass the inner room with its sealed chambers. But outside in the air once more, at the foot of the tower or standing on one of its open terraces, they will shout down towards the valley that cannot hear them, searching out with tight eyes their own home amongst the clusters of houses, pointing and smiling and shouting, feeling themselves glad to be there.

Important visitors will be taken to the tower and shown its wonders. When they leave the valley they will be given small models of the tower as gifts painted in bright enamels and gold-leaf. And when the people themselves go away from the valley they will take such models with them as gifts for their hosts. Or they will take scrolls, delicately painted, in which the houses of the valley will lie small beneath a towering hillside, and towering over the hillside, perfect in all its details and gigantic compared to the scale of the real thing, the tower, the people's tower itself. When they are asked where they come from they will smile and produce a model of the tower or unfold a scroll, so as to say, This is us, look. And if they are away for long periods of time, they will keep by them one of the scrolls or one of the models for themselves, to comfort their loneliness and to remind themselves of how perfect and how particular is everything about their home.

One of them, travelling abroad, will be forced by circumstance, by marriage, by sudden wealth, or by the deceptions of brothers who claim a right to his inheritance when he is away, to stay away and never to return to the valley. At first, he will live his new life in contentment, but as he gets older there will be a dissatisfaction in his life, like an itch that he cannot find. In time he will isolate the source of his discontent – what he had first thought was only an absence that could not be named – and it will take as its form the remembered image of the tower. All the stories that the tower brings to mind will come back to him and make him feel at peace once more. He will decide to devote the wealth that his new homeland has given him to re-create the tower that is the centre of all his happiness. It will become his obsession. His wife and family, all his neighbours, will think him crazy, but he will override all their objections to the waste and to the strangeness of the replica whose reconstruction he lovingly oversees. At his death, he will leave precise instructions for his funeral rites, remembered from his days of living in the valley, and

220

though his family will see this as a sacrilege to the ways of his adopted home, still they will carry them out. Knowing this, he will die a happy man, and his happiness itself will begin to persuade those around him that he was not mad, just as the associations that the tower will have for his widow and his sons will begin to make it a sacred place for them, as strange as they find it to be. A degree of charm will begin to attach itself to the man's reputed obsession, and a degree of grandeur to the stubbornness of his conception. When their time comes, his sons will certainly insist on having their own remains placed alongside his in sealed ash-pots inside the hidden chamber.

Or there will be a stranger, a visitor to the valley, or a widely travelled man who will fall into conversation with someone from the valley, and he will see the tower itself or an image of the tower and hear about the steady stream of joy that it creates amongst its people. He will determine to understand the source of this joy and to re-create it, if he can, in his own life. When he returns home, he will speak about the tower, and about a true joy, a true beauty and a true peace which belongs to it and which his own people have forgotten or have never known. He will become an apostle of the tower, bringing back scrolls and miniatures which he will leave behind when he departs on another journey. A few people will be persuaded by his enthusiasm, and they will set out to build a tower, or an image of the tower, in their own land – as if they, in their own home, were strangers, like the traveller. But, of course, the tower they build will share nothing except its outline with the tower in the valley, because for the people in the valley the tower is a nucleus for all that most distinctively belongs to them, whereas for the others it holds the significance of something strange, something incompletely understood – a monument to the restlessness of the traveller rather than to the love of home.

And in these small ways, through a filigree of chance meetings, the tower will spread across a world wider than the valley, borne like pollen on the backs of unexpected and sometimes unintended carriers, and transforming itself in shape and purpose wherever it grows up afresh.

For the tower itself, the first tower, it does not do to look too far into the future any more than it does to search too deep for origins. Perhaps in time the people of the valley will have reason to regret the games played by their guardians on the terraces of the tower. For there may come the time when an assault will be mounted from the far side of the hill, and the tower is taken by surprise – a night attack when the raiders come in a single wave and the first thing that the people know about it is the sight of their tower like a flaming torch against the blackness of the sky. This, or a daylight assault mounted by a larger force of men from different directions, who descend on the valley before a warning has gone out. And this will happen because the old enemy in the distant valley now have a tower of their own, standing atop its own hillside, with eyes that glare on the people's tower-man from afar and hands that are readier than theirs to strike.

It may happen on a holiday when a bonfire catches in the overhanging eaves of the terraces, or a spark lodges somewhere and only catches fire when the people have returned to the valley. There will be some ·efforts with water-jugs, but these will be in vain, and the people will stand and watch in dumb misery as their protector and, in a sense, their identity is consumed. Perhaps it will be lightning or a gale that brings the tower-man crashing down or burns him to a skeleton, and the sense of urgency to repair him or replace him will have gone, or even the skills that enabled the first builders to do it. The broken roof or the burned-out shell of the tower will be left to stand through the winter, and the terraces will begin to collapse inwards over the years. It will cease to be a place for people to go to. Certainly there will be voices that will say, The people nowadays do not understand the tower, they have even stopped paying their respects to the inner

222

chamber. If we do not look after the tower as it was entrusted to us to do, then what kind of people are we, and how can we ask the tower to offer us protection in turn? It will be better in that case if there had never been a tower, for we who have lived so long under the spell of its safety are no longer ready to live in a world that will be as it was before the tower came. For everyone, the destruction of the tower, however it comes – the desecration of its inner chambers by a youth crazed in the failure of his love, or perhaps no more than the slow sinking of old age – comes with an empty feeling like a death before its time, a glimpse of the painful new knowledge with which it must co-exist, that our eyes and our lives can no longer look up to the hillsides with a smile, but are now held down in the tedium and the daily fear of the valleys.

Repeat this a thousand times in a thousand different ways in a thousand other places. The boy on the sands, for instance. In the basic language, the place and the body are the same thing. If you can say what comes first, it is a man standing over against a tree, perhaps, giving orders for the tree to be hewn down to make room for his idea. Or perhaps just a man standing. The tower itself is, to begin with, what we say of it: a landmark, marking out the land as ours, as us, as where we both stand. We take our bearings from it, and then our identity. The idea of its power or mystery comes only by degrees. It will be a place to hide inside and to watch from. In times of threatened invasion, the villagers used to gather for safety in the church towers, to see and to be safe. It is reasonable to suppose that the height that presents itself to us as a sanctuary precedes in our conceptions the god who is raised on high, just as the inner warmth that is the mystery and identity of our being human – the warmth of the blood and of our shared blood in a huddle – precedes our conception of a divine mystery that inhabits the secret and the inner places. The body first, the idea of our own standing and of the womb inside the body, and the tower formed upon the instincts of our own flesh, terraces and chambers answering our own needs. And then the idea of the building coming only as the work is done.

In the end, of course, we are deluded by ideas. We become in our own eyes so many towers astride the earth, infinitely powerful, infinitely sacred. From our high places we look across into their eyes, the little men from whom we once huddled in fear, now huddled themselves in their own tower-tops, peeping out. And we will walk in like towers amongst these pigmies, smashing them down and their towers, and calling them slaves or worshippers of idols. Or what may be worse, we will carry home the strangers' towers where we defile them, renew them, set them up in our own land as quaint, incomprehensible, nugatory – and keep them not even as trophies of battle, but as pets. We may, in time, rob even from ourselves in the same way – from our own past, where we have become strangers to ourselves – and, in the safety that the tower has brought to our lives, build up fantastic towers that testify to the arrogance of security that allows us the leisure to imagine what would be delightful, as much as to our sense of delight. The dignity that the tower brings to its landscape is a faint recollection of the knowledge of power that the fortress brought to the land; the pleasure it inspires, a feeble afterglow of the magic warmth of a holy place. The power of the beautiful is perhaps no more than a watering down of other, earlier kinds of power which the tower has known. In the basic language, to fortify and to recall are the same word.

Perhaps it would be better to imagine the land free from all such layerings of creation and distortion, from all this tracking across of human ideas and human remains, which is always a process of forgetting and of loss – to imagine it as if all such things had never been. But to tell the story of the world as if there were no tower in it, you have to sit in the quiet of the tower's own circle of influence.

Perhaps in one of the smaller upstairs rooms, or in the spacious ground-floor hall whose cool marble and whose luxuriant pots of plants make inside and outside inter-mingle on a warm day with the doors and windows open; perhaps in the level grounds and intricate gardens that surround the tower. Wherever you sit and tell your tale – it may be at a great physical distance from the tower itself – still you will be aware of it, as you must be, or how else do you keep your eyes on the page and your mind on the story, and are not constantly looking up in fear to the hillsides in case the silhouettes of strangers are descried? If you do not share something at the centre, then how can you know what the story-teller means when he weaves his lovely images of a towerless world? There is a certain basic minimum, a shadow of the tower falling over the page, before there can be any work of the imagination at all, even the one about the tower not being there. To arrange words and to pile up stones, to do and to make, are, in the basic language, the same.

And besides, through all the deformations and forget-tings, the tower persists. So that even when we have gone from the defensive fortress and the sacred monument to the retreat, the private folly, the summerhouse in the pleasure-garden – to the squat exotic replica of the tower in an alien landscape – still there is a hint of recollection inside all the forgetting. Thus depleted of its functions, the tower at last stands in a sense as it first stood, something in a landscape over against the man who stands looking, without use or addition, without an idea, and without meaning. The merely beautiful may be the nearest that our teeming world can get to what it once was, bare and uninterrupted, with someone standing on an incline think-ing to himself for the first time what it would be like to pile up stones in such a place higher than he can reach.

It is because of this that your status as a stranger – a trespasser and an onlooker, peering around the edge of the trees from the end where the low bridge stands – is closer to the truth of things than the status of the owner, who still sees the little tower, for all the hands it has passed through, and as little as he understands anything about it, as a signal of himself and of his ascendancy within the circles of the county. Closer also than the status of she, the occupant, who bows and smiles when she hears what her guests are saying, about how lovely everything looks, and especially on a day like this, with all the flowers, and amongst such company! You, on the other hand, never see the thing entire, never clearly hear a word, but, standing at the bridge-end, you can endow the garden and the veran-dah with voices, just as you can fill out the interiors of the rooms and the unseen aspects of the building, imagining even the prospect as it must be viewed from the concealed window of an upstairs room. Here we are claiming to deal only with borrowings and trespass, everything at a third or fourth remove from what it was. And so the pagoda itself which is twice borrowed now, since it belongs to a point in time some two or three hundred years past, and then again is stolen from another, far distant, point both in time and space, is as suited to the enterprise in hand as a pagoda which is only ever partially seen. The pagoda's colour as well – the glowing pink in an afternoon of gold that made pink against green seem like a dish of jewels alongside the slender shadows of the trees – this too is a borrowing, for it is the pink of sweetness that touches the petal of the dog-rose, a shade away from white, touches the early-morning cloud with a flush, and makes it youthful, feminine, as it is also the sweet pink of mutton flesh close to the bone. Not a sugared, hardened pink, but a hinting colour, announcing the flow of blood beneath the skin, and endowing the stone walls of the pagoda with a sugges-tion of fluidity and warmth, the touch of life.

All this, you must imagine, comes together at a time of flux. Oh all times are such, but at a particular time when home, desire, purpose and belief, were all uncertain, all head-on to one another. You were mindlessly abroad,

226

walking, as your distracted habit was, at great speed, keeping to the paths but crashing down unexpected random turnings aimlessly. It was autumn. The estuary lay flattened in the sunlight below. Ahead and out of sight along the path were the quarries. Northwards to your right the parkland of the big house, whose symmetry of five bays would come into view past the clump of trees in front of you. Farther on lay the burned-out church. All of this was familiar, accustomed. The mind did not need to state such commonplaces, they formed a picture that unwound alongside, or rather a little ahead of, the reality. The dog was in a dense undergrowth of copse to the left of you, his presence little more than a clanging of leaves and branches, but weaving back between you and the scent again and again.

Then there came the decision – no, not a decision either, but an impulse, a shifting of the body in which the mind was pleased to acquiesce – turning to follow the downhill pathway to the right, a gentle slope never before pursued, leading you towards the foot of the parkland's steeper incline beyond. Whistled for the dog, bringing him swerving out of the copse and towards you. All at once, flinging himself in at the thick bushes beyond the oak tree, there is an upward crashing of alerted game birds from the shelter of the woods, and the inward crashing on the eye of a single magpie and a single stoat – at first it looked like nothing more than a rag of fur alongside the glossy coal-black mass – hanging pinned to the barbs of the fence. In what world do we walk that leaves such trophies – if they were trophies, or not warnings rather, talismans, offerings – stuck to the barbed-wired fence of a game wood? Voodoo in rural England (not that you thought of it as voodoo for a moment) chills and arrests the onlooker. They had been put there carefully, with some sense of glory, or display, or necessity, or mere custom – some sickening sense of adding to the fact of death. The eyes in them were opaque, drying, and the blood on them brown like mud. Mites and small flies were harboured there in great number. It is what they call magic.

Ignore the omens, move on. A partridge panics in your path, the dog bolts out after it. Blood in the nostrils, he lunges over-excitedly between the tightly planted trees. Only the slope of the path, and stubbornness, keep you from turning back. There is anxiety now treading the path alongside you, which, if it were to take shape, would come as whatever keeper it was who displayed the magpie and the stoat. Threatening you too now for being in his way.

And then it begins. Was it first the noise of the stream, or first the hints of a different lightness through the trees? The bridge comes into view, gated and blocking the path, and the lightness begins to take on the shape of a wall, a roof. There is a silence amidst all the frenzy of the dog behind you, and even the tune of the water is contained in silence. In the same long moment of silence your muscles contract, like the winding of a spring, and your breathing slows down, so that the time it takes to walk the next dozen paces is spun into a length of years. Not into an eternity, however, nothing loose and unspecific. It is a plain sequence of events that collapses into the ensuing minute, is braced by that minute, and held. First, it is the book, as you begin to range more widely across an undiscovered countryside, searching out walks, and this one more intriguing than most because of its inaccessibility and strangeness, and because of the terseness with which it is mentioned. It begins with a book. Next, there is the time that you approached, or tried to approach, from the north, with well-kept cottages and orchards beyond. You came away with the half-formulated, half-forgotten certainty that the place must be situated beyond the farthest point that you had reached, across an open tract of field you dared not broach. Next, the time you had approached the game-wood corner with a friend, spelling out the tantalizing message of the book then and there, and suggesting the detour that your instincts told you must be right. But the day was late and the wind already up on the river, so that home and tea and warmth were to be preferred to any more walking. You both agreed to make it another time, but there never was another time because of the fragility with which friendships exist, particularly those that arise to give heart and meaning to a time of flux. (And yet, it has to be said, there was an affinity between the pagoda and the friend, in that they both gave meaning without giving comfort. They stood, both of them, like a question mark against what was most taken for granted even in a time of trouble. They attracted by their strangeness. The difference was that the pagoda could never go away, or rather that the distance at which it was held was fixed in space, and it is because of this that there is a fidelity and a freedom in our relationships with places that we could never dare to ask for, or hope to achieve, in our friendships with people.) So you pocketed the project for another time, friend or no friend, and it became a physical determination to take the turning by the oak tree, and any idea or expectation of the place became entirely secondary.

It was this that your body had answered on a warmer autumn day, alone, thinking neither of the book nor of the friend, nor of anything but the pleasures of an untrodden path where the end of it is unseen and the direction that it takes turns away from home. Thinking nothing, in fact, but steering the body from a different centre, a pole of repulsion which says, I do not wish to return to a place where my identity is a foregone conclusion, where I am a protrusion upon the surface of the earth, built layer upon layer of intricate living, gone shell-like hard and impenetrable, as much to me as to others. It is this, more than any aim you had inside your rattled head, that explains the delight of the pink-walled pagoda-shaped octagonal-conical out-of-place out-of-this-world place, the secret and novel and inexplicable place, that then came into view. The vortex suddenly for a rush of sensations that came from the middle distance and from far away, from all over at once, and reached in the fact of the pink pagoda standing there a single, sharp, and almost arbitrary, point of focus.

These, then, are the ways in which the pink pagoda was first seen. As they are also the reasons which prevent you from ever truly seeing it at all. And it is at the intersection of these points, and in the gap between the pink pagoda as it was and the pink pagoda as it was perceived, that the Game, and the demand for a Game – call it imagination – arises. And to which the logic of the Game seeks to return. The Game exists in recognition of the truth that the point in itself is nothing, least of all an answer. It is the disappearing point for any number of perspectives, and the starting point for all the imagining, the convolutions and the contrivances which comprise the Game. But do not think that these are ideas only, and so of no account, for all of them are ideas which point to the need for a something, an object, a fabric with which to clothe the idea in time and space. There has to be, if not the pink pagoda, oh there has to be something – a way of giving a name to everything that converges on, and diverges from, that place, that moment, that idea – or all of it will carry on in parallel, never meeting, never touching. And the Game knows this, knows that it is only play which gives the language of time and space to what is happening. Knows itself only to be an approach in a world where nothing more than an approach is permissible. Knows too how every new possibility encrusts the point of entry and the point of vision alike with more matter, more obscurity, so that each successive attempt is the harder, and in the end we are self-blinded men beating out our lives against walls of our own construction – playing in the knowledge that it is only victory over the Game, and not victory in the Game, that counts, and that the winning move is the one which vanquishes play itself and not the other Players.

But I am convinced that there was another moment too, immediately prior to the one of which I have just spoken, before everything tumbled into the world of the Game –

before the pink pagoda, so to speak, was invented. In this earlier moment there was nothing but a figure in a landscape over against a building in a landscape, and all that private sequence of events which had been building towards this moment, all that substance – the thousands of inarticulable experiences that drop to form the sediment of a life and determine the shapes upon which its pleasures will be grounded – which we call an identity, and all of the future that would grow from this place at this time, and seek time after time to return, all of this was silenced by the building itself which was its crown and substance too, its own sufficiency. The form it took was that of a smiling gaze upon the face of the figure, a gaze, a smile, and a slight parting of the lips, having smiled, as if to speak. To say what? Smiling and gazing and opening the lips, and still knowing that, whatever could be said, more would remain to be said, and still more be left unspoken.

Acknowledgements

The Makers of the Game wish to acknowledge the help they have received from the following sources: the *Oxford Dictionary of Etymology*; *Webster's Third New International Dictionary*; the *Victoria County Histories of England*, ed. Ralph Pugh (Oxford University Press); Niklaus Pevsner's *Buildings of England* (Penguin); Patrick Conner's *Oriental Architecture in the West* (Thames and Hudson, 1979); Philip Wheelwright's *Heraclitus* (Greenwood Press, 1982); Thomas A. Clark's *Fly Patterns for Still Waters* (Moschatel Press, 1978); the landscape of a portion of North-east Essex; and the many hundreds of merchants, sailors, explorers and exploiters, who, over several centuries, have kept open that narrow channel between East and West without which the conception of this Game might have been impossible.